THE PRINCE

THE JESTER KING FANTASY SERIES:
BOOK 3

K. C. Herbel

Epic Books Press
RICHMOND, VIRGINIA

Epic Books Press
P.O. Box 358
Quinton, Virginia 23141
www.EpicBooksPress.com

Publisher's Note: This is a work of fiction. Names, characters, places, and incidents are a
product of the author's imagination. Locales and public names are sometimes used for
atmospheric purposes. Any resemblance to actual people, living or dead, or to businesses,
companies, events, institutions, or locales is completely coincidental.

Cover Artist: © Andrey Kiselev – Fotolia (use licensed through stock.adobe.com)

Ordering Information:
Quantity sales. Special discounts are available on quantity purchases by corporations, as-
sociations, and others. For details, contact the "Special Sales Department" at the address
above.

Library of Congress Control Number: 2017940783

The Prince / K. C. Herbel. -- 1st ed.
ISBN 978-1-944314-14-9

To my dearest, Mary Anne,
whose patience I have stretched beyond human limits.

GWYTHIA

CAITHNESS
SHIRE

ERIN

ALBION

DUMNONIA

LYONESSE

Book Three

THE PRINCE

*"Be not afraid of greatness. Some are born great, some achieve greatness,
and others have greatness thrust upon them."*

— WILLIAM SHAKESPEARE

No Peace unto the Wicked

"You cannot have it! The throne is mine!"

Ergyfel, King of Lyonesse, shot up in bed, awakened by the same nightmare that had plagued him for a week. His body trembled as he looked into the darkness and tried to orient himself. Before his eyes could focus, a cold shiver replaced the tremor. Sweat soaked his skin and night-clothes. A cool draft from the window tickled its way across his flesh, bringing his attention to the warm, gentle hand on his arm.

Ergyfel looked to his side. Lady Maeven, barely visible in the dim light, lay raised up on one elbow, her silky brunette hair draped loosely around her alabaster shoulders. Even now, with most of her delicate, pleasing form covered by bedclothes, her full dark lips were enough to make him hunger for the feel of her. He would have forgotten his troubles, willingly lost himself to instinct and her natural feminine wiles, had she not spoken.

"The same nightmare, my lord?"

"Yes." He pulled away from her and sat on the edge of the bed. She shifted position, and again the warmth of her hand fell upon him. "It's not enough that the king hid his crown and deprived me of a proper coronation?" He struck his leg with a fist. "Now the boy's got to deprive me of my sleep as well?"

"Billy?" Caution flattened her tone.

"Yes! Who do you think?"

"It was not your fault, my lord. How could you know that he was the king's son?"

"He's as much a burden to me dead as he was alive."

"My King." She squeezed his arm. "The guilt is not yours, but those who plotted against King William."

Ergyfel remained silent.

"Come." She tugged gently on his shoulder. "Lay with me for a while and forget. We have time before we are needed."

Ergyfel resisted her persuasions until her warm body pressed against his back, and her mouth brushed the side of his neck. Her silken hair, like wind, flowed onto his chest, and he fell back into her embrace. Even though she had shared his bed for a short time, she had come to have a hold over him. A hold more powerful than any succubus could hope for. For in her glance, her voice, her touch, there was a kind of magic that was beyond Ergyfel's prodigious knowledge of sorcery to define. It was like nothing he had experienced before, for he had a place in her heart, and she had a place in his.

Ergyfel's mind drifted with the gentle caresses of Maeven's hands. His thoughts strayed from the current turmoil of his heart and kingdom, and snuggled into a warm, comfortable place in his memories. He sifted lazily through the events of the past years.

He had come to Castle Orgulous a mere youth, whose only assets were his distant relation to King William and a secret talent for sorcery—*the only gift mother ever gave me.* Yet, by use of his keen intellect and his birthright, he had landed himself on the throne.

He marveled at how easy it had been to manipulate people and events with words and a little magic. Ergyfel smiled, feeling very satisfied, and mulled over his blackest triumphs. The masterstroke had been contriving to have his uncle murder his beloved wife, Queen Eleanor, with his own hands. It had worked so well, in fact, that Ergyfel had used it as a model for his other endeavors. Not that it was flawless; after all, their heir Billy had escaped. A sore point to be sure, but then in time Billy too became one of his shadow puppets.

A spell here, a word there, an assassination or two. A propitious accident to augment a handful of betrayals and lies. They all wove together to form the dark tapestry of his rise to claim the throne. He replayed the events in his head for amusement. He reveled in his deeds, watching with great pleasure as the little shadows of his play combined into one great shadow: his. He felt warm and safe within his darkness.

A figure emerged from the comforting darkness of Ergyfel's mind, growing larger as it approached, and bathed in light of an uncomfortable intensity. At last, it was directly before him. Two eyes stared back at him with icy intent. The eyes of King William—but no—they were those of the late king's son. Ergyfel brought his gaze away from the penetrating blue eyes and saw Billy's visage. The little man was somehow different. His habitual smile and cheerful demeanor were gone, replaced by hatred and determination. Without warning, the luminous form of Billy held up a long curved knife and slashed at his throat. Ergyfel gasped and awoke, his hand grasping his throat.

"My lord!" Maeven tensed, but still cradled him in her bosom. "What is it?"

Ergyfel looked up at her soft brown eyes and caught his breath. The first light of morning warmed her features. His thoughts turned and his eyes narrowed. "You!" He pointed at Maeven as he rose and stood beside the bed.

Maeven looked into his black eyes and froze, struck dumb by unknowable fear.

"You." Ergyfel shook with anger. "You harlot. You have weakened me."

The king struck his concubine with the back of his hand. Pain tore through the flesh of his left arm like fire on oil and exploded in his brain, consuming his anger. He fell to his knees, gripping his wrist as if he could choke off the pain and isolate it in his hand.

The pain ebbed, and Ergyfel opened his eyes to look across the room. Lady Maeven still lay on the bed, the side of her face red from his strike, and tears streaming down her cheeks. She sobbed and stared at her love, a mixture of concern and confusion in her eyes.

Ergyfel caught her eyeing his left hand. She had seen the odd burn on its back only once—a horrible, festering wound that turned the flesh grey—and yet her revulsion was plain. It had been several weeks now, and still Ergyfel wore a glove over it, even in sleep.

"The same wound, my lord?"

"Yes," he gasped.

She edged forward. "It still has not healed?"

"No."

"Perhaps it needs air, my lord."

"No."

"But in that glove—"

"No!" he roared at her.

Maeven fell silent and covered her still burning cheek with her hand.

Ergyfel rose to his feet and started for his wardrobe. Maeven left the bed and poured water into a basin. She applied the cool water to her tight, hot cheek. In the costly silver mirror, Ergyfel caught her watching as he struggled with his clothes. The wounded hand was an albatross.

"Please, my lord, allow me to help you."

Ergyfel stared. With her help, the task of dressing would be less painful. Further, she earnestly wanted to help him, and in fact, seeing her before him brought forth desire for her assistance, but then something in him twisted and hurt. He grew angry again.

"You've helped enough." His voice sounded more like a snarl. "Leave me. Now!"

Maeven bowed to her king and collected her things. Then, mute and with the utmost of humility, she left.

The door to the royal bedchamber closed, and Ergyfel turned to call to her but was stopped by his taut image grasping for her in the tall mirror across the room. His outstretched hand became a fist. He was shaking inside, as he approached the mirror. He splashed some water on his face and pulled off the glove with caution.

"Damned faerie curse," he muttered while he examined the wound.

Ergyfel had tried everything he could to heal the injury caused by Billy's ring. At first, it appeared to be an ordinary burn. He had used all his knowledge of practical medicine and alchemy, but nothing seemed to affect it. That is, nothing except magic. Unfortunately, with each spell Ergyfel cast, the wound consumed new flesh as if the magic fed it. Now, much of the hand had festered and become grey and swollen. Its smell turned his stomach, and he had to turn away. His gaze struck the mirror again and he saw that his fingernails were turning black, as if great blood blisters grew beneath them. A closer examination revealed long, thin streaks of grey coursing up past his wrist to his forearm. A turn of his limb confirmed his worst fears. The arcane cankerous disease was not going to stop with his hand.

Ergyfel cleaned the wound and pondered over his decision made the week prior—not to cut off the hand. The choice seemed no easier now, and indeed, it might be too late for that. There had to be another way. He was determined to find it. Ergyfel couldn't imagine continuing the rest of his life as a one-handed cripple. Somewhere, amongst all the tomes he had collected over the years, there would be an answer—a cure. There had to be.

If only I had the ring. Blasted faerie! If Billy hadn't taken it to the bottom of the sea ...

Ergyfel's mind circled around the image of Billy. Why was the boy invading his dreams each night? He was gone, swallowed up by the deep, and that was that.

Ergyfel completed dressing and left the royal chambers. He ignored or avoided all whom he passed, only offering, "Later, later!" to his cowed and feckless ministers. One of the less malleable toads persisted, but Ergyfel deboned him by saying, "You are fortunate I have something more important than you to dissect."

At that moment, a servant arrived and announced, "My lord, the king's funeral waits upon your presence."

Ergyfel halted his stride and turned his face to the daring servant. The others backed away, leaving the man alone.

"Don't you mean King *William's* funeral, Gullinburst?"

The man bowed hastily. "Yes. Forgive me, Your Majesty. My grief got the better of me."

Ergyfel demoralized the hall full of minions with his stare. He spun on his heels and left them dithering. Without turning back, he proclaimed, "William denied me a crown at my coronation; I am returning the favor." When he reached the end of the hallway, he added, "Do not speak to me until he's buried."

By the time he arrived at his study, Ergyfel's mind had wrapped around the first fragment of a spell—a spell that would allow him a tiny glimpse of the future. He had dared to use the spell but once before; for to gaze on the future, as one not born with second sight, could drive a man mad or cost him his life.

Ergyfel barred the door and crossed to the large stone table in the center of the chamber. He grabbed a large, angular crystal and placed it in the middle. Then he picked up an egg in one hand and a thin black iron blade in the other.

Ergyfel stared with contempt at his gloved fist. Then he gripped the knife with a scowl. "I must know."

Before he could change his mind, Ergyfel completed the spell and punctured the egg. Pain gripped his left arm, and the beat of his heart raced as blood ran from the small hole in the shell onto the crystal. He focused on the semi-opaque stone and allowed his mind to slip into the trance.

At first, there was stark whiteness and the lone sound of his quickening pulse. Then shadows formed and danced, coming together, growing and dissipating. His heart pounded in his ears until it became like the sound of the ocean and the shadows became waves. A large shadow in the rough shape of a ship loomed on the horizon. The ship sailed alone on a stormy red sea with a small pale figure on its deck. The ship sailed to Ergyfel, and Billy stood at the helm. He held a sword in one hand but, more importantly, he still wore the ring. The storm redoubled in intensity and Ergyfel felt his heart was about to burst. By sheer will, he forced himself away from the ship and flew across the sea, back to where there were no shadows. Light radiated all around with nothing to reflect it.

Where am I? Ergyfel's mind grew more frantic with each beat. *What am I doing here? I'm starting to forget! No! I—I...*

The image of a man flashed before him. He fought to maintain the image as it coalesced and developed detail. The man was tall and thin, with well-groomed raven hair, and eyes like inkwells. He wore clothing to match a moonless night and a glove upon one hand. Upon his naked hand, there was the large signet ring of a great lord.

I ... I am Ergyfel. I am Ergyfel, King of Lyonesse.

At that moment, he found himself back in his study, in Castle Orgulous. His knees wobbled and he half-fell, half-sat on the stone floor. Before him, on the granite table, lay his large, rough seeing-crystal, caked in dried blood. He remembered now what he had been doing, and the vision he had received came rushing back into his mind.

"So ... the brat still lives, *and* he's coming to me."

He savored the thought of having Billy and, more importantly, the ring back under his control. Eleanor's ring would be his salvation—the cure for his hand. And Billy would be an entertaining aside.

The king smiled and whispered to the air, "You are welcome to come home anytime, Cousin. And oh, what a welcome I shall prepare for you."

CHAPTER ONE

Introductions

Billy woke to a moist, rough tongue licking his cheek. The sweet song of birds flittered on the fragrant, fresh air. Still half-awake, he smiled and reached up to push the affectionate creature away. His hand felt soft, warm fur, long ears, and horns...

Horns! Billy's bright blue eyes snapped open.

A young buck stood directly over him. Billy stared into the deer's large, brown eyes and remembered that he was now in Tirn Aill, the land of faerie folk.

He looked beyond the beast's antlers and into the green canopy over them. The silvery trunks of trees reached up for hundreds of feet, stretching to touch the sapphire sky that peeked through their branches. Billy had never seen trees like these or smelled flowers as fragrant, nor seen a sky so blue. Nor had he ever felt such peace.

Being washed up on the shore of Tirn Aill, all alone, with only myths and legends to go by, Billy didn't know what to expect. *But then again*, he reminded himself, *ever since I left the Valley of the Yew, things haven't exactly been predictable.* The thought of his boyhood home brought back memories of John, the kindhearted innkeeper, who had raised Billy as his son and had paid for his kindness with his life. Billy had always known him as "Father," and now felt he would never know an end to the ache caused by his absence.

Still gazing at the trees, Billy tried to analyze his situation. Tirn Aill was the last place he had expected to wind up when he'd stowed away on the *Gyldan Mene*. The ship had been headed for Erin. Now he found himself in a strange land, with no one to help him and no idea of what he should do.

"It could be worse," he told the buck. "The shipwreck could have left me on Lyonesse."

It felt strange to hear himself say it. Billy had lived his whole life in Lyonesse and never imagined another place more to his liking, but that was before he had to run for his life and before he came to peaceful Tirn Aill.

He had heard many a yarn about the land of Faerie, but no tale could touch the truth of its serene majesty. None could have prepared him for the excitement of discovering its wonders. Everywhere he looked, from the pastel beaches to the glittering bark of the trees, something grand and unexpected confronted him. His greatest surprise had come when he learned that he could communicate with the birds and other animals.

Something tickled his foot, and he looked down to see the fawn that had befriended him the day before on the beach. It licked his toes in greeting. Billy pulled his foot away, and rolled over, but something hard and sharp at his side stopped him.

"Ow!" Billy reached under his shoulder to tug out the offending object.

As his hand wrapped around its handle, Billy recalled that he had left Sir Hugh's sword by his side in case he needed some protection in the night. Of course, it was ridiculous to think that he could wield it with any effectiveness, but having it close at hand made him feel safer. He still wasn't sure if it was safe for him in the woods. And though the wounds had all healed, the memory of his encounter with a forest dragon was still vivid. This sword, in the hands of Sir Hugh, had saved his life that day, and Billy yearned for his friend's company.

He put the weapon aside and sat up, then stretched and yawned, but froze in mid-stretch. The birds stopped chirping and were still. Billy lowered his arms slowly. He rubbed his eyes and scanned the area. All around him, an abundance of nature's creatures sat or stood, staring at him as if waiting for something. There were squirrels, hares, turtles, weasels, wolves, deer, foxes, and boars, to name just a few. They all eyed him expectantly. Billy picked himself up, putting his back to a large, rough-barked tree. All at once, the creatures of the forest crouched or otherwise lowered their heads to bow before him. The confused subject of their obeisance remained pressed against the tree trunk, not understanding what they were doing.

Finally, the friendly fawn sneaked a peek at him. Billy then bowed to the creatures, just as Malcolm the Magnificent had taught him. But still they humbled themselves to him.

"Rise, my friends."

The creatures arose, and an irresistible grin pushed its way onto Billy's mouth. As his lips parted in one of his knock-a-gargoyle-from-its-perch smiles, the creatures moved forward, each one in turn coming to nuzzle up against him or crawl and climb over his body. All at once, Billy found himself laughing, and all the birds and animals of the forest joined him.

***

"How much farther is it?"

Billy and the small – but growing – army of animals had marched inland for most of the day, stopping only to drink from cool, clear creeks and graze on the available vegetation. He had never tasted sweeter berries, nor seen them in such abundance.

A fox, which was the troop's guide, turned and yapped at Billy. It then ducked into a grove of old oak trees.

"That's good." Billy entered the thicket. "I was beginning to think we'd never get here. By the way, where is here?"

"This is my home," a voice stated from behind him.

The sound startled Billy. It had not been spoken by an animal, but a resonant human voice. It was the first time he had heard human speech, other than his own, since he had come to Tirn Aill. Billy spun around, only to find trees, birds, and animals.

"Who said that?" He felt uneasy and backed away.

One of the trees bent slightly. "I did."

Billy gasped and fell backward when the top of the tree descended towards him. Before he knew what had happened, two of the lower branches had reached out, grabbed his arms, and helped him back to his feet.

The large, rough hands of the oak released Billy, and he fell back to the ground. He stared at the tree and a shape emerged from its trunk; a gnarled and knotty face, which looked rather like the weathered face of an old man. A name popped into Billy's head.

"Quercus." He wagged a finger at the tree. "Don't ever scare me like that again!"

The wrinkled bark-face furrowed its brows and stared narrowly at Billy with one eye. "Do I know you, friend?"

"I don't think so." Billy was at a loss. How did he know the creature's name?

The tree twisted from side to side, watching all the animals that were still coming into the small opening between the trees. "I see you are a forest friend, for the animals love you, but I do not recognize your face. What's more, only one other has known my name."

"Two others," a third voice announced.

Billy turned to his left, looking for another talking tree, but instead found a little man, no more than a foot tall. This diminutive fellow had a bushy white beard and thick eyebrows, which framed his round mouth and sparkling black eyes. Over his perfectly proportioned, although some-what pudgy body, he wore a green and brown mottled robe, decorated with strange, dark figures and symbols. Atop his head, he wore a tall blue fez, and upon his feet, pointed shoes of the same color. The last item Billy noticed was the walking-staff the man carried in his tiny hands, which was nothing more than a willow twig.

The little man smiled. His numerous laugh-lines and cheerfully grown crow's-feet betrayed a long lifetime of good humor. He then looked to the oak and said, "Two others, Quercus—myself, and our young friend's mother."

"Who are you? And what do you know of my mother?"

"I am Elzgig, your servant." He bowed gracefully before Billy. "And it was my pleasure to know Her Majesty, Queen Eleanor, even before she was queen."

Quercus inspected Billy. "You are Queen Eleanor's son?"

"Aye." Billy nodded. "My father is King William."

He had never uttered these words to anyone before, and it made him feel strange to admit it, though maybe it was finally sinking in. He had only known for a short while, and he was still getting used to the idea, but it wasn't easy. It should have been a point of pride, but the concept itself was bogged down and tangled up in anger and self-pity. It would have been much easier to accept King William as his father had he not turned out to be his mother's murderer.

"I see." Quercus bowed as best a tree can. "Then I am also your servant, Your Majesty. Please, forgive me for not recognizing you."

The strange tree's words brought Billy back from his reflection. He tried to stifle a laugh. "Your Majesty? No, oh no. Just Billy."

"King Billy?" Elzgig looked amused. "Yes, I rather like it!"

"No, I'm not a king. I left all that behind, in Lyonesse. There's no place for me back there, much less a kingdom. I am just the son of Eleanor."

Quercus frowned. "What do you mean?"

Elzgig climbed down a thick exposed tree root. "He doesn't know, my old oak friend."

"What? What don't I know?"

"You don't know what import your mother was to us."

"What do you mean?"

"Your mother was Queen."

"I know that!" Billy put his hands on his hips.

"You see, Elzgig. He knows that."

"I know he thinks he knows, Quercus. But what he thinks he knows is not what you and I know."

Billy scratched his head. "Huh?"

"Allow me to make myself clear." Elzgig moved to stand between Quercus and Billy.

"By all means, Elzgig. Please, do explain."

"Billy." Elzgig nodded his way. "I know you know your mother was Queen of Lyonesse, but what you don't know is that she was also Queen of Tirn Aill."

Billy scrunched up his face. "What?"

"Your mother was Queen of—"

"Whoa—whoa—whoa—wait! Hold it right there." Billy put up his hand. "How could she be Queen of Tirn Aill, when she was Queen of Lyonesse?"

"She was Queen of Tirn Aill long before she left for the world of man."

"Then why did she go?"

"She was content to watch mankind in the waters of a magic pond; their triumphs and their wickedness. One day, she saw a young warrior wounded in battle and became strangely concerned. Every day, she returned to see how he faired and eventually fell in love."

"My father."

"She thought," Elzgig continued. "She thought she could influence the ways of men. She wanted to bring them understanding and peace." Under his breath, Elzgig added, "Was that ever a mistake!"

"What? Peace and understanding?"

"No. They are never a mistake. Her mistake was in thinking she could change the hearts of men."

"Men aren't all bad."

"No, that's true enough, but even as we speak, a war is boiling over between Gwythia and Lyonesse, and the first battle has been fought."

"How do you know all that?"

"I have the sight." The little man touched his fingertips to his forehead. "And so did your mother. Although, she left before I could teach her much. I suspect you have the sight too."

"Me? I ..." Billy stopped short when he remembered that many of his dreams had come true, and how he had touched the minds of others to relive their memories. He also had occasional haunting flashes of faceless thousands butchered on the battlefield, or frozen in an icy death.

Billy looked down at the ring on his hand. It had belonged to his mother. "I believe this has given me visions. Some horrible—"

"Yes, yes. You can tell me all about it later, but now it's time we were moving on."

"Where to?"

"There are a great number of others who will be 'interested' to meet you."

"Then let's go."

"First, let me warn you." Elzgig sounded serious for the first time in their conversation. "Some will be happy to see you. Others will not."

***

Billy and Elzgig walked alone in the forest until dusk. As the sun set, they broke through the trees. A lush valley lay just below them, and a river wound its way through the valley's floor and on to a sea, where the final rays of the sun glittered on the water like molten gold. Near the banks of the river, Billy spotted a settlement. It wasn't what he would have called a town or even a village. Just a few peculiar structures scattered around a large clearing that sloped down to the water's edge.

As the gilded rays of sunlight faded and the long shadows merged into night, strange floating lights appeared in the little village, bathing the whole in a bluish glow.

Billy pointed. "What's that?"

"That is your court, Your Majesty."

At that moment, music came up from the valley. Cheerful music, unlike any he had ever heard. He watched as more of the pale blue lights appeared in the hills of the valley and in the forest that surrounded it. Some bobbed and wafted slowly, while others flew like shooting stars—all migrating to the valley's floor.

Elzgig snapped his fingers and a light appeared above his head. Billy jumped back in surprise, but immediately felt at ease when he saw the calm, smiling face of his companion illuminated by the faint blue light. Billy examined the phenomenon as it hovered before him. It looked like a sphere of pale blue flame, which remained constant in size. He reached out a hand, but felt no warmth coming from the orb. As if to answer his curiosity, the light jumped into his palm and rested there.

Elzgig gaped at him, and then threw back his head with a laugh. "Aye, you are Her Majesty's son, sure enough."

Billy looked up from the light to the little man and smiled. "Why do you say that?"

"Because your mother was the only other who could do what you just did."

Billy felt somewhat confused. "What did I just do?"

"Why, move a light belonging to another."

Billy looked at the small blue light in his hand. The sphere had no weight or tangible boundaries, yet it tickled his hand.

"I'm sorry."

He offered the light back to his new companion, but secretly wished he had one of his own. At once, the orb of light brightened and split into two. One light floated back to Elzgig, while the other remained in Billy's hand.

"Say, you learn quick!"

Billy examined the light in his hand again, and then looked out at the multitude of little lights moving through the valley. "And all of them are ... ?"

"The same." Elzgig nodded. "Many go to your court tonight."

"Then let's go."

"Yes, Your Majesty."

They walked down the hill, and Elzgig turned to Billy, who continued to toy with the light in his hand. The little man's face again took on an unexpected solemn expression.

"What?"

"Your Majesty, I feel I must warn you again. Some of your kingdom may not be happy with your appearance at this time."

"Why?"

"When your mother left, many came forward pressing their claim to rule."

"Like who?"

"Well, the goblins, hobgoblins, boogles, boogies, gremlins, and pixies, to name a few."

"So, what happened?"

"Nothing. You see, they can never agree on anything and always fought amongst themselves, and so the rest of Faerie could hold them at bay. But they are still dangerous."

"Now that I'm here, won't all that change?"

"Yes. But I fear it will get worse."

Billy stopped in his tracks. "Then maybe I shouldn't go."

Elzgig smiled at him and shook his head. "I'm happy to see you have not greed in your heart. That is the way it should be with kings. No, my young friend, you must go. It is your destiny."

Billy looked at the ring on his finger. In the short time he had worn his mother's ring, he had come to understand what it meant to have a destiny. He had lost everything: his father, his friends, his country, and even his identity. *What will my cursed destiny cost now?*

Elzgig cut Billy's reflection short.

"Your most dangerous enemies will undoubtedly be those some call dark elves."

"Dark elves?"

"Aye." Elzgig frowned. "They are by far the strongest of those who would usurp your throne. And I hear they have made secret pacts with the goblins and hobgoblins to gain their support."

"What can we do?"

"Your timely arrival may be enough to upset their plans, but they will not simply roll over because you are Eleanor's son. Come, we have dallied long enough. Your subjects await."

At that moment, a blue light came through the woods and passed between Billy and Elzgig. Beneath the tiny bouncing light, a small humanoid creature ran at an alarming speed. It stopped, tipped its hat, and then was off again. With that, Elzgig increased his pace towards the faerie court. Billy followed close behind him. His anxiety intensified with each step.

The enchanting music grew louder when they approached the river. Billy listened to the voices as they joined in the song. Some were birdlike twitters while others lowed like cows. The song of crickets joined them, and underneath it all, the river mumbled a counter-melody.

Most of the blue lights had already reached the court, but occasionally, Billy caught one or two filtering in from the hills. At last, they arrived at the edge of the large clearing beside the river. Billy blinked his eyes in an attempt to clear his vision. All around him were fanciful creatures and dancing lights. And though he was now in the land of Faerie, he could scarcely believe his eyes. People of all description surrounded him: some big, some small, some with wings, some with antennae like bugs, and some were almost animal in appearance, while others had the countenance of cherubs. Beauty danced with repugnant, old sang with young, fat feasted with skinny, and blind-drunk drank with tipsy, all together in joyous revelry.

The rabble surrounded a table, which was nearly a quarter furlong in length. At the far end sat a large wooden chair decorated with gold, silver, and gems.

Elzgig led Billy through the throng of revelers to the end of the table with the throne. No one seemed to pay them any attention until Elzgig jumped up onto the table and struck it with his tiny walking stick. Lightning shot from the end of his staff into the sky. A thundering boom shook the ground and echoed throughout the hills. All present then turned their attention to the end of the table, and at the diminutive mage standing there. Billy peered at him from behind the throne.

Elzgig stood tall and smiled with his eyes at those around the table. "My brothers and sisters, I have great news!"

The former revelers shifted nervously, mumbling to each other.

"Our noble ruler," Elzgig continued, "has come home from the land of man."

A clamor erupted from the mob. Elzgig held up his hands in an attempt to quiet them, but they continued to shout and argue and rant. Finally, he struck the table with his staff. Again, lightning spewed forth and near deafening thunder filled the air. When the noise receded, only quiet remained.

"Queen Eleanor is dead!" a female voice from the edge of the crowd shouted. "What sort of gnomish trickery is this?"

Several tall, dark figures stood in the half-shadows on the fringe of the clearing. They had been so still that Billy hadn't noticed them before. One of the figures stepped forward. She wore an elegant black cloak embossed in an intricate knotwork of gold. A slender gloved hand protruded from the cloak and pushed back the hood. The woman had a pale, narrow face with high cheekbones and almond shaped eyes the color of violets. Billy shuddered at the coldness he perceived in her eyes. Her features were nearly identical to those of the Night Queen—the nightmarish creature he had narrowly escaped in Lyonesse.

The woman brushed back her hair, revealing pointed ears. Her thin dark lips parted in a venomous smile before she spoke. "I said, what kind of trick is this, Elzgig?"

"It's no trick, Malkry. Eleanor's heir has come."

"She had no heir!"

"Ah, but she did, and you know it!"

"What?" Malkry took a step forward. "The son of that mortal?"

"King William was not wholly mortal, Malkry."

"Even if the boy did exist, he's dead now."

Billy stepped from behind the chair. "No, I'm not."

A gasp went up from the assembled denizens of Faerie. Billy felt their eyes upon him, boring down on him, staring at him like some monster. The brief silence crumbled under an avalanche of whispers and muttering.

"What kind of trick is this?" Malkry shouted over the hubbub. "Who is this ... this boy?"

"This is William, son of Queen Eleanor and King William of Lyonesse."

"You lie, gnome!"

"No! He is Her Majesty's son."

"Ha! This is some shallow trick of yours. The boy is dead."

"Then you admit to the boy's existence."

"Fine, but that boy is dead!"

At that moment, a short but very stout man stepped forward. Thick, wiry brown hair covered his face and arms. He had a scar running down his leathery cheek that became a white streak in his beard. Steel-plate armor covered his torso, and bracers of gold his wrists. A large, well-used war hammer hung at his waist. Behind him were three others of his approximate size and build, similarly armed and just as rough-hewn in appearance.

The leader of these gritty little men approached, his grey eyes locked on Billy's. He set his cup down on the edge of the table and held out a hand. Billy examined the man's dirty hand. While he was close to Billy's size, his hands were very different, for they were short fingered and gnarled. Billy was blessed with elegant hands.

"Let me see your hands," the man said in a gruff voice.

Elzgig nodded to Billy, and he warily held them out. Without hesitation, the rough little man grabbed his right hand and held it up to his eye. He touched the ring and it tingled.

"He bears the ring," the squatty man hissed to his companions. At once, they all went to one knee and bowed their heads. "Your Majesty. I am Thortan. The dwarves of Tirn Aill are yours to command."

"Thortan!" Malkry rushed down from her vantage point. "What is this? What is this? This is some kind of conspiracy, isn't it? You dirty little hole dwellers have joined against us. Is that it?"

"No." Thortan rose to place himself between Billy and the angry elf.

Malkry's companions fell in behind their leader, and Thortan's dwarves behind him. The two sides stared across at each other. Malkry bared her teeth and hissed at the little men. Before she could reach for her weapon, Thortan's hammer was an inch in front of her nose. She stepped back, surprised to have the weapon thrust in her face.

"He wears the ring, elf!" Thortan waved his hammer at Malkry.

"What ring?"

"Don't play thick with me, missy! The ring my forefathers wrought when the world was yet new. The ring my people gave to the first rulers of Faerie. The ring that Queen Eleanor and all the kings and queens of Tirn Aill before her wore on their coronation day!"

"Oh, that ring."

Thortan glared at the dark elf. "Yes, that ring." He then turned and faced the rest of those congregated at the court. "I, Thortan, do pledge my life and service to this boy, for he is our rightful king." He turned to Billy and whispered, "What's your name, boy?"

"Billy."

"I pledge myself to the wearer of the ring, King Billy!"

"King Billy!" the other dwarves shouted in unison.

A small number within the crowd followed suit and hailed Billy as king. However, many more remained silent or mumbled amongst themselves.

Malkry smirked. "You see, not everyone is so eager to believe this ... boy is who you say he is."

Elzgig turned to a beautiful winged faerie and asked. "Faenor, will you support the boy?"

The faerie looked away from the gnome, as if too shy to speak her mind.

"Onian!" Thortan shouted.

An elf standing near the edge of the mob with others of his kind, all dressed in leafy-green clothes, looked up from his companions. "What do you want, Thortan?"

"Will you not support him?" the leader of the dwarves asked. "Surely you will not deny the wearer of the ring."

The elf stared across at the dwarf with clear green eyes. "We need more proof."

"Proof? He wears the ring!"

Malkry crossed her arms and cocked one eyebrow at Thortan. "I think you'll find that most here do not put as much stock in that ring as you dwarves."

"Because you do not understand its power as we do."

The arguments went on for hours with nothing decided.

At last, Onian the elf stepped forward. "And what of the other citizens of Tirn Aill? Many of our fellow faerie are not present tonight. Are we to decide on this matter without them?"

"There is nothing to decide!" Malkry threw her arms up.

"I agree with Malkry," Elzgig said.

All eyes settled on him, and a hush fell over the assemblage. Malkry scanned the little wizard suspiciously.

"I agree. There is nothing to decide. Either Billy is our king, or he isn't."

Instantly, the mob resumed shouting and arguing. They jeered and hurled insults at each other. Many glared at Elzgig and called him an old fool.

Once again, Elzgig struck his willow twig on the table and lightning shot into the sky. While the thunder rolled in the distant hills, Elzgig crossed down the middle of the great table to its center.

"My friends, allow me to make myself clear. We are all agreed that Queen Eleanor was our rightful ruler, are we not? And that her offspring would, in turn, become our rulers, would they not? Then, I put it to you plainly: either Billy is Eleanor's son and our rightful king, or he is neither."

Elzgig's words seemed quite logical to Billy, all the dwarves, and even to Malkry, but to many others, his words were like wind to a stone. After an uncomfortable silence, the discussion restarted. The discussion became a debate, which digressed into an argument, and several times resulted in blows before the two parties could be separated. And then it would start all over again.

This up and down process continued throughout the night and into the next day, and again into the night. For three days, this went on, with neither side of the argument making progress and many faeries changing sides repeatedly. At times, it was as though some were arguing out of some perverse pleasure it brought them; to be contrary or simply to hear themselves talk.

Billy, like many others, had grown bored with the entire mess on the second day, and only stayed because he had to. A break in the tedium came when several satyrs showed up.

Billy marveled at the unusual creatures as they appeared one by one from the brush. He couldn't help but stare as they approached on their two cloven hooves.

"Good day, Your Highness." The lead satyr gave a slight bow.

"He's not our prince yet."

The satyr regarded Malkry and then smiled; a rather toothy horse-like grin. "Whatever," he said with a flip of his wrist. "My name is Sylvys, and these are my brothers, Fylvys and Elvys."

The other satyrs bowed as Sylvys named them.

"Welcome to Tirn Aill, Your Highness."

"Yes, welcome home, Your Highness."

"What have satyrs to gain by siding with dwarves?"

"Gain?" Sylvys stared at the dark elf. "Why, nothing. And we do not side with anyone but ourselves, and our new Prince here." He indicated Billy with his hand.

Gulch, the goblin leader, leaned out from behind Malkry. "Why have you come, Sylvys?"

"And why now?" Malkry added.

"To stir up more of your wild trouble?"

Elvys crossed his arms. "We heard that Queen Eleanor's heir had returned home yesterday."

Malkry wagged her finger at him. "He hasn't proved that he's the heir!"

"Yeah, whatever," Fylvys said. "But we heard he was here, and here we are, and there he is ..."

"But he hasn't proven—"

Sylvys cut Malkry off. "We're not here to argue with you, elf." Then the satyr turned his attention back to Billy. "Your Highness, we are here to deliver a very important message."

"Please, proceed."

Gulch groaned. "Yes. Get it over with, so we can get on with our important business."

The rather impressive satyr stared at the toady little goblin. Gulch swallowed hard and darted behind Malkry's warriors.

Sylvys cleared his throat. "Your Highness, these are probably the most important words I'll ever say—" He stopped abruptly, his attention and that of his brothers drawn to something in the distance. They stood high on the tips of their hooves, extending their torsos and stretching their necks, like curious, startled deer.

Billy turned to look over his shoulder. At the far end of the clearing, a dozen nude, young women appeared from the bushes. They danced and sang their way into view, unaware of their audience. Then all at once, they giggled and whispered and pointed towards the other inhabitants of Faerie.

"Nymphs, Sire," Elzgig whispered in Billy's ear.

Billy was aware of nothing but the frolicking girls until he felt the point of Elzgig's staff pushing his slackened jaw closed.

"Uh-m ... yes. Where were we?"

At that moment, the three satyr brothers sprinted past Billy toward the nymphs. Their prey squealed with delight and scattered like a flock of frightened birds. They ran, giggling, back into the woods.

Billy blinked as if wakened from a daydream. He watched in dismay as the satyrs disappeared behind the nymphs.

"What about your message?" Billy shouted to the vacant meadow. "Who was that?"

The wizard smiled. "That, Your Majesty, was Sylvys, the leader of the satyrs. That is, he's sort of a leader."

"What do you mean?"

"Satyrs are seldom lead by anything except their *prolific urges.*"

Billy looked back to where the unusual creatures had vanished into the trees and nodded. "What do you suppose their message was?"

"Oh, could have been anything." Elzgig shrugged. "But we'll probably never know. The important thing is they're behind you."

On the evening of the third day of arguments, after the meal had been served, and after Gulch, the fat, self-important leader of the goblins had droned on for an hour about goblin traditions and goblin rights, Billy rose to his feet. His boredom had transformed to frustration, and now to smoldering anger.

"Shut up!"

All eyes were on him. The only sound came from the babble of the nearby river.

"I've been sitting here for three days, and not a one of you has said anything new in two! You've been arguing the point endlessly, and in truth, I think you'd argue for eternity and never get anywhere.

"Elzgig is right, either I am Queen Eleanor's son and heir, or I am not. It's that simple. Now, surely there is some way you can tell whether I am who I say I am. Test me. Examine me. Use a spell. I really don't care how you do it, but do it without any more of this meaningless blabbering!"

When Billy had finished, many looked down and kicked the ground or otherwise avoided his eyes like scolded children. One by one, the faeries suggested ways to "test" Billy.

Elzgig winked at Billy and whispered, "That's it, Your Majesty. They just needed you to lead them to it."

After a round of somewhat more civilized arguments, all save Malkry agreed that Billy should undergo a thorough examination by the wizards of Tirn Aill. Their findings would determine what claim, if any, he might have to the throne.

CHAPTER TWO

The Gallant Fall

Hugh drove himself onward. He had left Castle Orgulous consumed with one thought: *save Myrredith.* She was the only woman he had ever loved. For all he knew, it might be too late. Still, he drove himself on, only stopping long enough to change horses, and then he was off again. Luke, the royal page, told him that the army of Gwythia had already defeated Earl Cairmac in Wyneddhamshire and was headed straight for Myrredith in Dyven.

Many years before, when Gwythia tried to invade, Hugh had stopped them. That day, few stood against many and drove them back into the sea. Hugh's heroism had saved the nation, but it had cost him Myrredith's hand. Now the Gwythies were about to take her away again. In the pit of Hugh's stomach was the agonizing fear that he couldn't defeat them again. Though he found praying helpful, there was more comfort in speaking to the dead.

Hugh looked toward heaven and sighed. "Billy ... I fear that my sin against you will weigh heavy against me in the battle to come. I wish there were some way I could undo what I've done. I'll need what strength the Lord will grant me to defeat them this time. But more, I wish you were here by my side."

Hugh doubted Myrredith would want to see him again, but she was in danger, and all that mattered was saving her. He rode on—his heart a tangle of guilt, fear, and love.

How many days have I been gone? Seven? Ten? I don't know anymore. Only a few days ago, I was Sir Hugh, the King's Champion and First Knight of Lyonesse, but now, Hugh. Simply Hugh. I haven't been that since ... before Father died.

Hugh pondered the darker days of his youth. His father, Sir Sedgmore, had disappeared along with the king's infant son. In his absence—unable to defend himself, he was declared a traitor. Hugh and his mother, Lady Galawyn became hostages against Sedgmore's return; but he was never seen again. From that point on, it was a daily struggle to be something other than "Hugh, the traitor's son."

More than a year later, on Christmas Eve, Lady Galawyn persuaded Sir Rudthar to take Hugh as his squire. Hugh did well at Cyndyn Hall. He even fell in love with Myrredith and found happiness for a while, but before the next Yule, his mother was dead.

With no other prospects, Hugh dedicated himself to his training under Rudthar, and strove to be the best squire in Cyndyn. Having accomplished that and earning his spurs for valor, he was forced to leave Rudthar's service. He wandered the land, serving the kingdom wherever he was needed. In this way, he hoped to prove his father's innocence.

In time, Hugh's devotion made him the King's Champion. Even so, there was a constant, unspoken pressure for perfection. Nothing else would be tolerated—not by Hugh, and not by the long memory of the court. Worst of all, his calling had separated him from Myrredith.

Now I'm free to do as I will, when I will.

In the few moments he took to reflect on this, Hugh discovered that his newfound freedom was both blessing and curse.

My former duties always gave me purpose and direction. Now I am beholden to no man. But this autonomy could be dangerous. I will only answer to God and myself. After all, a man without direction could surely lose his way, and his soul shortly thereafter. I must be careful!

He made a quick oath to be true in all things, and never again to allow another to detour him from the path of righteousness.

At that moment, several smoke plumes in the distance drew Hugh's attention. He hoped he was wrong about their origin. Without hesitation, he spurred his mount forward in the direction of the smoke—in the direction of Dyven.

Hugh had crossed vast stretches of the kingdom in only a few days. He was bone tired, sore, and hungry. Dyven lay no more than three miles hence, but to Hugh, it seemed like thirty. Myrredith's face was the only thing that kept him from collapsing.

By traveling through the wilderness, Hugh had hoped to escape the eyes of any Gwythian spies, but when he came to the King's Road, his mind thought only of reaching Myrredith. He spoke his mind to the world, "Spies be damned!" Then he urged his horse up the road.

Movement caught his attention as three men on horseback darted from the woods and onto the road. Hugh reined his mount to a halt. He stared down the road at the men. Soldiers—wearing the colors of Gwythia.

"Damn! I should have known."

His mind raced to a full gallop. *Should I try to lose them in the woods, or take on all three here on the road?* His hand moved to his side. The sword that usually hung from his hip was painfully absent. Hugh's strategy was decided for him. He had no sword, nor any other weapons. He wore only tattered clothes and no armor. All had been lost to the sea.

He charged into the forest. A moment later, a crossbow-bolt shot by his ear and horses crashed through the bushes behind him. The brush was thick with many low-hanging tree limbs; something he hoped would give him cover until he could lose his pursuers. A glance over his shoulder showed that only two Gwythies had followed him into the woods.

Ssswat!

Hugh's horse let out a whinny and missed a step. Hugh knew, without looking, that a bolt had struck her in the hindquarter. The tired mount would be hard pressed to outrun a pair of fresh horses, but now, wounded, there wasn't a chance.

He had to think fast. He chanced another look back and saw the closest man rapidly gaining on him, his sword held high to strike.

Ahead, a narrow path led through some thistles. A large elm stretched out a branch just above the trail beyond. Hugh turned his horse up the path, forcing his pursuer to fall in behind him.

Without further thought, Hugh grabbed the overhanging branch. His momentum pulled him from the saddle and swung him up over the bough. The first soldier gaped in stupefied amazement as Hugh revolved around the limb and dropped onto the back of his horse. Before the Gwythie could recover his wits, Hugh smacked him with his own sword, then gave a slight shove and his stunned opponent dropped into the thistles.

Hugh spun his new mount around and charged the second soldier. This man, who was still coming at a gallop, was so befuddled by Hugh's sudden turn that he spontaneously shot his crossbow into the sky. Before he could draw another weapon, Hugh raked him from his horse with an outstretched arm.

Hugh took out the third scout when he came looking for his comrades. As the youth leaned over their bodies, Hugh jumped out and spooked his horse. A tree branch did the rest.

The three Gwythies had nothing to say when Hugh relieved them of their weapons. They wore no armor, and so a crossbow, a heavy broadsword, and a shield were all that interested him. Had he more time, Hugh would have tied them up and questioned them.

"My thanks for the loan of your weapons, gentlemen," Hugh told the unconscious soldiers. "Have a nice day."

A moment later, he was back on his way to Dyven. He bounded through the forest with his fresh horses, deciding it was better to stay off the King's Road to avoid any other patrols. By evening, he came to a small, shady creek that wound through the hills. The last time he had traveled down it, he was Squire Hugh, hunting boar with the late Lord of Cyndyn.

"God rest his soul," he muttered.

Hugh's mind flashed to Myrredith. He picked up his pace. His mind again filled with worries about her safety. In a few minutes, he would see Dyven. From there, he would know what his chances were.

The scent of smoke grew stronger as he got closer to the city. He turned his horse away from the creek and headed up a densely wooded hill. As he crested the summit, his heart sank.

Below him, nestled around Kelmyrr Bay, lay the remains of Dyven. Smoke rose from every district of the city, making the evening dark and gloomy. Gwythian soldiers strode through the streets, pillaging what they didn't vandalize. Their campfires flickered like stars in the surrounding orchards and fields, while the masts of their dark ships crowded the sky over the harbor. The sound of their drunken singing floated up to Hugh's burning ears. Their words of victory turned his stomach as he retreated from the hilltop into the trees.

This was truly a dark day. In the whole history of Lyonesse, no invasion had ever been this successful. Thanks to men like King William and Hugh, the nation had never had to face a war on its own soil. The people had never known the fear of such destructive violence. All of that was about to change. Gwythia, their ancient enemy, had arrived, and by the looks of it, they meant to stay.

By the size of their army, the Gwythies must have planned this invasion for months ... even before Gaelyn's assassination.

His blood boiled as he descended from the hill and headed for Cyndyn Hall. It was too late to do anything for Dyven, but perhaps he could still save Myrredith.

Hugh saw nothing on the ride to Cyndyn Hall. The anger within him grew with each step, until the only image his mind could conjure was blood. Rivers and oceans of Gwythie blood.

He found the enemy camped in the woods and fields east of Cyndyn Hall, which gave them control of the main road and high ground overlooking the drawbridge. The tents furthest east were in orderly square arrays in the fields, while the tents of the woods were coarse and strewn like seed, in an arc around the castle. He sneered at these and muttered to himself, "Mercenaries." The outmost of the mercenary camps looked across at the north wall of Cyndyn Hall, just yards from the entrance to a hidden hunting trail.

By the time the sentries spotted Hugh, it was too late. He swept into the Gwythian camp like a flood, cutting down every man that got in his way. Many who saw him simply ran. Some would never forget the image of Hugh slaughtering their comrades with wild abandon. Others wouldn't live long enough to remember it at all.

A cheer went up from the ramparts of Cyndyn Hall as Lady Myrredith's men saw what was happening. The sight of a lone warrior raining such destruction on the enemy camp gave them hope. They hurled missiles and insults at the soldiers below and picked them off with bows as they left cover to confront Hugh.

***

The Lady of Cyndyn heard the commotion and ran to the battlements, accompanied by Malcolm the Magnificent.

"What is it, Captain?"

"Milady, you should not be up here!"

"Never mind that. Why are the men cheering?"

"A warrior, milady." The captain pointed. "I don't know who he is, but he's down there in the Gwythies' camp, and madder than a wet hornet."

Lady Myrredith looked over the wall at the chaos below. The battlefield swarmed with mercenaries running every which way. In the center of this scene was a single man on horseback. In the dim light, she could see that he wore no armor or colors, yet he sat his mount like a nobleman. He fought with merciless rage; the ferocity of a hungry wolf.

At that moment, a company of archers commanded by the mercenary captain launched a volley of arrows at the warrior. His shield bristled like a porcupine from all the arrows in it, but he never slowed down; he merely swept off the arrows with his sword. Suddenly, Lady Myrredith caught a glimpse of his face.

"Hugh."

"What?" Malcolm said.

"It's Hugh!"

The men on the wall, upon hearing this, called out Hugh's name.

Myrredith clasped her captain's shoulder. "Ready a force for a mounted attack on that camp. Force their archers back! And order our archers to protect Hugh."

"Milady. We don't dare lower the drawbridge!"

Lady Myrredith placed her hands on hips and looked the captain in the eye. "We must help Hugh. We *will* help Hugh!"

"Yes, milady."

"I will lead that charge, milady. If you will allow me."

Lady Myrredith eyed Malcolm, the man who was both warrior and juggler. She had come to trust him and even count on him in recent weeks.

"I must go, milady. He is my friend."

In truth, Myrredith wished she could run to Hugh's aid herself, but she could not. She nodded, and Malcolm left.

Myrredith returned her attention to the battle. Aided by many volleys of Cyndyn arrows, Hugh continued his brutal punishment of the Gwythian troops. He cleaved flesh and steel like a man threshing wheat. He smashed down the mercenary captain as he rushed in, and his men scattered and fled. The leaders of the besieging army were helpless to halt their retreat.

***

A great cheer rang from Cyndyn Hall when Hugh toppled a siege tower still manned by Gwythian soldiers. He drove his mount around the wreckage and charged towards another siege tower near the moat of the castle as the drawbridge lowered.

His way to the siege tower was clear. The men who operated it scrambled to get out before he and Lady Myrredith's men arrived. They joined the scores of Gwythian troops fleeing into the woods or felled by arrows.

Hugh came to an abrupt stop. Through the smoke and dust, he saw a young boy standing in his path. The boy stood erect and defiantly tossed back the unruly hair from his face. He glared at Hugh with his piercing blue eyes.

Stunned, Hugh lowered his guard. "Billy?"

Many eyes were upon them. The boy stood his ground, without a sound—a lonely David to Hugh's Goliath.

"It can't be," Hugh muttered. "Billy is dead." He wiped the sweat from his eyes to clear the apparition from his vision and noticed a broken arrow jutting from his thigh. He stared again at the brave boy, and a wave of remorse destroyed his anger. Without warning, the long journey to Dyven took its toll, stripping Hugh of his strength. The shield fell from his arm. "I betrayed you."

Suddenly, the boy flung a rock and struck Hugh's head. A hush fell, while Hugh swayed and rolled from the saddle.

"Hugh!" Myrredith cried out, as he fell to the ground. Her voice hung on the air. It was a lonely, haunting sound.

***

A moment later, the retreating Gwythian army cheered and turned around to attack the warriors who had sallied forth from Cyndyn Hall. With newfound courage, they fell upon them and overwhelmed Lady Myrredith's men before her archers could respond. She scanned the battlefield for Hugh and Malcolm but could find no sign of either man.

"Raise the drawbridge!" Lady Myrredith yelled. "Now!"

Before it could be raised, Gwythian soldiers toppled their siege tower onto the drawbridge. The army poured across the lowered bridge and smashed through the portcullis. The attack was so sudden and effective that the castle fell before Lady Myrredith or her staff could escape into the secret passages.

Within the hour, enemy soldiers dragged Lady Myrredith into the main hall and presented her to the conquering general. The three men needed to restrain her tossed her to the floor before the dais that she had sat upon as master of Cyndyn Hall.

Lady Myrredith's eyes came up from the floor to stare at the man lounging on her throne. He was a well-groomed, comely man dressed in fine chain mail and rare silks. A red eagle—the crest of Gwythia—blazed across his yellow doublet and a well-crafted long sword rested in his hands. While Myrredith had never laid eyes on him before, his features seemed eerily familiar.

"So, you are the wench responsible for my brother's death." The man pointed his sword at Lady Myrredith. He spoke with the Gwythian accent she had expected, but much stronger than she had heard before.

Myrredith pushed the hair back from her face and attempted to stand up. The guard behind her shoved her back to the stone floor. She snapped a harsh look back at the man, who grabbed her soiled, crimson hair and forced her to face his commander.

The man rose from the throne. "That won't be necessary, Rhyfelwr."

Lady Myrredith remained kneeling and faced her captor. Again, his features struck her as familiar. "I don't know what you're talking about."

"Come, come, Lady Cyndyn, let us not fence around truth." Her conqueror made sparring gestures with his sword in her direction and descended from the dais. "You know it as well as I that you planned and carried out my brother's murder."

"I'm afraid you have me at a disadvantage."

Myrredith's captor stepped on her hand and placed the point of his sword at her throat. "Aye, that I do." He laughed, and his men joined in.

Her hand burned under the man's boot, but Myrredith fought back with all the dignity she could muster. "I am a lady! How dare you treat me this way?"

"I will treat you as I will." The man released her hand. He then used his blade to lift her face up. "As for you bein' a lady, that has yet to be decided."

Again, the men laughed. Myrredith flushed with embarrassment and rage at the insult.

"You are no gentleman!" Myrredith forced the words through clenched teeth. "Who are you?"

The man glared at her. "I am Prince Hereweald, brother to Prince Gaelyn, and you are my prisoner."

CHAPTER THREE

Eleanor's Enchantment

Billy was poked, pinched, prodded, rubbed, scratched, sniffed, squeezed, tickled, tweaked, turned upside down, and finally bathed by the three strange creatures known to him only as "the Witan." Elzgig had left Billy in their dubious care, simply asking them to "test him."

Elzgig explained that he should do as they say and all would be fine. "The Witan knows what must be done." The little mage then left Billy alone with his examiners.

The Witan lived in the heart of a great tree, accessed through a narrow door at the top of its stair-like roots. Inside, nature had carved out a spacious compartment. The hollow was dark and musty, illuminated only by a greenish fire in the center that burned without heat or smoke. Aside from the books, jars, and peculiar objects jammed into rough niches honeycombing the walls, it reminded Billy of a cave.

He found the Witan's unique domicile an equal match for their quirky appearance and character. Each was no taller than three-and-one-half feet and hunched over with age. The skin of their vaguely elfish bodies, including their long, pointed ears, had passed the leathery stage and now resembled tree bark. In fact, they were so bent, gnarled, and wrinkled, that Billy couldn't tell if they were male or female. They were a little creepy.

Each member of the Witan seemed to conduct their own "tests" on Billy, unmindful of the others. They continuously mumbled to themselves, occasionally stopping to nod and say, "Yes, of course."

After an hour of this behavior, Billy reached the end of his patience. "What?"

His examiners stood back and stared at him, their heads all cocked to one side. Billy made contact with their sparkling green eyes and, for the first time, noticed a distinct characteristic in each. The eyes of the first faerie studied Billy with discerning intellect, the second set regarded him with patience, and the third set of eyes smiled knowingly.

Billy held out his palms. "Who are you?"

Together, the Witan answered Billy, each speaking in turn.

"We–"

"are–"

"the Witan."

The method of their reply confused Billy. "What is the Witan?"

"We are scholars–"

"physicians–"

"wizards–"

"advisors–"

"protectors–"

"and friends."

The Witan's tandem speech threw Billy off balance. It was like talking to someone who keeps jumping about the room.

"What are your names?" He hoped to gain some clue as to their gender.

The first ancient faerie gestured to the others and said, "This is Gwylid, and this ... Gwylain."

"I am Gwylain, not Gwylid."

"And I am Gwylith."

"I suppose that makes me Gwylid."

"Quite so."

"Got it right the first time–"

"and we didn't have to help ... much."

Billy, seeing that this was going nowhere, decided to forget learning names and get back to the purpose of his visit. "What have you found?"

"Found?" the third Witan asked.

"Yes. You keep saying, 'yes, of course.' What do you mean?"

"Yes, of course." The first Witan nodded. "You mean what have we found–"

"with you."

"Yes," Billy said.

The first Witan stepped forward and scratched its chin. "Well, you've been enchanted–"

"by Queen Eleanor–"

"and you are quite short,"

The first two Witan looked at the last, who shrugged.

"What he means–"

"Yes, what he means–"

"What *I* mean, is that you are short, for someone your size."

Billy tilted his head. "For someone my size?"

"Yes," the first Witan said.

"I don't understand," Billy said.

"You should be taller." The third Witan waved its hand over Billy's head.

"But ... I'm ... not."

"Precisely," the second Witan said.

Billy tried to keep the Witan primed. "Why not?"

"Queen Eleanor."

"Her enchantment."

"Probably there to hide you."

"Hide me?"

"Yes–"

"from your enemies–"

"both here and in the land of men."

Billy felt excited by the prospect of being a "normal" height. "So, I'm really much taller than this?"

"Much?"

"Much."

"Maybe."

"How much taller?" Billy asked.

"We don't know," the Witan answered in unison.

"But there's more," the first added.

Billy looked at the first. "More?"

"Yes," the second answered.

The third Witan came forward and tweaked Billy's ear. "Eleanor's enchantment does more than just hide you."

"More?"

"Yes. Eleanor left more than a disguise upon you."

"Oh yes."

"Very powerful."

"Very powerful."

"Very powerful."

Billy looked at the three creatures, whose appearance and manner were less alien and threatening with each passing minute. They seemed worried about something.

"Can you remove the enchantment?" Billy asked.

The first Witan turned to the others. "Can we remove the enchantment?"

"Yes, can we?"

"Dare we?"

After a brief pause, the first turned back to Billy. "Why?"

"Why not?" Billy asked.

The third Witan smiled. "You ask good questions."

"Thank you," Billy said. "Well?"

"Well, what?"

"Can you remove the enchantment or not?"

"Oh yes–"

"the enchantment."

"Very powerful."

The Witan folded their hands. Finally, the third said, "We don't know."

Billy waited for more, but his hosts weren't volunteering anything. "You don't know?"

"Very difficult."

"Could be dangerous."

"Could be fun!"

Once again, the first two faeries glared at the last and grunted their disapproval.

The third leaned towards Billy. "Those two never admit when things are fun."

"How would it be fun?" Billy asked.

"Because, if we succeed, it is the beginning of a big journey."

"For me?"

"Yes."

The first two Witan stood with their backs together and their arms crossed. They tapped their feet and stared at their colleague.

"What?" The third Witan shrugged. "He asked!"

"Is there something I should know?" Billy said.

"You don't need to know any of that!"

"No, no, no–"

"but you must know–"

"it will be dangerous–"

"if we remove the enchantment."

Billy looked at his hosts and asked, "How dangerous?"

"Very."

"Very, very."

"Very, very, very ... but fun!"

Billy stared at the first two Witan. "Please, explain."

"If you survive–"

"it will be a most memorable experience."

"*If* I survive?" Billy said.

"Yes."

"Not removing the spell–"

"but what will follow."

Billy was almost too afraid to ask, but he had to. "And what is that?"

"We cannot say," all three Witan said.

"What we mean is–"

"you will have to find that out–"

"for yourself."

"It is your destiny–"

"your path–"

"your journey."

"Your task–"

"your mission–"

"your adventure."

"And what if you don't remove the enchantment?" Billy asked.

The Witan looked at one another, then back to Billy, and shrugged.

At that moment, the jagged, narrow door flew open and sunlight blasted in. The light struck a crystal dangling in one of the niches, spraying flecks of light around the chamber like sparks from a blacksmith's anvil. The room's occupants were still blind from the flash when several silhouettes charged into the doorway.

Billy squinted at the door and saw one of the short dark figures raise its hand. He detected the glint of metal just as the creature threw something at him. He ducked down and the object sliced by him with a choppy whirling sound. He looked up from the smooth wooden floor and saw a crude steel axe embedded in the wall where he had stood.

Billy returned his attention to the door. Three armored hobgoblins wielding axes and long curved knives stepped into the room, grinning at

Billy and clicking their teeth. The Witan had vanished, leaving Billy alone.

One of the gloating hobgoblins cast about the room with his large black eyes. "They have run away, as she said they would." He laughed until slobber ran from his toothy maw.

The would-be killers ambled towards Billy, shifting their weapons in their hands. He glanced around the room for some means to protect himself. The only thing in reach was the axe over his head.

Billy jumped to his feet and grabbed hold of the axe as his attackers stepped forward. He tugged with all his might, but the weapon remained buried in the wood. The hobgoblins closed in. The largest of the ugly brutes raised his axe, intending to split Billy in half. Suddenly, he stiffened and dropped his weapon to the floor behind him. His mouth and dark cow-like eyes opened wide, and then he collapsed in a heap, an arrow jutting from his back.

For a moment, the hollow tree was quiet as Billy and the two remaining hobgoblins stared at the downed assassin. The killers returned their gaze to Billy. He could see the wheels turning behind their eyes. The stillness grew heavy as they sized up their situation.

In the blink of an eye, both hobgoblins acted. They drew back their weapons and charged. Billy heard a hissing sound, and before they had taken two steps, the remaining assassins were struck down from behind.

Still in shock, he stared at the three bodies at his feet. Each lay with a single arrow protruding from its back. The arrow shafts and fletching were bright leaf-green, but Billy couldn't tear his eyes from the near-black blood that oozed from the wounds.

Once again, shadows blocked the light from the doorway. Billy looked up to see Onian and a second male elf step through the door. The proud, thin elves stared at Billy and bowed.

"We tracked these three from Malkry's camp," Onian said in his crisp manner.

"We knew they were up to no good."

Onian noticed Billy's preoccupation with the corpses. "Are you feeling ill?"

"Oh, I'm fine. Thank you." Billy forced his gaze back to the elf. "And thank you for saving my life."

"The Witan has not yet told us who you are," Onian said. "But I think Malkry put these worthless scum up to this."

Onian's companion kicked one of the hobgoblins and knelt to remove his arrow. He looked back at Onian and said, "These warts haven't enough brain amongst all of them to come up with this on their own."

"Aye, Shaldra. And if that dark-hearted wench is behind this ..." Onian turned to Billy and grinned. "Then she must be afraid of you."

"Me?"

Shaldra nodded. "Aye. It's the only thing that makes sense. If you were not a threat, then she would not have tried to have you killed."

Onian poked one of the hobgoblins with his bow. "Malkry knows something she's not sharing with the rest of us. That's enough for me to crash her little party."

Shaldra examined the sticky black point of his arrow and asked, "But why use these useless toads? One of her warriors would have a much better chance."

"Ah! But using one of her own would lead straight back to her. Besides, she didn't exactly count on us showing up."

"Precisely." One of the Witan appeared from a dark corner.

"Gwylith!" Onian turned and knelt.

"Onian, I see all that jumping about in the forest with Shaldra has not weakened your grasp on strategy."

Onian replied while still kneeling, "Thanks to my teacher, Gwylith."

At that moment, the other two Witan materialized from dark cracks in the wall. They circled the dead hobgoblins and one of them approached Billy.

"The fun has already begun, and we haven't even removed the enchantment from you."

Onian shot a glance at the faerie. "What enchantment, Gwylid?"

"Eleanor's enchantment."

"Queen Eleanor?" the elves said in unison.

"The very same."

Shaldra and Onian eyed Billy with suspicion. He felt very uncomfortable under their stare and backed into the shadows.

"Is it the ring?" Onian asked.

"It *is*–"

"Eleanor's–"

"ring."

"No. Is the spell coming from the ring?"

"No."

"Definitely not."

"Not a chance."

"But while he wears the ring–"

"we cannot remove it."

"The spell, that is."

Billy examined the ring on his finger. Its simple design was just as beautiful as the first time he'd laid eyes on it. It was the only thing left of his mother. The only tie he had with her. He didn't want to take it off. What's more, he had made an oath to the spirit of his mother that he would never remove it.

Billy returned to the light. "I can't take it off."

"Can't–"

"won't–"

"or shouldn't?"

"I made a promise," Billy said.

"What's so important about this enchantment, anyway?" Shaldra asked.

"Aye," Onian said. "And why remove it?"

"It's a disguise. It's made me shorter than I really am."

"And more–"

"much more–"

"much, much more."

Onian leaned forward on his bow. "What more?"

"We foresee–"

"that he shall never be king–"

"while the enchantment is in place."

"Tirn Aill needs a ruler!" Onian said.

"Aye." Shaldra nodded. "Without a king, we are doomed."

Onian looked hard at the Witan and asked, "Is he Eleanor's son?"

"He wears the ring," Gwylid said.

"What is that supposed to mean?"

"The ring knows," Gwylain said.

"Knows what?" Shaldra asked.

"The ring chooses," Gwylith said.

Onian rubbed the tip of his ear. "What does that mean?"

"If you had paid attention to your magical studies ..." Gwylith wagged his finger.

"Yes, yes, yes. I know! It's yesterday's sun." Onian gave a heavy sigh. "Please, just tell me what you mean."

"Yes," Gwylith said.

Onian waited for more, but once again, the Witan were not very forthcoming with information. "Yes, what?" the frustrated elf warrior asked.

"Yes–"

"he is–"

"Eleanor's son. You really should pay more attention."

Onian scanned Billy and shrugged off the Witan's scolding. His keen emerald eyes took in every detail as he asked, "If you remove the spell, the boy will become our king. Is that right?"

"Only time will reveal whether 'tis so–"

"but he cannot rule Tirn Aill–"

"while Eleanor's enchantment is bound to him–"

"and he to it."

"If this boy is our king," Shaldra said, "then you *must* remove the spell!"

"That is for him to decide–"

"not the Witan–"

"not you."

Shaldra and Onian stared at Billy.

"What?" Billy looked from one to the other. "You want me to let them remove the spell? The enchantment my mother put upon me for protection? The spell that has kept me alive for all these years, and may have very well just saved my life not five minutes ago?"

"Yes."

"Are you crazy? That spell has been on me since … since forever! And—and—and they told me that I'd be in great danger if they removed it."

"You're in great danger now." Onian kicked a dead hobgoblin.

"But—but—but it would be even more so, right?" Billy turned to the Witan.

"Possibly."

"Probably."

"Undoubtedly."

Onian glared at the Witan. Then he frowned at Billy. "We need you."

"Get someone else."

"Tirn Aill needs you." Shaldra held his gaze.

"There's got to be someone else!"

"There is," Onian said.

Shaldra and the Witan turned to Onian with great interest.

"Who?" Billy asked.

"Malkry."

"Malkry?" Shaldra spat on the floor. "That treacherous wench has no right to the throne!"

"Aye. But unless we put the rightful heir on the throne, she will take it."

"Aye." Shaldra nodded. "And by bloody force too."

"I like having my body in one piece," Billy said, half to himself. "In fact, not having it chopped into little bits is my favorite pastime."

With slow, measured steps, Onian approached Billy. He stopped just inches away and leaned towards him. Just having the imposing elf that close made Billy uneasy.

Onian glared down at Billy and whispered, "If you are truly a son of Eleanor, you will take up this challenge. If not ..." Onian glanced at the dead hobgoblin assassins. "I will not risk lives to protect a coward."

Billy stared at the three bodies and the axe in the wall. *I was lucky this time*, he thought. *I know that. There will probably be more attacks, whether or not Mother's enchantment is removed. It would be nice to have the protection of Onian, but what of the protection of the spell? Hasn't it protected me my whole life? What might happen if it were removed? The Witan keep saying that it's more. What do they mean? I wish they were clearer!*

Onian, seeing that Billy was thinking it over, took a step back to give him some room. Billy looked into his stern eyes and detected a glimmer of hopefulness. He allowed his eyes to stray back to the dead hobgoblins.

That might have been me, he thought, and turned to face the wall. *If not for Onian, I would be dead already. What should I do? I wish Mother were here. She'd know what to do. No. I have to start making my own decisions. If I am to become anything, I must make the decision. No more will I be the victim of my fate. Either I am king or ...*

Billy turned around to face Onian, Shaldra, and the Witan. Sweat coated his palms and his heart pounded. He took a deep breath and said, "Remove the enchantment."

Onian knelt before Billy and bowed his head. Shaldra knelt just behind him.

"I pledge my devotion and loyalty to you, Highness." Onian looked into Billy's eyes. "The elves of the forest are yours to command."

"Command?" Billy grimaced and looked at the Witan. "I don't know anything about giving commands."

"You will–"

"in time."

Onian rose. "Trust the blood that flows in your veins, and the courage that lives in your heart. I will be here should you need any help. Right now, I think we had better do something about your safety."

While Onian and Shaldra discussed what steps to take to protect Billy, the Witan surrounded them and prodded them out the door.

"You can discuss strategies–"

"out there."

"We have a spell to unravel!"

Billy removed his ring and forced a smile. "Let's get this over with."

***

Three days later, Billy emerged from the Witan's hollow, hungry, exhausted, and feeling a strange melancholy loneliness. He had been alone before and felt longing, but this was different. Some part of him was missing, as if the world was somehow closed off to him. Even when he placed his Mother's ring back on his finger, the usual comfort he received did nothing to dispel his mood.

Everywhere Billy looked, the surroundings seemed less vibrant, less alive. The ground was wet from a rain that had started the moment his melancholy descended on him. He looked up at the grey sky and let the cold drops of rain strike his face.

Onian stepped out of a dark crevice in the tree and stood next to Billy. He then spoke to the Witan, through their still open door. "He's no taller."

"Yes–"

"but he will be."

"Give him time."

Billy examined himself. It was true, Eleanor's enchantment was gone, but he was unchanged, physically. "How much time?"

"Who knows?"

"Perhaps you will need to grow like an ordinary boy–"

"or perhaps not."

Billy had hoped to gain something from the removal of the spell, but at present, it seemed like he had only lost. The words of the Witan were disheartening after having his hopes built up for a change. Again, Billy felt the ache of separation from that part of himself which had been severed.

"What have you done to me?" Billy asked the Witan.

"We have started you on your journey," the third said.

"It's all up to you," the second added.

"Your destiny is in your own hands."

"Be you king–"

"or–"

"fool."

"We will be here–"

"when you need us–"

"but now we must rest."

With that said, the Witan closed the door. Billy looked at Onian and sighed. His tired, hungry body was now cold and it showed on his face.

The elf placed his hand on Billy's shoulder. "Come, we must get you to shelter where you can rest."

Suddenly, a flash of lightning blazed and illuminated dozens of elves clustered in the forest. Billy fell back against the huge, hollow tree.

"It's all right, Highness. These are my—your—warriors. Forest elves all, and handpicked by me to watch your back."

Billy came down the root steps and greeted his new bodyguard. Each of the elves bowed, then took up a position around him. Billy felt a little bit crowded.

"Why so many?" Billy asked. "My back isn't that big!"

Onian grinned at Billy's joke, then became very solemn. "All of Faerie is aware of what the Witan found. And this strange storm that gathered while you were in seclusion with them. ... We've never seen a storm like it. Many of them are afraid."

"Afraid? Of what?"

"Of the storm ... of each other ... of you."

"What about Malkry?"

Onian's eyes snapped to Billy at mention of the dark elf. "That one," he said. "That one is the reason for all these bodyguards."

"Why? What's she done?"

"Nothing, *yet.*" Onian frowned. "But she's planning something."

CHAPTER FOUR

When Faith is Lost

Hugh woke with a start. "Billy!" He grabbed his head and thigh in pain. A pair of firm hands stopped him when he attempted to sit up. The room was dim, and the man attending him was seated in shadow.

"Who are you?" Hugh's voice was weak.

"It's me, Malcolm," the man whispered. "You must be quiet."

"Malcolm? I can't see. Are we in Cyndyn Hall?"

"No."

"The battle?"

The highlander sighed. "Lost."

"And Cyndyn Hall?"

Malcolm shook his head. "When you went down, they overwhelmed us. The drawbridge was compromised. It was all over in a matter of minutes. I only escaped because I was knocked into the moat. When it was fully dark, I swam back and found you. The Gwythies were too busy celebratin' and lickin' their wounds to see me, or look for you. I think Lady Myrredith was captured."

"Myrredith," Hugh whispered. "My fault."

"No, laddie." Malcolm shook his head. "You did your best, and that's a damn site better than most ..."

"No! Don't you see? I failed because I am no longer fit!"

"Shh. You must be quiet, or the Gwythies will find us."

"I have done evil to another."

"Evil? I know you, Sir Hugh, and that cannot be."

Hugh furrowed his forehead—his lips twisted as he fought to contain his emotions. A tear escaped from the corner of his eye and ran down his cheek. He hid his face and sobbed. "My soul is on fire. I am damned."

"Damned?"

"I betrayed my friend. Now I must pay." Hugh straightened. "'A life for a life.' My worthless life for his."

"What are you talking about?"

"If not for my sin against him, Billy would not have brought about my defeat."

"Billy? … I saw what happened. That boy was not Billy. Now, please, be still."

"I know," Hugh said. "But Billy was there, in that boy. He reached out from the grave."

"Who? What grave?"

"Billy."

"Billy … is dead?"

"Aye." Hugh shook with sorrow and bitter shame. "And I am as responsible as any who plotted against him. I have dishonored myself."

Malcolm kept silent for a moment while he tried to grasp this news. Billy had been the best student and juggling partner he had ever known. He had come to think of Billy as a son, and now for him to be dead was unthinkable. At last, he asked the only thing his stunned mind knew how to ask. "How did it happen?"

"Billy was killed in a shipwreck."

"You found his body?"

"No."

"Then he might still be alive."

"No." Hugh spoke as if the words were not his own. "The storm was far too great, and I saw him … struck by a mast, just before the ship broke up and went down. I and one other—a crewman—were the only survivors."

"Then you were lucky to survive."

"Lucky?" Hugh raised his eyebrows. "That was the most unfortunate day of my life, until today."

Before Malcolm knew what was happening, Hugh had commandeered the dagger from his hip and raised its blade up with both hands above his own heart. Malcolm's hands flew to the weapon. If not for his honed reflexes, he would not have been able to stop Hugh.

Malcolm struggled with him to gain control of the dagger. Despite his grievous injuries, Hugh showed remarkable strength. The point of the narrow blade descended towards his chest. Malcolm pulled with all his might, but only managed to hold his own.

"No!" Malcolm grunted. "Myrredith. ... Think about Myrredith! You've got to rescue her."

A tiny rivulet of blood ran from the point of the dagger as it pierced Hugh's skin. Malcolm looked into his friend's eyes. In them, he saw no anger or fear, only his own reflection.

Without warning, Hugh's strength gave out. Malcolm jerked away with the dagger and fell back on his rear. Hugh laid on the tiny cot, staring at the ceiling. Malcolm sheathed his weapon and sat down across from him in the dim room. He rested and waited until Hugh fell asleep.

Malcolm got up to find some food and hide his weapons out of Hugh's reach. "She really does need you, my friend," he told the sleeping warrior. "You're the only one in the kingdom who can save her."

CHAPTER FIVE

Condemned

Lady Myrredith paced the length of her narrow cell. She looked through the tall embrasure at every turn. With each hour that passed, her footsteps had grown heavier until they sounded like marching. She tried to sit and calm herself, but within seconds she was back on her feet, pacing with more vigor and venom than before.

Myrredith stopped once more beside the slender window. At the end of her taut arms, both hands balled into crushing fists, pointed towards the floor. Since her husband's death, she had worn mourning colors, which accentuated her long, fiery hair. Because she had no access to maid or mirror, she now wore her hair in a simple, thick braid that fell straight down her back.

As she stared out the window, a tear found its way to her cheek. It waited there, unattended, before falling to the grey stones of the floor. She closed her tired eyes, trying to blot out the image she had seen. For two days, new columns of smoke rose up through the trees as the conquering Gwythian army laid waste to Dyven.

At that moment, the door to Lady Myrredith's cell opened and Prince Hereweald strutted in. He seemed content to look at the lonely, dark figure by the window.

"Don't cry for Dyven, Madam. Their punishment is just, as will be yours."

Lady Myrredith spun around and faced him.

*

Her green eyes bore down on him with such fierceness that he froze. Prince Hereweald was an expert at reading faces and master of his own; skills he had learned from his dispassionate father. Lady Myrredith's ability to affect him so readily caught him by surprise. The prince examined the details of her face and saw that her hateful glare was not just for anger, but an attempt of pride to hide frailty. Her puffy, reddened eyes, the lines of worry on her brow, and the hint of fear on her quivering lips gave her away.

"How long are you going to allow this crime to continue?" She spat her words.

"This 'crime,' as you call it, is nothing of the kind." Hereweald took a step toward her. "It is repayment for their treachery against my brother."

"Treachery?"

"Yes, I know the truth about his murder. The wedding, the talk of peace … all a ploy by you and your king: a cowardly strike at the heart of my family! Well, you'll pay for your foolishness now: every city, every town, every farm in my path!"

"No! It's not like that at all. Can't you see?"

Hereweald stared at his prisoner. She did not have the face of a murderer, and yet the reports said otherwise. He shoved his observations aside. "All I see is the harlot who killed my brother."

He watched while Myrredith forced down her rage. He knew all the reasons she hated him: He brought death to her countrymen, destruction to Dyven, and threatened everything she held dear. He knew, yet felt guiltless.

She clenched her fists at her sides. "Gaelyn was my friend."

Prince Hereweald struck Lady Myrredith with the back of his hand, knocking her to the floor. "You lying witch! Don't ever say his name again. Or so help me, I'll tear out your tongue with my own hands."

Myrredith placed a hand over her bleeding lip and looked up at the prince. Tears welled in her eyes, but she did not allow them to fall. "Please," she whispered. "Stop this now."

Hereweald once again looked into her expression. She was not unlike the women of his homeland. He recognized that she possessed strength and courage, but there was more. She was also very beautiful, much more beautiful than he had thought she would be. The prince blinked and realized that he had stepped toward her. He stepped back, feeling disgraced and betrayed by his thoughts.

"To answer your question: Dyven will be punished one day for each year of my brother's life."

"No."

"Your country will burn, as long as my blood burns for revenge."

"Please. I beg of you ..."

"Do not beg to me, harlot." Hereweald took another step away. "You should be beggin' for your god's forgiveness, for in twenty-eight days, on the first morning of Dyven's new life, you shall be taken to the market square where your head will be struck from your body."

Prince Hereweald turned and left the room, slamming the door behind him.

*

A moment later, Myrredith heard the bolt slide into place. This sound had a certain finality to it that eroded her strength.

"Prince Hereweald!" she cried. "Prince Hereweald! Your Highness!"

Again, the door opened. Prince Hereweald stood in the doorway with arms crossed. His eyes still smoldered.

"What is it?"

"Your Highness." Myrredith dropped her gaze. "I ..." She wanted to plead for her life, but hesitated. She looked into the eyes of her enemy.

The stone-like orbs mocked her. "I ..." Just then, she remembered all the other lives at stake and threw down her weakness and fear. If she just rolled over, if she allowed them to kill her, then she couldn't stop Hereweald. She didn't give herself much of a chance, but she wasn't going down without a fight.

Lady Myrredith straightened her shoulders and said, "I have not bathed in two days, or had a change of clothes. This room is cold and the bed uncomfortable—"

"So?"

Myrredith lowered her eyes again. It appeared that she was being submissive, but in truth, she was girding up her strength.

Lady Myrredith renewed her subtle attack. "I would ask Your Highness to allow me to return to my own room. Your Highness could keep me prisoner there just as easily as here ..."

Prince Hereweald listened to her words. Each time she addressed him as "Your Highness," his brow furrowed. She'd said it with the proper regard due a person of his station but still managed to sound superior. With each repetition, the prince's title took on the qualities of an insult.

"Therefore, Your Highness." Lady Myrredith ignored his deepening scowl.

"No." The prince shifted his weight to the other foot.

She finished her thought, as though he hadn't spoken. "I would be most grateful—"

"No!" Hereweald flexed the muscles in his jaw.

Myrredith bowed her head in a way that could seem condescending to Hereweald, and he left again, this time not only slamming the door but also stomping his feet as he marched down the corridor.

Lady Myrredith listened to Hereweald's heavy footfalls until he was out of earshot. A faint smile crossed her lips. If nothing else, she could upset this arrogant prince. It wasn't much, but it might be enough to keep him unbalanced. It might even save her life or spare Dyven. Myrredith's smile faded as the window drew her attention. *If I were a man*, she thought. *I'd do more than upset him.*

***

For the remainder of the day, agitation plagued Hereweald, Second Prince of Gwythia. He was quick to rebuke each soldier, servant, or advisor who approached him. Quite unusual behavior, in light of his recent victories. At last, it rose to the attention of his newly-arrived advisor, Lord Snegaddrick, who found the prince in his quarters.

"Your Highness—"

"What is it, Snegaddrick?" Hereweald snapped.

"If it pleases, Your Highness ..." The former ambassador threw about extraneous gestures. "... would you address me as 'Lord' Snegaddrick? I do so like the sound of it, having only recently acquired the title."

Prince Hereweald shot the impudent little man a dark look. He took in the man's chubby face and bloated body and chortled. "*Lord* Snegaddrick," he said with a grin. "You are the only man here with enough cunning and *gall* to talk to me that way. My father was right to send you."

"Are you sure my years as ambassador to Lyonesse didn't have something to do with that, Your Highness?"

"Perhaps, but I believe it was your ... character, that landed you in that role as well."

"Quite so, quite so," the newly ennobled lord said. "After all, a man's character does more for his duty than all his former titles."

"I had no idea you were a philosopher."

"Oh yes indeed, Your Highness."

"But I doubt it's philosophy you have come to discuss."

"In a manner of speaking, it is, Your Highness."

"Oh?"

"Well, my prince." Snegaddrick hesitated. "It has been brought to my attention that you have been quite ... short today."

"Short?" Prince Hereweald scowled. "To whom?"

"Well, to everyone, Your Highness."

"Oh." Hereweald grudgingly accepted this judgment.

His advisor seized the opportunity to continue. "And, as your advisor, it is my duty to know what it is that is troubling you so that I might better advise you."

"I see."

"If you don't wish to talk to me about it ..." Snegaddrick sounded apologetic.

"No. It's quite all right."

Lord Snegaddrick clasped his hands together and moved to the prince's left side. He sat next to his chair and waited there for Hereweald to begin.

Though it was the customary position for an advisor, Hereweald felt uncomfortable with Snegaddrick by his side. This was his first campaign with full command, and having advisors of this nature was something new to him, but there was something more. Something about the cheery, gluttonous man bothered him. Rather than controlling his instincts, Hereweald allowed them to propel him across from the little man. He wanted to see his fat, round face and know what he was thinking.

Snegaddrick got up to follow his prince, but Hereweald's pale eyes rebuffed him. He resettled himself across from Hereweald, and once again clasped his hands together.

"What is it that's troubling Your Highness? I hope I have done nothing to offend."

"No, no." The prince noticed his new advisor's hurt expression. "Sometimes I think better on my feet."

Hereweald wondered about this man before him. How could this soft, emotional, easily slighted creature get so far with no birthright whatsoever? *He must possess a great wealth of cunning for my father to send him. Perhaps all these weaknesses are affectations to deceive.*

Hereweald took a deep breath and released it. "What's troubling me ..." He pointed towards Lady Myrredith's cell. "Is that woman!" He stopped himself when he realized that his voice had already risen higher than he had intended. Just the mere allusion to her made his blood boil.

"Woman?"

Hereweald sighed. "Lady Myrredith."

The prince was almost too busy controlling himself to notice a change in his advisor's expression, but it still pulled his attention. Snegaddrick's eyes had shifted and narrowed in response to the woman's name but quickly returned to the prince.

"I don't see why she should bother Your Highness. She is guilty of your brother's murder. When she is executed, she will trouble you no more."

"You say that with such certainty."

"I have found that dead enemies are soon forgotten, Highness."

"No. You seem so certain that she is responsible."

Lord Snegaddrick scanned Hereweald's face and said, "As were you, my prince."

"After hearing your report, aye. But now I am not so sure."

"Don't let her bewitch you, Your Highness." Snegaddrick sat up straighter. "She is no less guilty of Gaelyn's murder than the cursed elf that wielded the knife!"

"Yes, yes, so you've said."

"Believe me, Your Highness ..." Snegaddrick leaned forward. "The sooner that witch is dead, the sooner your brother will rest easy."

"Won't her people rise against us if we kill her? She is a noble, and quite popular."

"Not when they are told she is the reason for this war. The reason for their suffering."

"Is she?"

"Is she what?"

"Is she really the reason for this war?"

*

Snegaddrick started to answer with a pat affirmative, but then saw that Hereweald was after something more. The ex-ambassador recognized that Prince Hereweald, like his father the king, had a keen intellect and keeping something from him would be a challenge. Not wanting to give up too much at once he asked, "What are you getting at, my prince?"

"It's probably nothing." Hereweald crossed to the window.

The prince's advisor was relieved that his young master hesitated, this once, to follow his instincts. The line of questioning he had started could lead a young man, even a prince, to falter in his duty.

"I understand completely. It is only natural that you should be *unsure*. This is your first command of such a campaign, and your brother's murder must weigh heavily on your heart." He wanted to bring the conversation back to where he was comfortable—to a place he could manipulate the prince, and correct any misgivings he might have about the enemy. He stood and walked to just a pace behind Hereweald. "You and your brother were quite close, weren't you?"

"Yes." Hereweald's focus was far away. "We are—were—less than two years apart."

"And now they've taken him from you." Snegaddrick placed a hand on the prince's shoulder.

Hereweald spun around to face his advisor. His eyes were cold and dark as the sea that hungrily drowns sailors. Snegaddrick swallowed hard.

The new lord realized that he had made a mistake. He had meant to reinforce Hereweald's anger with Lady Myrredith and Lyonesse, not to bring it on himself. *You fool,* he thought. *You moved too soon. Let your new title go to your head, didn't you? He doesn't quite trust you yet.*

"Leave me!" Prince Hereweald bit off each word. "I wish to be alone!"

"Yes, of course, Your Highness." Snegaddrick gave a deep bow.

*

As the cowed advisor bowed and scraped his way to the door, Hereweald turned back to the window and scanned the lush countryside. The blue shadows of evening were merging into night. "We've been at war with Lyonesse for so long, and peace was in our grasp! Why would they … ?"

Snegaddrick hesitated at the door. Finally, he chanced to answer. "Arrogance, jealousy, vengeance ... The list is long, my prince. I think it is simply because they hate us so much."

"So much," Hereweald mumbled, staring at the soft glow from Dyven's fires. "I wish to be alone."

"By your leave." Snegaddrick gave a final bow.

Alone, Prince Hereweald stewed over the situation late into the night. As he stirred the fire, something he liked to do himself, he glanced around his new quarters. A pleasant, albeit feminine suite of rooms. Not surprising, since they *had* belonged to the Lady of Cyndyn Hall.

The Cyndyn family crest, carved boldly in reddish stone, presided over the hearth. On the adjoining wall, there hung a large tapestry in vibrant hues, depicting wild animals in peaceful coexistence with men. A rose-floral cloth draped the large canopy bed—something that Hereweald had never seen before. Its down mattress felt uncommonly soft and warm. In fact, it was too soft for Hereweald, who was accustomed to a barracks cot or the ground. The remaining furniture, all of dark wood, was also quite comfortable except for a tall chair that sat behind a rather imposing walnut desk in the entry room. Near the large double window, next to the large wardrobe and wash basin, stood an extraordinary mirror, which allowed the prince to see his entire person at a glance; a treasure unto itself.

Prince Hereweald found himself standing in front of that mirror. For an instant, he panicked, not recognizing the face staring back at him. It was the same every time. He thought it peculiar that no matter how many times he saw his reflection, his own countenance was, at first, strange. It was as if he expected to find a different face. But as soon as he saw his own constant features, whatever image he had in his head evaporated. The thought made him feel uncomfortable and he wondered if others might have the same odd experience.

Hereweald focused on his body. He had a well-favored physique—tall and trim like his brothers, only more muscular. He attributed this to his extensive martial training. His older brother, Brendyn, had been groomed for the throne all his life while he himself had been schooled and practiced in the ways of war. Little Gaelyn, expected to be married off to some foreign hussy, as he was, had been offered only scraps of both disciplines.

The thought of Gaelyn brought Hereweald back to his campaign. Seeded deep in his heart was a hatred of all that was Lyonesse. As a boy, he was taught they were the enemy, and as a man—a warrior—he had grown to know what that meant. But now, it was more than the lessons he had learned from history or on the battlefield; it was personal. The murder of his brother had riven the chain that held his primitive instincts at bay, and catapulted him beyond the narrow, carefully constructed walls of civilization. He burned for revenge. He wanted to see the whole of Lyonesse put to the torch and its inhabitants trampled into the ground.

Once again, the prince's image in the mirror distracted his ranting mind. The regal clothing on his person seemed out of place for the man who, only days before, had butchered countless soldiers and citizens in the streets of Dyven. On that horrible day, his hands were not his own. His mind was not his own. His heart was not his own. He wished that his eyes had not been his own, for the sights that they witnessed were abhorrent to him now. He could scarcely believe what he now knew he was capable of, what he was still capable of doing. The reflection stared back at him with calm, civilized, princely poise. The monster within was not visible. *I am truly two people: a beast and a man. But which one is stronger? Which one will rule?*

Hereweald felt a slight chill and stepped away from the window. As he stretched out on the comfortable furs before the fire, he was reminded of whose room this had been, and how cold and barren her current accommodations were. Part of him relished the thought of her shivering in the dark, dank cell. He allowed himself to smile, but then another part of him asserted itself. It was the part that remembered the tears held back in the eyes of a woman too proud to cry, the part that recognized a woman with strength and courage...

"As fiery as her lovely hair," he mused.

***

"Your Ladyship," a kind voice said.

A gentle hand rested upon Myrredith's shoulder. She turned and looked behind, groggily. The room was dark, but she could make out the silhouette of Eadwig, her elderly Chamberlain.

"I'm sorry to wake you, milady," he offered.

"Oh, Eadwig." Myrredith sighed. "I had the worst dream …"

At that moment, Eadwig raised the hood on his lantern and his gaunt face resolved into the new light. His forehead flaunted a dark bruise, the result of a bashing he'd received from Gwythie soldiers for protecting his mistress. His ancient, loyal eyes stared at her apologetically, and the twinkle she had known since childhood was gone. Myrredith thought he was going to cry.

"It's all right, Eadwig." She placed a hand on his shoulder.

Eadwig took her hand, in his fatherly manner. "You must come with me, milady."

Lady Myrredith looked over his shoulder, and in the dim yellow light saw three Gwythian soldiers waiting at the door. "Where are we going?"

"You have new quarters, milady."

"Oh?"

The old chamberlain continued. "They brought me out to prepare the room."

Lady Myrredith sat on the edge of the bed. "Where are they keeping you?" She kept her voice low.

"We're all in the stables, milady."

"Push off!" one of the guards said. "That's enough claik! Get a move on."

Lady Myrredith and Eadwig shuffled to the door and fell in behind the leading guard. Her ladyship became despondent when she saw the condition of her ancestral home. Much of it was now barracks and hospital space for the dirty, uncouth occupiers. All the symbols of Lyonesse and her family, proudly displayed for generations, had been torn down, broken off, or burned from the walls. Standards and banners, bearing the predatory eagle of Gwythia, rose in their stead. The air reeked of sweat and smoke, and a hint of urine. Myrredith could not help but weep at the blatant disrespect for her home and family.

Even if this is war, she thought, *certain things should be sacred.*

Eadwig noticed her tears and placed a supportive hand under her arm. "Do not worry, milady, these brigands will be gone soon."

"Shut up, old man." The guard shoved him from behind. "Or do you want another clout?"

Lady Myrredith spun and faced the man. "Coward."

Without hesitation, the guard slapped Myrredith across the face. The force of it knocked her back, but she did not cry. Instead, she tossed the hair from her face and stared at her assailant.

"Coward."

The guard's face puffed up. He drew back his arm and backhanded Lady Myrredith, this time sending her to the hard stone steps beneath them.

"Lyonesse cow!"

Suddenly, the ruffian straightened and pulled off his belt. Eadwig gasped as the man hauled his arm back to strike his mistress. Without thought for his safety, Lady Myrredith's oldest retainer stepped in the way of the whipping belt. Eadwig winced after the stinging blow, but kept his body between the brute and his mistress.

The two other Gwythian soldiers evidently intended to do nothing. The older of the two wore a satisfied smile that, due to a long, jagged scar, stretched up to his left eye. The third guard was little more than a boy, who stood with his back against the wall, his wide eyes windows to confusion.

Still stunned, Lady Myrredith blinked and saw Eadwig leaning over her. She attempted to rise, but instead of helping her, his gentle hands held her fast. Then there was a loud crack accompanied by a forceful grunt as the guard lay into his back once more. The sound brought her back to her senses and she screamed out for help.

Again and again, the villain whipped the old man's body, in mindless frenzied repetition, while the others stood by. Lady Myrredith tried to protect Eadwig but only received a welt on the arm for her efforts. Her cries for help echoed through the castle unanswered.

"Aneuch!" a voice shouted from the top of the stairs.

All three guards stopped what they were doing and looked up. They snapped to attention. Lady Myrredith and Eadwig held their awkward position, too frightened to move. The only sound in the broad stairwell was that of someone slowly padding down the steps, one step at a time.

The footsteps came to a stop in front of them. Then silence again. Lady Myrredith and Eadwig dared a quick look. Prince Hereweald stood in front of his men.

Without warning, the prince slapped the faces of the two spectator-guards. The sound of his hand on their cheeks reverberated in the stairwell. Then he approached the guard who had beaten his prisoner and her servant.

"Forgive me, my prince, but—but this Lyonesse cow insulted us … and you … an-an-and Gwythia!"

Prince Hereweald's face was blank. Not a shred of hatred or anger or any other emotion was present. Even his hands and body seemed quite relaxed.

Like a stroke of lightning, the prince struck. His hands and feet moved together to throw the guard down the stairs in one movement. Hereweald flew down the stairs and kicked the man before he could stop his tumble. His target sailed down the stairwell out of sight, and the prince followed him.

Lady Myrredith listened as her captor beat his own man down the steps. For a moment, the sounds brought her a small amount of gratification, but each additional blow caused her to cringe and wish it would end. A moment later, it did.

Once again, the slow, plodding footsteps of the prince came towards them. When Hereweald turned the corner, Myrredith was surprised to see his face in its usual placid condition.

"My apologies, Lady Myrredith." The prince helped Myrredith to her feet. "I assure you, that man's actions were not my intention." Hereweald's eyes shifted to the two remaining guards. "And their like will not be tolerated again."

Much to Myrredith's surprise, the Second Prince of Gwythia bent down to help her elderly chamberlain to his feet. It seemed incongruous that this pompous, violent foreigner would do such a thing. For a brief moment, the enemy was gone and she saw in him Prince Gaelyn's likeness.

Hereweald steadied Eadwig. "There now. Can you continue to her ladyship's quarters?"

"Yes. My thanks to Your Highness."

Prince Hereweald led the way up the stairs, followed by Lady Myrredith and Eadwig, who supported each other. The two guards took up the rear. Myrredith had grown up in Cyndyn Hall. She knew every turn and twist, every room and hallway, and to the best of her knowledge every secret passage, but on this night she was surprised when she found herself in Cyndyn Hall's master bedchamber.

Hereweald gestured to the room. "Your new quarters."

Although Eadwig was shaky, he went about his duty without pause, examining the room and taking note of any needs. Unlike elsewhere in Cyndyn Hall, this room was undamaged. The heat from the fire and her family crest, which survived unblemished above it, gave Lady Myrredith comfort. She turned to thank Prince Hereweald, but then his cold, dispassionate eyes met hers, and she knew him for what he was. She remembered what he had done to her home, her people, and the man she had loved. Nothing the prince did could erase that.

All of a sudden, Eadwig collapsed to the floor. Lady Myrredith rushed over to him, followed closely by the prince.

"Eadwig?" Myrredith cradled the old man's head in her lap. "Eadwig? What's wrong?"

Eadwig's eyes fluttered open and stared at his mistress. The prince came near, and he sat up. He closed his eyes and rubbed his forehead.

"Forgive me, milady. I appear to have passed out."

"Quite understandable."

Eadwig made motions to rise, but Lady Myrredith held him down.

"I must see to your room, milady."

"No, Eadwig, the room is fine. You need to rest right here." She took a large pillow and placed it under his head. "That's not a request."

Lady Myrredith got up and motioned for Hereweald to follow her to the door. He hesitated, eyeing Eadwig as he lay before the hearth. The prince offered to get Eadwig a doctor, but Myrredith insisted on tending him alone and showed Hereweald the door. He raised his finger, but then gave in to her will. He took a last glance over her shoulder at the chamberlain, and then bowed and departed with his guards.

Myrredith closed the door behind the prince and returned to Eadwig's side with a washbasin and a towel. As she applied the cool, damp cloth to his forehead, Eadwig's left eye popped open and glanced about.

"Is he gone?" Eadwig whispered.

"Yes."

"Good."

Eadwig rolled to his feet. Before Lady Myrredith realized what was happening, her old retainer pulled her to her feet and ushered her to the wall nearest the fireplace.

"Eadwig!"

"No time to talk, milady." Eadwig placed a hand on a small stone sconce, which was part of the hearth. "You've got to get out of here."

Eadwig tugged on the sconce, pulling it out a few inches. Then he gave the stone a quick twist. A soft thump sounded, followed by a low grinding sound, and the corner of the hearth moved to reveal a small doorway.

"Go, milady." Eadwig thrust a candle into her hand.

Myrredith started into the opening, then stopped. "You're not coming with me?"

"No, milady." Eadwig shook his head. "I will make good your escape."

"But—"

"No." His frown melted into a smile, and she saw again the familiar twinkle in his eyes. "Don't worry, daughter of my heart," he said. "I know more ways out of here than they know in."

Myrredith looked at the man who was so much to her: friend, surrogate-father, teacher, caretaker, and conscience. She placed her hand on his and squeezed. "Thank you. You will leave as soon as …"

Before Lady Myrredith could finish her thought, the door opened. Both she and Eadwig looked up to see the prince striding into the room.

"Forgive me, Lady Myrredith, I—" Hereweald stopped cold, his eyes widening uncharacteristically, and his head tilting as he spotted his prisoner halfway into the secret passage.

All three stared at each other for a moment before Eadwig pushed Lady Myrredith through the opening.

"Guards!" Hereweald shouted. "Guards!"

Eadwig pushed on the hearth to close the opening. The secret passage had diminished to a crack when the blade of a dagger thrust into it. Eadwig spun to jam the sconce and met Prince Hereweald's fist head on.

Lady Myrredith struggled to move down the narrow steps of the passageway. She knew this "secret way" well, but her candle had been blown out when Eadwig forced her through the door, and in the darkness it was rough going. The steps were more uneven and the corners further apart than she remembered. Myrredith now wished that she had practiced descending this escape route in the dark. She stumbled past one turn, then another.

Just then, a low grinding reverberated through the passage. Myrredith held onto the wall and listened. Heavy footsteps and voices from behind told her that Eadwig had been unsuccessful in stopping her pursuers. She hoped the kindly old retainer had not been injured again, but did not allow herself to dwell on the unhappy thought. Eadwig had risked much to help her, and she wasn't about to let his sacrifice be in vain. She hurried down the passage as swiftly as the gloom would allow her.

The sounds of her pursuers grew nearer and Myrredith looked over her shoulder. The dim yellow glow of a lantern leapt across the far wall of the previous corner. With one hand on the wall and the other extended before her, Lady Myrredith raced into the darkness.

Without warning, the wall that had guided her down the passage disappeared from under her touch. Lady Myrredith tried to stop, but it was too late. She smacked into the opposite wall. Dazed, she rebounded down the corridor, trying to regain her balance. Her feet were unable to find the proper footing on the narrow steps and again, she banged into a wall. Her foot caught sideways on a step and she tumbled down the corridor.

The next thing Myrredith knew, two men yanked her to her feet. The back of her head pounded like an angry war drum. She wanted to rub the ache away, but her captors held her arms tight to her sides. Myrredith blinked her eyes to clear her vision, and in the amber lantern light, she saw the fuzzy image of Prince Hereweald strutting down the thin passage to her. She focused on the large red eagle on his chest, which appeared to soar toward her.

The prince lifted her chin gently, to look into her eyes. Lady Myrredith frowned as the pain became sharper.

"Are you well, Lady Myrredith?"

"Yes," she answered. "I think so."

The prince struck Myrredith across the face. The sting of his hand snapped her out of her daze, but any anger in her drained before a sudden wave of nausea.

"You made a fool of me! I showed you courtesy and generosity, and this is the thanks I get?"

Myrredith's legs shook, her head spun, and her wrathful stomach knotted like a fist.

"I should have you executed now. I should have you drawn and ..."

Myrredith vomited. The two guards dropped her, but not soon enough to protect their master's clothing. Myrredith fell to the stones, holding her stomach. She remained there until there was nothing left in her gut to eject.

"Pick her up, you fools!" Hereweald bellowed.

The prince's men dragged Lady Myrredith up the steps of the secret passage, back to her chambers, and dropped her on the floor before the fire. Eadwig still lay facedown near the hearth, surrounded by several Gwythian soldiers who waited for their commander.

"You." Prince Hereweald pointed at a pair of his men. "Pick up the old man and take him out with the others. And you—" He pointed to four others. "—I want you in that passageway. You will stand guard, here at the top, while you two search for the other end. When you find it, report to the sergeant and show it to him. I want guards at either end at all times. Standard watches."

The soldiers jumped to their ordered tasks. Myrredith, though still nauseous, watched in amazement. She had always been told that Gwythies were uncivilized, undisciplined barbarians, but now she realized this was propaganda. While they might be uncivilized, their soldiering was far from undisciplined.

When the room had emptied of soldiers and the secret passage closed once again, the prince turned to Lady Myrredith. He stood over her with his arms crossed. The fire's reflection flickered in his lithic, unblinking eyes. Then, without a word, he left.

Lady Myrredith crawled to her bed and dragged herself onto it. Though her body hurt from stem to stern, there was no ache like the empty pain in her heart. Her people were suffering, and she felt guilty. She, like her father and his father before him, had sworn to protect the good people of Lyonesse. And her beloved Hugh had given his life for them. This sacred duty was more than an oath or an obligation to her. It was at the core of her soul. It was all she had left. By failing to make good on her only chance for escape, she felt she had failed her people, her father, and her love.

Love? Yes, love. Despite all that had passed between them, she could finally admit that she loved Hugh.

Myrredith glanced around her room. It had been a refuge since her childhood when it had been her father's, but it seemed desolate now that it was her prison. *Oh, Hugh, how I need you. How can you be gone? Perhaps if our last words had not been in anger ... I'm sorry, my love.*

Unbidden, a tear slipped onto her cheek. It traced a thin line that smiles had created and fell to her pillow. The loss of Hugh and her fears for the future overwhelmed her. Myrredith turned her face into her pillow and, for the first time in many years, cried herself to sleep.

CHAPTER SIX

The First Leaf of Autumn

His days with the Witan left Billy spent. The elves of the forest took him in, but for the first few days, the only hospitality he was up to sampling was a forest bed under the stars and a few simple but tasty meals.

In the days that followed, Billy spent most of the waking time with Onian and his children, discovering the secrets of the forest and *tree-listening*—a faerie ability Onian awakened in Billy. With it, he learned quite a bit from the trees, about wind, water, elves, and time.

"What about Quercus?" Billy asked.

Onian grinned. "It's better just to speak with the oak-men."

"How is it that he can speak?"

"How is it that I can speak? Or you?"

The elf children laughed; a sound that reminded Billy of anxious sheep bells.

Billy smiled. "I don't understand."

"Quercus is our kin, as is the willow and the elder, the hazel and thorn, to name a few."

The trees *talked*, and Billy listened. They taught him that all trees had an innate desire to live and to nurture life, to provide home and shelter, and even food. The oldest had the strongest desire and the longest memory.

"In the lands of men," a humble hazel whispered, *"the old ones still remember a time when faeries frolicked under the sun, in their roots and branches. They loved the faeries like children, and the trees' lament at their loss can be heard on the wind; as far away as Tirn Aill."*

On another occasion, a kindly elder tree asked, *"Be you fate-born, child?"*

"I don't know what that is."

"It's rare, but some elf mothers see the fate of their child at the moment of birth. Rarer still when they tell anyone. These children are the fate-born."

"And their mothers *tell* them?"

'When the time is right, in accordance with elf wisdom."

"So, they know the day they will die?"

"Not the day, but the circumstances. In truth, all are fated for a certain end, but the fate-born carry the burden of knowing what it is."

"Why did you ask if I was fate-born, mother elder? I'm not an elf."

The tree seemed to smile. *"You listen like an elf. I asked, dear child, because I sense a force drawing you like a great wind. So it is with many of the fate-born."*

In sleep, Billy dreamt he visited Lyonesse and strolled along the familiar pathways of his homeland with old friends. He came to a wide meadow, hosting a merry picnic. The celebrants at this feast had all been close to Billy, and all had passed on.

Of the dead, he saw John, the only father he had known. Then Duncan – his first juggling teacher – entertained them while they sat with Princess Kathryn and Prince Gaelyn. But the most interesting guest of all was Queen Eleanor.

Billy took her hand, and they walked until they came to a garden with an extensive hedge-maze. Mother and son entered the labyrinth and traveled its narrow high-walled passages. At last, they came to an opening that was a garden unto itself. Billy recognized this garden as the "Queen's Garden" in Castle Orgulous, and suddenly they were boxed in by the tall white walls of that glorious fortress.

Eleanor stood by Billy's side and pointed at the far end of the garden. They walked around the reflection pool and approached the site of

Eleanor's grave. Billy examined the simple, black stone enveloped by a thorn tree. He looked to his side, but his mother was gone. Then, to his amazement, the thorns swallowed up the gravestone.

Billy reached out to push away the obtrusive plants but stopped short when he heard someone calling his name. He turned around to see who had called him. There was no one and nothing behind him but a barren plain. Dark clouds raced across a red sky and again, the voice called to him.

"Help me, William," it wailed on the wind.

Billy turned once again and found that the plain surrounded him. His mother's gravestone had been replaced by another. It was the only object visible for miles. The smooth granite stone had a name carved upon it: Lady Myrredith of Cyndyn.

"William." This time, the voice seemed much closer.

Lightning danced across the sky, like blood pulsing in the veins. It plunged to earth, striking the headstone with a fierce boom. The rock split and the ground opened in a jagged trench. As the maw-like fracture widened, Billy saw the body of Lady Myrredith. She lay prone, unmoving, and dressed in black. She looked ever so beautiful.

"Lady Myrredith!"

Myrredith's eyes snapped open and she extended a hand up toward him. "Help me, William."

Billy dropped to the ground and stretched out his hand, but he just couldn't reach her. He inched his torso into the trench and reached for her again, but she only seemed farther away.

"Help me, William."

Billy looked into her eyes. A tear bled from the corner of one as she strained to touch his hand.

Billy redoubled his efforts. Their fingers almost touched. The lightning struck again, and the rift in the ground started to close.

"William!" Myrredith slipped farther away—drawn down into the earth.

Billy didn't give up. He tried to reach her even when the earth threatened to swallow him. At the last second he withdrew his hand, and the surface of the desolate plain returned to its flat, barren appearance.

"No!" Billy pounded the hardened, rock-strewn ground with his fists. He screamed Myrredith's name until it reduced him to tears.

He awoke, lying on a patch of thick, soft grass, surrounded by red toadstools and bluebells. His heart beat against his ribcage like an angry prisoner. He inhaled sharply. The scent of flowers and grass wet with dew filled his nose with a richness he had never experienced before. It was intoxicating—calming. He rolled to his back and looked into a high canopy of metallic colored leaves—some silver, some gold. They fluttered and glittered on the fragrant breeze as dull light from a cloudy sky winked between them.

"Tirn Aill," Billy muttered.

At that moment, he heard someone running through the brush. He pushed up on one elbow, but saw no one. An uneasy stillness rested on the clearing.

Am I still dreaming?

As soon as he relaxed, the sound of running returned. He concentrated and heard the steps coming closer.

Something caught Billy's eye. He turned and saw Onian's face reflected from the silver leaves of a nearby tree. The image shivered and writhed in a dozen disjointed fragments. The breeze gusted, and Onian's visage disintegrated.

"Onian?" Billy whispered.

"Shhh. Someone comes. Listen."

Billy always thought he was a good listener until Onian taught him *spirit-listening.*

Billy calmed his heart, quieted his mind, and stilled his spirit. He listened once more for the sound of the running feet. They were subtle and muted, yet now unmistakable to him, as if they were very close. He concentrated further and could hear the runner's breathing. A question formed in his mind, and his heart beat a tiny bit faster. Then, he lost the sounds of the runner, and instead heard the rustle of the leaves, and the chirping of birds, and myriad sounds he could not identify. All the sounds of the forest and its inhabitants seemed to pour into his ears until they became a roar like thunder.

Billy sat up like a fired catapult. "Myrredith's in trouble!"

The clearing remained silent.

Onian stepped out from behind the tree and bowed to Billy. "Your Highness."

Billy jumped to his feet. "Myrredith's in trouble."

"So you said."

"You don't understand. She's in real danger. She needs me ..." Billy stopped when he observed Onian leaning on his bow like a farmer watching his crops grow.

"Please continue, Highness."

"You're not really interested, are you?"

Onian paused. "I try to focus on the dangers nearby."

"Nearby?" He scanned the woods surrounding the clearing and hunkered down. "You said someone was coming," he whispered. "I believe I heard them too."

"Yes. That's good."

"If someone is coming, why did you come out?"

"I thought it might be one of Malkry's assassins."

"Then why aren't we hiding?"

"Because it's only Shaldra."

Billy scanned the small clearing but, this time, caught glimpses of a dozen elves hiding in the trees. Had they been there all along? Why had he failed to see them? It was as if they were out of focus.

Onian noticed Billy's expression. "What is it, Your Highness?"

"Is that faerie magic?"

"Magic? I know very little magic, as I'm sure the Witan will attest."

"Your elves have been here all along, but I didn't see them until just now."

Muffled laughter drifted out from the trees. It lilted on the breeze like flutes.

"Oh, that." Onian gave Billy a crooked smile and looked from side to side. "Just a trick. I'll show you sometime."

"Yes, please."

At that moment, Shaldra appeared. As he approached, Billy listened to his footsteps. *Yes. The same footsteps as before.*

Shaldra bowed to Billy. Although he breathed hard, his jaw was set in a determined manner and his green eyes remained grim.

"My lord."

"Yes," Billy and Onian answered in unison.

Onian bowed to Billy. "Excuse me, Your Majesty. Habit, you know."

"Quite all right."

"My lord." Shaldra gave another bow.

"Yes, what is it?"

"Your Majesty—" the elf began.

"Please. Will all of you just call me Billy? It will save a great deal of time, and me some discomfort. Maybe later, once this mess is all cleared up, you can give me a title."

"Yes, Your Highness—uh—Billy." Shaldra bowed again.

Onian tapped him with his bow. "You were saying."

"Yes." Shaldra straightened. "I was on my way back from Malkry's camp..."

"What news of Malkry?" Onian asked.

"Nothing. She keeps council with her warriors in seclusion."

"And the hobgoblins?"

"Still in her camp as well."

"Interesting."

"I have found something even more interesting." Shaldra reached inside his vest. "I think it is important."

Billy and Onian watched in expectation as Shaldra withdrew a large brown leaf and held it out to them. Billy leaned over and examined the dead leaf, looking for something unusual. He could see nothing on its broad, wrinkled surface, or anything about it that seemed out of place.

Before Billy could say anything, Onian snatched the leaf and held it up to the light. The elf leader rubbed it and squinted.

Billy felt somewhat baffled by his behavior. "What?"

"I've never seen this before." Onian tilted his head to one side.

"It's a leaf," Billy said.

"Yes." Onian frowned. "But I've never seen one like this before."

Billy took the leaf in his hand for a closer examination. It looked to him very much like any other dead leaf he had seen. He looked at the ground around him and noticed a lack of loose leaves. And those few that were on the ground were still green or bright in color.

Shaldra frowned. "There is more. The tree this came from … it looked … bad."

Onian touched Shaldra's arm. "Come. Show me where you found this."

The two elves turned and left the clearing at a jog. Billy chased after them. At once, the elves hiding in the trees slipped into focus and fell in around him. Onian and Shaldra stopped and turned to face him.

"Your Highness, you should stay here where we can better protect you. We'll report back to you shortly."

"Protect me? Must I stay hidden in the woods forever? If I'm to rule this kingdom, I must take stock of it, know the lay of the land, and learn its secrets—and I can't do that sitting around. Besides, I feel that I might be able to shed some light on this mystery."

Billy felt curious saying these words, but he was also proud. He was finally taking his destiny into his own hands, and it felt good. His usually stoic guards smiled approvingly.

"Very well." Onian inclined his head. "Who am I to argue with the future king?"

The small faerie troop loped through the forest undetected. Billy felt very much at home amongst the elf warriors. They ran like ghosts through the brush, and moved in the same fashion he had taught himself when, as a boy, he snuck through the woods in the Valley of the Yew.

At last, they came to the site where Shaldra had found the leaf. A tall maple-like tree stood circled by evergreens. Yellow, red, and brown leaves carpeted the forest floor and hung from the central tree.

Billy waded through the ankle-deep leaves. When he arrived at the thick trunk of the only leaf-bearing tree, he turned and saw that none of the others had followed him. Instead, they stared in wonder at the tree.

Billy once again looked at the tree, then back at the elves. "What's the matter?"

None of the elves seemed able to speak.

"Onian. Onian!"

"Yes."

"What *is* the matter?"

Onian stared back at Billy. His emerald eyes narrowed. "There's something wrong with that tree. I think it may be ill."

"What do you mean?"

Onian wet his lips, but had no words to express his feelings. Billy bent and picked up several of the leaves at his feet.

"Is it these leaves?"

"Aye."

"What about them?"

"They're not green."

"So, you've never seen autumn leaves before?"

"What kind of leaves?"

"Autumn."

"I don't know that word. Is that a kind of malady?"

Billy laughed. "Heavens no. Autumn is the season between summer and winter."

"Winter?"

"Yes, winter." Billy was puzzled by the elf's apparent ignorance. "You know, winter ... when it gets cold ... and the water freezes ... and snow falls from the sky."

The elves scanned the sky with suspicion.

"I'm afraid you're wasting your time, Majesty."

He turned and saw Elzgig leaning up against the central tree. The diminutive wizard bowed and took Billy aside to continue his discourse.

"You see, Tirn Aill has never seen a winter or an autumn."

"Never?"

"No, and its inhabitants have seldom traveled anywhere, especially these young ones."

Billy looked to his bodyguards. They congregated closely together, deep in a discussion of their own. "Never?"

"Not since ..." Elzgig scratched his head. "Well, since Dagda sired the tribe you call Celts. At least not much."

"But *you* know. And what of all those faerie stories?"

Elzgig frowned. "Yes, yes, yes. A handful of undesirable misfits and exiles."

"And what of my mother?"

"I told your mother about the world of men. A bit too much, I suppose. A mistake, I'll grant you, and I've regretted it ever since, so you don't have to flog me with it. But we're losing sight of the problem."

"What is the problem?"

"What's the problem?" The tiny wizard looked at the huddled elves and lowered his voice once again. "The problem is that Tirn Aill has forever existed in spring and summer. It's never had an autumn or a winter, and if it does. ... Who knows what will happen?"

"What do you mean? 'Twill be autumn, and winter, and then spring will come again."

Elzgig looked into Billy's eyes. "Will it?"

"You think it won't?"

"I've already read the signs elsewhere."

"Have you listened to the trees?"

"Aye, a number of them."

"This one?" Billy pointed to the autumn-tree.

"I tried, but it kept falling asleep. Trees do not fall asleep, not in Tirn Aill!"

"And Quercus … ?"

Elzgig shook his head. "Tirn Aill is slumping into autumn, and I don't know if it can be stopped."

Billy knelt down by Elzgig and examined the leaves in his hand. He glanced over at the elves and said, "Don't tell the others. Not yet."

Elzgig nodded. "Wise choice, my king."

"And don't start with that king stuff. 'Twould be nice to know there's a kingdom to rule first."

"Agreed, Your Highness, but until you *are* king, I think it important to keep up appearances."

"Aye, perhaps."

"Then come, Your Highness." Elzgig raised his voice. "Let us consult the Witan. Perhaps they can explain what has happened."

When Elzgig, Billy, and his elf guard arrived at the huge, hollow tree that was home to the Witan, a few citizens of Faerie already waited outside. They clustered together with others of their kind, mumbling and grumbling—the whole sounding like a hive of angry bees.

A lone satyr sat to one side, cross-legged, on a flat rock with his head in his hands. Occasionally, he sighed, shook his head from side to side, and moaned.

Billy approached him. "Sylvys?"

With sorrowful eyes, the satyr raised his head to look at Billy. His lower lip protruded like a tiny shelf. His habitual buck-toothed grin was gone.

"What's the matter?"

"Oh … nothing that would interest Your Highness."

"No, no. I'd like to know."

"Well, when I—And I—Well, I used to—But now I can't. Oh, it's just too embarrassing, Your Highness."

Sylvys slumped back to his original position and resumed his moaning. He was so pitiful that Billy just didn't have the heart to ask him any more questions.

Elzgig motioned Billy down to whispering range. "I've known Sylvys for a long time, Your Highness. Maybe he'll tell me what's troubling him."

"No, no. Leave him be."

"This could be important, Your Highness. If it's what I think it is, we should know."

Billy thought for a moment. "Well, if you think we must."

Elzgig approached Sylvys and placed his tiny hand on the satyr's shoulder. He leaned close, whispered in his ear, and then waited until Sylvys replied in kind.

"Nothing's ... come up?" Elzgig asked.

Sylvys shook his head in the negative.

"Nothing at all?"

The satyr shook his head more fervently.

Elzgig returned to Billy's side. "It's worse than I thought."

"Worse, how?"

"The whole mess. The whole blasted mess. And if we don't do something fast ..."

"What? ... *What?*"

"Remember what I said before?" Elzgig whispered. "Winter. All over. Ice and everything."

"But we still don't know if that would be permanent."

"You don't understand. ... Of course, he doesn't understand," Elzgig muttered. "He hasn't been here long enough. He hasn't learned anything yet."

"What must I learn?"

Elzgig gazed into Billy's eyes. For the first time since Billy had met him, the wizard's sharp, birdlike eyes contained fear. They searched Billy's face, seeking out something beyond his reckoning.

"What must I learn, Elzgig?"

"You must learn what every bird, tree, and animal in Tirn Aill knows. You must understand what most of your subjects only sense. In short, you must learn to be king ... and quickly."

CHAPTER SEVEN

The King's Disease

"How dare you come to me with this disgraceful news?" Spittle flew from King Ergyfel's mouth. "I warned you not to fail me, Cairmac! And now you disappoint me, not once, but twice?"

"But, Your Majesty ..." The Earl of Wyneddham paled.

"There is no excuse for your bungling!"

Cairmac bowed his head. "Yes, Your Majesty."

Ergyfel shifted his eyes to the elderly lord, Finnalaghe, standing next to Earl Cairmac. "And you, what do you have to say for yourself? How can you defend this wretched weakling's failure?"

The white haired Earl of Hillshire stepped forward and bowed. "My lord," he began in calming tones. "As you know, I have fought the Gwythies many times. From Earl Cairmac's report, I can only believe that they have been planning this invasion for some time."

"What difference does that make?"

"They have emptied the Saxon mercenary halls and brought their entire army to our shores."

"Again, what difference does that make?"

"The difference, my lord, is that in both battles, at their sea-landing and outside Dyven, the Earl's troops were so badly outnumbered that he could not possibly win."

The Earl of Wyneddham stepped forward. "Yes, Your Majesty, as I tried to explain—"

"Shut up, Cairmac." Ergyfel scowled.

"Yes, Your Majesty." The cowed earl bowed like a scolded chambermaid.

The Earl of Hillshire stared at his compatriot, the Earl of Wyneddham. Despite the man's loose morals, Finney had always held Cairmac with some regard and, at times, even respect—but now all he felt was pity. The man who governs all of Wyneddhamshire should not be such a coward that he could not confront his king with the truth. Ergyfel had reduced him to a frightened slave in fancy clothes.

"What about your men, Finnalaghe? Are they ready to attack the enemy?"

"Before you recalled me, my lord, I gave orders for my men to lay ambushes and set up other delays for the Gwythies, but I ordered them to retreat in the face of an all-out assault."

"Retreat?" Ergyfel's face turned red. "You ordered them to retreat?"

Earl Finnalaghe allowed the echo of Ergyfel's voice to die before he resumed. "My lord, I do not have enough men to stop them, much less attack successfully."

"I do not want your excuses, Finnalaghe! I want results!" Ergyfel pounded the arm of his throne to punctuate his demands.

"Yes, my lord." The Earl of Hillshire inclined his head. "And I can give them to you if—"

"If what?"

"If you release half of the army you have here, to me, and grant me command of your knights."

"*Half* my army? *And* my knights?"

"Yes, my lord."

"Impossible!" Ergyfel wiped his lips. "We need those men here to defend us."

"The enemy landed his entire force in Wyneddham ..."

"We need them here!"

Finnalaghe stepped forward. "My lord, the remainder of your army and the castle guard can hold off any secondary attacks to Orgulous and Nyraval, but unless I have more men to confront the Gwythies, the rest of Lyonesse will fall. Then the fate of Orgulous will be sealed."

"Enough!" Ergyfel rose to his feet. "You will not say such things again. Do you understand? I alone know what is best for the kingdom."

Silence filled the great hall as Ergyfel descended from the dais and looked at the faces of his lords. The more capable lords of the realm were in the field, preparing to battle the invaders. Most of the men present were young, foppish weaklings, inexperienced in the ways of war, but they had one quality that gave them standing here: they were loyal to Ergyfel and his new order.

Billy is on his way. Ergyfel's nightmares still plagued him. *And I need my army to fend off his army. But I can't tell them that. They must never know that he is alive, or I'm finished.*

King Ergyfel cleared his throat and, in an authoritative voice, announced, "There is another threat to Orgulous, on its way now ..."

A murmur rippled through the assembled lords and swelled into a panicked rumble.

"Silence!" the Earl of Hillshire shouted.

Ergyfel nodded to him and continued, "And we must be ready to defend against it."

"Who is it?"

"Enemies, Finnalaghe. Enemies that would take advantage of our current state."

The earl frowned. "Who?"

"Do you doubt me, Finnalaghe?" Yet more spittle flew from Ergyfel's mouth, as he moved to within inches of the Earl's face.

"No, my lord." The earl stood his ground. "I only wish to know from which direction this new threat will come."

Ergyfel frowned at the elderly lord and turned away. He rubbed his temples as he paced towards the dais. "Because of diplomacy, I cannot reveal to you who may be involved. However, my *source* tells me that they are massing as we speak. They will, of course, come by sea, but we know not where they will land. I only know that they plan to strike here, at Orgulous."

"My lord, give me the army now, before this new enemy strikes, and I will defeat the Gwythies. Then we can concentrate—"

"Finnalaghe! Be silent. I warned you not to speak of this again."

"But it's the only way."

"I said, be silent!" Ergyfel was fuming. "It is *not* the only way!"

Earl Cairmac looked up from the floor. "I will do it, Your Majesty."

"What will you do, you simpering twit?"

"I will take Finnalaghe's men and attack the enemy."

Ergyfel and the Earl of Hillshire turned to view Cairmac. The king wore an expression of surprise and delight, but Finney only sneered.

"Well, well, well. Cairmac." Ergyfel grinned. "So, you're not the coward I took you for."

"You fool!" Finnalaghe hissed. "What do you hope to prove?"

Ergyfel strode directly to Finnalaghe and struck him with his fist. The old man fell to the floor.

Ergyfel kicked the venerable old lord as he shouted, "Did you not see … the men outside … in the courtyard?"

Finney got to his hands and knees. Pain was written on his face, but it was more than physical pain in his eyes: it was sorrow. All his life, he had faithfully defended the kingdom. Now, many of his fellow lords turned away while he was beaten, and Ergyfel's zealous pets gorged their eyes on the spectacle.

"I asked you a question!" Ergyfel gave the earl another kick. "Did you see the men?"

"On the gallows?"

"Yes, on the gallows, you feeble-minded fool! All of them failed me, and for their treachery, they have been properly rewarded."

"You're mad," Finnalaghe whispered.

"You disappoint me. You fail me before you even try. In fact, you fail me because you refuse to try."

Ergyfel straightened and walked away from the earl. He motioned to two guards who stood near the dais, then pointed to Finney. "Take him away."

"Yes, Your Majesty. Where shall we take him?"

King Ergyfel watched the guards pick up the aged lord; his dark eyes completely void of emotion. He then shoed them away with a wave of his hand. "Hang him with the others."

Ergyfel's command caused the guards to drop their charge. They stood motionless in shock. The men Ergyfel had hanged, up until now, were nobodies—but this was Earl Finnalaghe, a celebrated hero of the people.

"Are you deaf? Take him away!"

The guards bowed and ushered the Earl of Hillshire from the great hall. The assembled lords watched, with eyes open and mouths shut, each one fearful that they could be next.

That should keep them in line. Ergyfel watched the doors of the great hall close. He then returned his attention to the Earl of Wyneddham. "So, you will rid me of these invaders?"

"Yes, Your Highness." Cairmac nodded. "I pledge my life on it."

"Funny you should put it like that." Ergyfel smiled at his little joke. "That is precisely what it will cost you to fail me again."

The King looked to the back of the hall and the lone figure lurking in the corner shadows. The man had been present throughout the assembly, but had gone unnoticed to all but Ergyfel's keen, sorcerous eyes.

Ergyfel raised his voice and called out, "Hengest, please, come forward."

Several guards flinched as the thin, grey figure emerged from the darkness. Ergyfel held up his hand as a sign to let him pass, and the guards relaxed.

Again, all eyes were to the back of the hall as the mysterious man strolled to the dais. He seemed quite ordinary as he passed into the light streaming from the high windows. He wore breeches, a tunic, and a hooded gorget that could be described as common or even low, and no visible jewelry or weapons. His face remained unseen, obscured by the hood's recesses.

The stranger bowed before the dais and pulled back his hood. Long hair, like fine brass wires, flowed over his head, terminating in a tidy warrior's knot. A short, well-groomed beard with a narrow white streak adorned his chin.

"Your Majesty," the man murmured.

"Hengest, stand up." Ergyfel came down beside him.

As the man stood and turned, he made eye contact with each of the assembled lords. His blue eyes froze their hearts with the chill of an unforgiving sea.

Ergyfel placed his arm around the stranger and said, "This is Hengest, my half-brother. After Sygeon died, I realized how important it was to have family around, so I asked Hengest to come. I am naming him as my First Counselor, and you are to address him as such. Hengest will know my thoughts on most matters, and will at times be my eyes and voice. I want you to look upon him as an extension of me."

The lords bowed to Hengest.

"Good. I believe you understand me perfectly. Now, Cairmac, you will return to the field. Collect what's left of your men and take control of Finnalaghe's army. Levy every able boy and man between here and there to fill your ranks, and attack. I want you to destroy the army of Gwythia. Crush them and drive them into the sea. Make them wish they never set foot on our soil."

"Yes, Your Majesty." The earl bowed. "It shall be done."

"Yes, Cairmac, because I order it. And to see that it is done, Hengest shall accompany you. Now leave us."

Earl Cairmac chewed his lip and eyed Hengest. "Yes, Your Majesty." He turned to leave, but his master's voice stopped him.

"Remember, Cairmac," Ergyfel said in warning tones. "Hengest will be my eyes and my voice."

"Yes, Your Majesty."

As soon as the Earl of Wyneddhamshire had left, the remaining lords surrounded Hengest. Each one engaged in degrading and more than obvious ploys to ingratiate himself to the new First Counselor.

"Leave us," Ergyfel said over the din. "Leave us. I know you are all anxious to meet my brother, but you will have to wait. I have important things to discuss with him ... alone."

Ergyfel dismissed his guards as the young lords bowed and scraped their way from the great hall.

Ergyfel called, "Gullinburst."

"Yes, Your Majesty." The house servant bowed his way to the throne.

"Prepare a room for my brother; something near my own."

"Yes, Your Majesty."

"And, Gullinburst?"

"Yes, Your Majesty?"

"Have you found my crown yet?"

"Well I-I don't have the, uhm, that is the exact, but I. ... No, Your Majesty."

Ergyfel coaxed Gullinburst close with his finger and whispered, "If you don't find my crown in a fortnight, I'll cut off your fingers one joint at a time. Now, find my crown!"

Gullinburst fled from the great hall, slamming the doors behind him. When they were alone, Hengest let out a guffaw that reverberated in the rafters.

"My, my, my, Brother, what an odd flock you have there."

Ergyfel chuckled. "Yes, but their combined influence and affluence are enough to keep me in power."

"Brother!" Hengest threw wide his arms.

"Brother!" Ergyfel answered in kind.

The two half-brothers embraced, then turned and, arm in arm, climbed up the dais. Ergyfel took his seat on the throne while Hengest sat on a bench beside him.

"If Mother could only see you now."

"And how is Mother?" Ergyfel's face scrunched in distaste.

"She's dead, Brother."

"Oh, what a shame." Irony dripped from his tongue. "And how did the dear old witch die?"

"She was killed."

"Oh?"

"Beheaded by angry villagers, who claimed she put a hex on their cattle."

Ergyfel chuckled and placed his hand on Hengest's shoulder. "You wouldn't be telling a tale just to cheer me up now, would you?"

"No, no. Every word of it truth."

Ergyfel arched his eyebrows and sighed. "And I was so looking forward to choking her with my own hands ..."

"Ergyfel!" Hengest's mouth dropped open. "She was our mother!"

The king looked at his brother. "She may have bore me, but from that day forward, she gave me nothing!"

The reunited brothers stared at each other in silence.

Suddenly, Ergyfel became quite animated. "Well ... enough reminiscing for now. I have a mission for you."

"Yes, Brother."

Ergyfel reached into the folds of his robe and pulled out a round copper disk, held up by its chain. "Take this."

"What is it?" Hengest examined the spinning necklace.

"It's a gift, Brother. With it, I will see what you see and hear what you hear."

Hengest gazed warily at the amulet. As its spinning slowed, he could see that upon one side there was a gem very much like a cat's eye, and indeed, it was set in-between two copper eyelids. On the reverse, there were strange inscriptions about the circumference, spiraling into an intricate knotted symbol in the center.

Hengest reached out to take the amulet. At that moment, Ergyfel mumbled something incomprehensible, and a small spark leapt from the amulet to Hengest's fingers. He jumped back with an oath. Still holding his hands close to his chest, he stared at his brother.

Ergyfel smiled. "If I had told you it was going to do that, you wouldn't have touched it, would you?"

Hengest relaxed, but still refused to come closer or take the amulet.

Ergyfel betrayed some frustration. "Oh, please." He tossed the necklace at his brother, who caught it with a delayed flinch as if expecting another jolt, but none came.

Ergyfel watched as Hengest put the amulet around his neck and slipped it inside his tunic. "Very good. Now, for your mission ..."

"Yes, tell me, Brother." Hengest slid back to his former position beside Ergyfel.

"As you know, I want you to go with Cairmac to take charge of Finnalaghe's men. He will try to levy the troops we need, but he is soft. See to it that he is not. Use pressgangs where necessary. This is the first part of your mission."

"Yes, Brother."

"For the second part, you must keep order amongst the troops and ensure their bravery by executing all deserters and cowards; preferably by hanging."

"Yes, Brother."

"Despite what you may have heard, Gwythia's army is as well-equipped and organized as the former legions of Rome. We will need all our cunning and discipline to defeat them. That is why Cairmac failed: not because he was outnumbered, but because he was weak-willed."

"I will be as steel."

"Good." Ergyfel patted him on the arm. "The final part of your mission is to kill Cairmac." Ergyfel paused a moment to observe his brother's reaction. He smiled at Hengest's unchanging features. "If he falters in any way, kill him and take command. When the battle's over, Cairmac will be counted among the dead."

"If we should win, Cairmac would be a hero."

"*When* you win." Ergyfel frowned. "Cairmac shall be a dead hero."

"I understand, Brother."

"Good, there's nothing like the understanding that comes with family. Now, come with me. I have an urge to see how long Finnalaghe's neck has become. Oh, and I want you to meet Maeven."

King Ergyfel rose and descended from the dais, accompanied by his brother. As they approached the dimly lit rear of the great hall, a figure lunged from behind a column. There was a flash of steel as Hengest pushed Ergyfel back. The long blade of the assailant slashed the king's robe, just missing the royal face.

Hengest grabbed the man's sword arm and kicked his midriff. The would-be assassin let out an explosive grunt and dropped his weapon. Hengest whirled around, with the newly acquired sword flashing in his hand.

"Stop!" Ergyfel yelled, but it was too late. Even had he wanted to, Hengest could not pull back the strike that removed his target's head.

Hengest finished his follow-through with a flourish. Abruptly, his head jerked to the side to look at Ergyfel. "Stop?" He noticed a few flecks of blood on his brother's face and glanced back to the decapitated body at his feet. "Very well. If you insist."

Ergyfel chortled. "Hengest, you always make me laugh."

Hengest placed the sword next to the body, eyeing the king like a reluctant child returning some forbidden treat. Ergyfel laughed again and examined the dead assassin.

"Now, how am I supposed to question him?"

Hengest scratched his chin. "I don't know. Know any good doctors?"

The two brothers laughed and playfully pushed each other. Then Ergyfel noticed that the head was missing. "Where's the head?"

"Oh no!" Hengest put his hands to his mouth in mock terror. "Now he's really lost his head."

Both Ergyfel and Hengest searched the area. The King's First Counselor found the missing gourd behind the same column that had hidden the assassin before the attack.

"Now, where do you think you're *heading*?" Hengest reached down and grabbed the head. "Chin up, old bean ... the king wants to talk to you." He then held it up for Ergyfel's inspection. "Know him?"

"Aye. Lord Angall."

"Well, milord ..." Hengest held out the head so he could bow to it. "... You really shouldn't have tried such a *heady* deed. You just don't have the stomach for it. Now, don't get a-*head* of me. Just tell us, who put you up to this, eh? Did you put your head together with someone? Come now, who heads the organization? Humph. The strong, silent type."

Hengest then held out the head to Ergyfel. "For you, Your Majesty. Two heads *are* better than one."

Hengest's gruesome performance increased Ergyfel's mirth until he laughed uncontrollably. "It's good to have you here, Brother. No one around here has your sense of humor. Oh, there is one more little problem I want you to take care of, but the little faerie bastard can wait 'til after we've properly celebrated your arrival."

Hengest dropped Lord Angall's head and exited the great hall with his brother. "That Lord Angall. Has he always been so headstrong?"

Ergyfel threw back his head and guffawed.

CHAPTER EIGHT

Sir Who?

Hugh woke with a start. Cold had crept into his bones until its grip shook him from his sleep. A sleep plagued by accusing images of a friend betrayed.

The former knight surveyed his surroundings. The last thing he remembered with any clarity, was ordering a drink at the Blood and Slobber Inn for a Gwythie sergeant who promised not to toss him out if he paid. Now he was in a garbage-filled alley, sitting in muck and ankle-deep water, a bottle of cheap wine in his hand. His head pounded like an angry landlord while his gut pondered the feasibility of ejecting its contents past his thick, pasty tongue.

The filth reeking in the gutter coaxed his stomach in favor of ejection and he fought to keep it down. Hugh brought the wine bottle to his nose, thinking that it might help cover the smell. Like the hair-trigger of a finely crafted crossbow, the odor of stale wine caused Hugh to retch.

With his stomach empty, Hugh pulled himself up and stumbled out of the alley. As he skulked through the muddy backstreets and putrid alley-ways of Dyven, his heart wept. The once bustling city-port he'd enjoyed in his youth had become a black, sooty nightmare, and the dreams that had built it—ashes. The smell of burnt timbers which had lingered on the air for days was now faint, thanks to recent rains. Unfortunately, this only made the stench of the bodies more urgent.

Gwythia's soldiers were still everywhere. They bullied those with anything of value, taking what they pleased, including the innocence of daughters. Anyone who got in their way was severely beaten, or lashed to death in the market square and had their home burned to the ground. The Gwythies banned funerals and burial rites, and forbade starting a fire to all but the occupying troops.

Cruelties heaped upon cruelties as the piles of corpses grew. Each act was more malicious, more savage than the last, until the spirit of Dyven's people was broken. Captive in their own city, they wandered its dying streets in a trance.

Onto this grim tapestry, shambled Hugh—dirty, faceless, beaten—his wounded thigh still cursing him. He watched from the safety of an alley as several previously human creatures, dressed in tattered rags, picked a fresh corpse clean of all dignity and belongings. He remembered thinking the previous night that he must be in hell. In the grey, rain-streaked light of day, he saw nothing to change his mind.

A few streets away, Hugh witnessed the ghoul-like stripping of another body. The rag pickers flocked around their prey, picking and tearing, circling and bobbing like carrion birds, unfettered by judgments of humanity. They never seemed to consider that the corpse had been their neighbor, or that they might be next. Hugh felt dizzy. He turned and limped away.

Suddenly, a man grabbed Hugh and dragged him into a doorway. The assailant then flung him inside the abandoned building. Hugh struggled, but in his state, it was futile.

"Sir Hugh." The man's face was veiled in shadows. "Thank God I found you."

Hugh squinted, trying to pierce the darkness. "Who?"

The man stepped forward to reveal his handsome, slender face.

"Malcolm ... the Magnificent." Hugh felt indifferent. In truth, some part of him wished the juggler had been a murderer. "What do you want?"

"What do *I* want?" Malcolm exclaimed. "Not a fortnight past, you were on your deathbed, or so I thought. I awoke to find you gone, along with my dagger. Where have you been? You look ... and smell horrid!"

"Don't worry about me." Hugh scratched his chin stubble and sat against the wall. "I'm fine. But I had to sell your dagger."

"Sold? Why?"

The morning he'd escaped the little shack where they had hidden, he'd risen before the sun while Malcolm still slept. The exhausted highlander had done his best to hide the weapons from his suicidal friend, but the veteran warrior knew that he would keep something in reach. It was a simple matter to find the dagger and slip away into the darkness.

"Why? Why did you sell it?"

Hugh still did not answer him. Instead, he stared at his hands. The cuts where he had gripped the dagger's blade were still angry. *A moment's hesitation,* Hugh thought. *An infinitesimal moment ... to think, to feel one's pulse. ... Then the moment expands, and you are still alive, still breathing, still staring at the means to end all your pain. It would be so easy. Then comes another moment.*

"The sun rose at that moment," Hugh said.

"What?"

Hugh glanced up at his companion. "I hadn't the courage to use it, so I sold it."

"You needed money?"

"Aye. Well, not right away. After I was kicked out of the Blood and Slobber, the first time ..."

"The tavern?"

"Aye."

"With the whole place crawling with Gwythies? Are you trying to get yourself killed?"

Hugh made no comment save a short grunt.

"Good God, man. What's the matter with you? Why, look at yourself. You're a stinkin' mess! You should be making plans to rescue her ladyship, and you're out drinkin' and carryin' on with the damned enemy!"

Hugh glared at Malcolm, but a guilty conscience would not allow him to maintain eye contact. *He's right.* He turned away. *He's so bloody right. Billy. I'm a coward. What can I do?*

Hugh struck the wall with his fist. When the pain registered, he leaned into the wall. Tears of frustration and self-pity streamed down his face. He felt trapped and ashamed.

"I'm such a coward," Hugh said into his arm.

"A coward? You're certainly not that."

Hugh stood. "No. I am the worst kind of coward. I betrayed the gentlest, most caring person I ever knew, and brought about his death. Me: Defender of the weak."

"No, my friend, you are the one wronged. I, too, miss the lad. Just knowing that he's dead; the world seems less bright. But we cannot live in the past. That was yesterday's battle. Today, we must save Lady Myrredith."

Hugh started for the door. "I can't help Myrredith. I can't help anyone."

Malcolm stopped him. "You're the only one who can."

"Don't you see?" Hugh wished Malcolm would just let him leave. "Everything I do must fail! I betrayed my friend, and God was watching."

"No." Malcolm shook his head.

Hugh's own words caused his frustration and self-pity to tangle and twist together. They fed on each other, growing and churning. "I am damned. Billy's blood is on my hands, and I can never make that right."

"Punishing yourself will not bring him back."

"God is punishing me. God!" Hugh spun around and smacked Malcolm with a vicious punch. The juggling-master fell to the floor like so many dropped balls.

Hugh started for the door. He looked back and saw that Malcolm wasn't moving. He crouched down beside him and placed an ear to the entertainer's chest. The pulse was strong and regular.

Hugh found himself staring at Malcolm's purse. It was tucked neatly into his belt, but otherwise was free. Hugh sat up and turned away.

"No. I can't. I won't."

Struck by a sudden thirst, he eyeballed the purse. He licked his lips while he pondered how many drinks he might buy with the coins it contained. His mind, unsteady in purpose, began to tread down the road that he had seldom ever glanced.

Outside, the rain increased, and its hiss seeped into Hugh's consciousness. "*Drink,*" it whispered seductively. "*Drink and forget. Forget and find peace.*"

Hugh snatched the purse from Malcolm's belt and dashed out the door. He ran on, driven by the rain. He was not mindful of his destination or whereabouts until he stopped at an alley behind several charred buildings. Fire had gutted all but one in the entire block. Hugh glanced about and noted numerous barrels stacked in the muddy alley. Over the back door of the remaining structure, the painted words "Blood and Slobber," looked down and beckoned.

Hugh stared at the door as the cold rain trickled over his body. He examined the small pouch in his hand. It clinked as he turned it over. A stroke of lightning illuminated the three gold circles that made up Malcolm the Magnificent's personal crest. There was another flash, and Hugh saw with his mind's eye an image of Billy and Malcolm juggling for Lady Myrredith.

Hugh threw the purse to the ground with disgust and collapsed to his knees. He sobbed and fell forward, his hands sinking into the muck.

Hugh straightened and blindly shook his filthy fists at the sky. With his energy spent, he sank back to his knees. He opened his eyes and stared at the mud between his knees. From the corner of one eye, he caught the glimmer of metal and looked over to see Malcolm's purse. Several silver coins had spilled out onto the soggy earth.

"Silver," Hugh muttered. "For Judas."

The rain whispered, "*Forget all that. Doesn't your leg still hurt?*"

"No." Hugh moaned. "I can't."

"*Wash away your troubles. Drink and forget.*"

It would be something to forget. To lose myself, if only for a moment.

"*Yes,*" the soothing rain whispered. "*That's it.*"

Trancelike, Hugh placed the silver back into the purse and put it in his shirt. He used a barrel to pull himself to his feet, and then headed around the tavern and in the front door.

Shortly, there was a disturbance within the Blood and Slobber Inn. The door burst open, and Hugh sailed through it. His feet hit the slick muddy stones of the street and down he went. A husky, ruddy-faced soldier filled the doorway, surrounded by his exuberant comrades.

"I told ya to stay out," Hugh's ouster bellowed. "Ya stinkin' bucket of biswail!"

Hugh pushed up to his knees and spat out a bit of turf. His eyes came up on his assailant as the man stepped out the door.

"He's spittin' at ya, Sergeant," one of the Gwythies said.

The ruffian stepped forward. "I guess ya haven't learnt yer lesson yet."

Hugh held up his hands to block the large fists coming at his head, but then the man kicked him in the gut. He doubled over, and the sergeant pounded his ribs and back. The spiteful blows knocked Hugh to the stone paving.

Just then, a buxom woman pushed her way between the men at the door and ran out. "Stop it, stop it!"

"Heather, no!" the barkeep shouted from within.

The pretty barmaid paid no heed to her employer and continued into the street. She put herself between the Gwythie sergeant and Hugh, then knelt beside the latter to give him aid.

"This stinkin' meddwyn spilled my ale and got his stinkin' puke all over my best tunic," the sergeant snapped. "Now he comes back in here stinkin' and drippin' filth. The good-for-nothin' lout should be horse whipped."

Heather lifted Hugh's head from the street. She looked up through the rain at the grumbling soldier. Tears filled her eyes. Despite the fresh bruises on her cheek and breast, she was quite luscious. "This is Sir Hugh."

The sergeant grabbed her chin. "Sir Who?"

"Sir Hugh. He's a knight ... a noble."

The sergeant released her. "That pile o'dung?"

She stroked Hugh's hair then said under her breath, "And I love him."

The sergeant turned to his men. "Hey, lads, this wench says we got ourselves a real hero here. Let me introduce you to the Butcher of Sceula Tor!"

One by one, a score of grim soldiers filed out of the tavern and into the street. They circled around Heather and the fallen Hugh.

"Help me." Heather looked up at them. "Help me get him up."

"We'll help ya." One of the men grabbed her wrist and pulled her to her feet.

Immediately, the mob of soldiers tossed Heather over their shoulders until she was outside their ring. Like wolves attacking a sick deer, the soldiers descended on Hugh. Each man struck the former King's Champion once or twice, shouting "for my father," "for my brother," "for Gaelyn," or "remember Sceula Tor," then fell back in line to allow the others their turn. The men in back kept Heather on the ground as she struggled to reach Hugh. The brutal, ritualistic beating continued until the sergeant, who remained in the middle of the circle, drew his gladius and pointed its short blade to the sky.

"Gaelyn! Your enemies fall before us."

Heather screamed out as the sergeant plunged behind his men. There was a moment of silence, and then the soldiers turned their backs on Hugh and filed back into the Blood and Slobber Inn. They laughed and chatted about the rain as if nothing had transpired.

Heather crawled to the body of the king's former champion. She lifted him up and rested his head in her lap. "Hugh! Why?"

One of the Gwythian soldiers stomped back into the street and grabbed Heather by her hair. She screamed and kicked as he tore her from the body of her secret love.

"Hugh!" Heather shouted again and again.

"Shut up, wench. There be real men inside, an' you've got servin' to do."

The door of the inn slammed shut, and a ragged figure of a man appeared at the mouth of the tiny alley across from it. He kissed a small charm hanging around his neck and slipped it back into his shirt. With marked trepidation, the beggar stepped onto the street. The second step was more laborious, as the accompanying walking stick was necessary to complete it. Watchful, the bent man crossed to where Hugh lay.

The beggar prodded Hugh with his stick, then looked up and down the street. He knelt beside Hugh's body and searched it with haste. He scanned the street again, and then with great difficulty, dragged the body off the street and disappeared into the alley.

CHAPTER NINE

Apprentice

"So, what's been happening to Tirn Aill has something to do with my mother's spell?"

"Quite so," the first Witan said.

The second nodded. "Yes, indeed."

The third Witan pinched Billy's cheek. "You are as bright as your mother."

"Perhaps brighter."

"Even more so–"

"but it wasn't really a spell."

The Witan had been talking around in circles for nearly an hour. Just when Billy thought he was catching up, they would spring a "not exactly" or "not really" or "yes, but" on him, and the whole thing would start over.

"Wait right there." Billy held up his hand. "Was it or wasn't it a spell?"

The Witan glanced at each other then back to Billy.

The first Witan scratched its chin. "It's hard to explain."

"Yes, quite." The second added.

The third frowned. "No, it's not."

Billy turned to the third Witan. Even after spending three days and a bit with the Witan, he still had trouble telling them apart. "Gwylid?"

"Aye."

"You tell me."

"Yes, you tell him, Gwylid."

"Yes, by all means, Gwylid."

"Don't listen to us–"

"we don't know anything."

"Please, I don't mean to offend you, but Gwylid says he can explain it, so I want to hear what he has to say."

"Thank you, Highness." Gwylid bowed. "Your wisdom besets your noble brow, as a crown."

Billy returned the Witan's bow and gestured for him to proceed.

"You see, Highness, your mother, Queen Eleanor, set upon you a kind of spell. Not an ordinary spell. Oh no, no, no! And not just one—that is for sure …"

Gwylid looked up at Billy before continuing. "You see, every ruler of Tirn Aill has powers—that is, they can control—their will is absolute! Yes, that's it. Over all things: flowers, trees, grass, the animals and birds. All Faerie, in fact, is subject to their will."

"The weather?" Billy asked.

"Oh yes."

"Quite."

"Very astute, Highness."

Billy nodded to them. "So, what's gone wrong?"

"Well, you see–"

"the enchantment we removed–"

"wasn't really a spell."

"Then what was it?"

"A spellbinder," the Witan said in unison.

"A spell-binder?"

"Very important thing to understand–"

"if you are to weave a lasting spell–"

"a permanent spell."

"Most mortal wizards–"

"search their whole pitiful lives–"

"but never find it."

"And my mother knew how?"

"Oh, yes."

"Taught her, we did."

"But we never expected … you."

"Me?"

"Your royal mother must have known that she was to die."

"So, she placed in you all her power."

"And bound it to you."

"In you–"

"all your life–"

"was the power to rule Faerie."

"And you took it away!" Billy shouted. "Why didn't you just leave it alone?"

"Use it … you could not."

"Locked away it was–"

"like a bird in a cage."

"We have unraveled her spells and opened the cage."

"You must catch the bird–"

"and tame it."

"What? You mean the magic that rules Tirn Aill is … loose?"

"It's still here–"

"it's just …"

"wild."

"And you want me to catch it."

"In a manner of speaking."

"It's your destiny–"

"to be king."

"How am I supposed to catch it? I can't even see it!"

"Ah, but you will–"

"you must–"

"if you are to succeed."

Billy shook his head, wanting to deny what amounted to an impossible task. *I can't. I don't know anything about magic.* He looked up at the Witan and sighed. "Even if I do learn to see the magic, how will I catch it?"

"If you see it–"

"you will know how–"

"and your will is the means to tame it."

"Very well." He still believed that the task they set for him was impossible. "What then?"

"Then you must bind it."

"Bind it? Won't that lock it away again?"

"Not to you."

"How will I bind it?"

"That is for you to decide–"

"no one else."

"It must be personal."

"You must choose something to be the binder."

"Almost anything will do–"

"but not just anything."

"Something special to you."

"Your mother chose you."

"Most amazing."

"Never been done before–"

"a living person."

"A very wise choice for one so young."

"Very wise." Gwylain nodded.

"Very insightful."

The Witan nodded approvingly to one another.

Billy nervously spun the ring on this finger. "Then, what should I use?"

"Only you can say."

"Something special–"

"something dear."

Billy sat on the solid wooden floor of the Witan's home. He placed his face into his hands and rested his elbows on his knees. "But I don't know where to start. I know absolutely nothing of magic, little of Tirn Aill, and I doubt that there's much time!"

"True–"

"too true."

"'Tis pity."

"What is?"

"That we cannot teach what is needed."

"That the time is short."

"That you must go."

"Go?" Billy lifted his head. "Where am I going ... and when?"

The first two Witan frowned at the last, who shrugged.

Then Gwylid looked at Billy. "We have foreseen it–"

"but only you can know–"

"where and when."

"Perhaps you will think of something–"

"or dream of somewhere–"

"then you will know."

"And when I leave on this mysterious journey to somewhere, will I also know what I need to bind the magic?"

"Perhaps, no."

"Perhaps, yes."

"Perhaps, you will know, but not know you know."

"Listen to your head."

"Listen to your heart."

"I always listen to my gut."

Billy looked to the three ancient and gnarled faces of the Witan. Their wise, understanding, and kind eyes stared back. He felt like he might burst. There was so much at stake, and he felt so inadequate for the job.

Billy took a deep breath. "Will I be able to save Tirn Aill? Will I figure out how to bind the magic in time?"

"You are our best hope."

"You alone may have the power."

Billy tilted his head. "*Best* hope? Is there someone else who could do it?"

The Witan glanced at each other, then down at the floor.

"What are you three hiding? Who else could do it?"

"We didn't want to mention it–"

"didn't want to distract you."

"You thought I might just give up—let someone else rule Tirn Aill."

"Well ..."

"What would be the harm in that?" Billy asked.

"She would be worse than–"

"no ruler at all!"

"If she figures out–"

"what has happened–"

"and she probably has ..."

"She will try–"

"to grab the power–"

"for herself."

"Malkry." Billy scowled.

"Yes–"

"but you can beat her to it–"

"and perhaps we can help."

"How?"

Gwylid placed a gentle hand on Billy's shoulder and gestured to the numerous cubbyholes and nooks in the walls. Each was stuffed with books, scrolls, and strange—sometimes beautiful—objects.

"If you cannot find it in your heart, then perhaps our little collection will help."

Billy stood and scanned the walls. "Where should I begin?"

"You have too little time to begin at the beginning–"

"so start in the middle."

"Where's that?" Billy couldn't discern any difference in the wall or the materials stuffed into it.

Gwylid took Billy by the hand and made a broad sweeping gesture to the room. "Anywhere you wish."

Still confused, but not knowing what else to do, Billy took a scroll from the wall. When he unrolled it, he saw that the writing was something he had never seen before. He glanced up at the Witan, who had retreated to a discreet distance across the room. They were huddled together, mumbling.

Billy cleared his throat. "Excuse me, but I can't read this one. Are they all like this?"

Gwylith looked back over his shoulder. "Yes-"

"but you *can* read it-" Gwylain said from around Gwylid's side.

"*if* you use the ring," Gwylid whispered with a wink.

Billy examined the ring. "How can the ring help me to read a language I don't know?"

"The ring knows that language."

"Quite so."

"Maybe better than us."

The Witan, satisfied that they had answered Billy's questions, turned and continued to mumble amongst themselves.

Billy looked at the scroll again and concentrated. Still, he could not read it, so he spread the document on the floor and placed his hand to his head with the ring touching it. Again, he was unsuccessful, but he did not wish to disturb the Witan for something that they thought was simple. Billy tried and tried to read the scroll, looking at it from different sides and angles, concentrating with all his heart to read the message written on the parchment.

Finally, frustrated and tired from his efforts, Billy decided to rest. He rolled over on the wooden floor and looked at the ring, wondering what he was doing wrong. *Maybe it just doesn't work for me.* Billy slipped off the ring and examined it in the light. The smooth, curving surface and the beautiful liquid-like stone reflected the dim light; with the sparkle and clarity of water.

The ring slipped from Billy's fingertips and landed on the open scroll. He reached for it but stopped short when he saw a tiny image in the center of the ring that was familiar to him.

"How did I miss that?" He leaned over the scroll to have a better look.

When he snatched up the ring, the symbol changed. Billy eyed it, but now he didn't have a clue what it meant. He scratched his head, and then moved the ring back over the symbol. This time, he watched very carefully as the center of the ring circled the character. As before, Billy recognized its meaning.

A thought formed in Billy's head. The symbol's image hadn't really changed shapes but, by placing the ring over it, the meaning became known. He put the ring to his right eye. With his left eye closed, he stared through the ring at the parchment. Magically, the images on the page became thoughts, words, and complex concepts.

Billy read the scroll, then another and another. He read voraciously, like a starving man set before a feast. His thirst for knowledge seemed unquenchable. As he read, he found bits of Tirn Aill's history, herbal remedies, innumerable references to magic, and actual spells. He scanned the documents, searching for any mention of spellbinders or their use, and came up with only a handful of vague references.

Day became night and then day again, and Billy continued to read, refusing both rest and food. Soon, he had finished all the scrolls and began poring over the books in the Witan's library. He turned the pages ravenously, seeking the kernels of knowledge he needed, driven by the thought that hidden somewhere in the parchments was the salvation of Tirn Aill.

Billy closed the cover on one manuscript, then realized that he had read the last quarter and learned several spells without looking through the ring. In fact, the ring lay on the table where he had set it down. Curious, he picked another volume and found that he now understood the mystical symbols. Freed from this restraint, Billy tore through the library with renewed vigor.

Occasionally, he would stop, and the Witan would clarify or demonstrate the things he had just read. They explained that verbal instruction was the preferred method, but that exposure to the material in written form would have to suffice, given the short time allotted him.

On one such occasion, Billy enquired, "What is meant by 'those who are free of their tongues'?"

"Ah, very interesting question."

"Very important question."

"Well ... ?"

"First, let us explain–"

"that most mortals are servants to their tongues."

"They cannot cause a thing to happen–"

"without wagging their tongues."

"The words are not the source of their power–"

"but only a gateway for the mind–"

"to release the power."

"This is true–"

"for wizards–"

"and ordinary people."

"So, when mortals use magic, they need words to make it happen."

"Precisely."

"But not everyone needs words?"

"Ah, you're getting ahead of us."

"Second, comes those who are slaves to the tongue."

"Slaves? Who are they?"

"Creatures not of this world–"

"nor of the world of men–"

"not normally."

"What do you mean?"

"Spirits, demons–"

"and other creatures summoned to this world–"

"by magic–"

"though often seeming powerful–"

"can be subjugated by words."

"Names in particular."

"Mostly their own."

"Well, of course."

"That is what I meant."

"We're sure you have read–"

"or will be reading about them–"

"soon."

"So you better get to it!"

"Start reading–"

"unless you're hungry?"

"No, no. I'm not hungry. But what of those free of their tongues?"

"Ah yes."

"That is in reference to true wizards–"

"those who cause change by will alone."

"Very few will ever attain this–"

"especially amongst mortals."

"It takes years–"

"too many for most."

"Better get to it!"

Without another word, the Witan turned and went about their business—a business that was still a mystery to Billy. And so, with the discussion closed, the royal apprentice went back to his studies.

Billy finished a short book of magical history and was about to grab another smallish book when he spotted a dark alcove in the back of the Witan's home. A large, black book sat in the shadowy depths. It seemed odd to him that he had not seen it before, and so he approached. When he neared the book, Billy saw that the cover was of fine, smooth leather with iron bindings.

He reached to pick up the tome, but stopped short of touching it. The hole felt cold. Something chilled his spine. There was an emotion, like that when receiving some long awaited prize. But the emotion was not his own.

Billy leaned forward and examined the book. It was huge in comparison to those he had been reading.

Surely a book this big must hold the answers to many questions. Billy reached for it again.

A flash and a smacking sound accompanied something striking Billy's hand. He pulled back and looked up to see Gwylith standing over him, a willow switch in hand.

"Not that one." He sounded more authoritative than Billy had heard him yet.

"Please, never that one," Gwylain said.

"Anything but that one," Gwylid said with a grim face.

The sting in Billy's fingers was the only explanation he needed. He blew on them and stared at the frowning Witan. They seemed in unison on this one topic more than on anything thus far and, oddly enough, they hadn't said a word to one another. They were bewildering, but if they were so set against his reading this book, then Billy couldn't see arguing the point. After all, there were still plenty of other books to search.

Without a word, Billy turned and took a book from a cubbyhole between two giant, twisted knots. As he cracked it open, he glanced over it to the Witan, who had returned to their nearly constant mumbling.

Billy searched and searched and searched. In his entire life, he had never read so much, nor had he ever had so much material at his disposal. Bits and pieces from different sources joined together as he waded through the extensive collection. However, throughout this search, his eyes frequently sought the black, yawning cavity where the mysterious forbidden book rested.

At first, Billy snuck peeks at the hollow, between turning pages. Then in the middle of each page, and then after each paragraph or spell. Finally, he could think of nothing else. He read the same sentence over and over again, like some nodding, sleepy reader in bed.

It became late, and the Witan offered Billy a place to lie down and rest. Again, he graciously declined their hospitality, claiming that he wasn't tired and wanted to continue reading, but in the back of his mind was the great black book. Gwylain, Gwylith, and Gwylid wished him a good night and retired, disappearing to wherever it was they disappeared to at night.

When Billy felt certain the ancient faeries were out for the night, he crept over to the alcove that housed the big black book. He knelt before it and scanned its smooth, seductive back and dark iron bands. Like before, he felt an emotion that wasn't his own—a presence. It was cold yet friendly, eager yet patient, and foreboding yet desirable.

The Witan's words of warning stung at the back of his mind. *Surely, they wouldn't want to deprive me of anything useful this book contains. And I'll bet it contains something on binding magic. They're too careful. They don't know what I'm capable of. They think I should learn the old way, the slow way. But I don't have time for all that. What if it has what I'm looking for? Why are they holding me back?*

Billy's curiosity exploded beyond his control and he grabbed the giant volume. It felt like a warm handshake, and as he pulled the heavy book from its lair and into the light, he felt gratitude and joy. The book felt eager to help him—to answer his questions—to make his life easier.

He set the book on a table and examined the cover. On its back and face, three fine seams creased the smooth black leather in a scooping pattern, resembling rows of ocean waves. Attached at each point was a tiny, hooked claw that stabbed back into the leather.

Billy pulled back the face and thought he heard an audible "Aaahhh!" He glanced around, but the three Witan did not stir. He returned his attention to the book and found the first page was blank, except for a strange text scribbled in a strong but fevered hand, diagonally across the page. Billy tilted his head level with the writing and read.

"Beware! He who opens this tome opens a tomb, for in it resides the knowledge for ..." The text became an illegible scratch and ran off the page.

He scrutinized the line, trying to decipher anything more. "Beware?" he whispered. "The knowledge. Beware the knowledge? The knowledge for doing what?"

Billy closed the large book and pushed it away. He was very tired, but the excitement brewing up in him would not let him rest. The book beckoned him. He stared at the tome's dark cover and pondered the warning on its first page.

Who wrote it? Could it be a ploy to keep simple folks from reading it? Or is it honest? In either case, what can be further inside the book to provoke the warning?—The secret of binding magic?

Again, the book beckoned. Billy's infallible curiosity was piqued. He thought about the warning one last time, then reached for the book and flung it open.

***

Billy woke with a start, haunted by the same horrible nightmare that had roused him when last he slept. He had seen his mother and others who were no longer among the living, and again, he had been unable to save Lady Myrredith from her devouring grave.

"Lady Myrredith!" He glanced around and saw that he was still at the table in the Witan's home. The Witan themselves were busy with something in the corner and didn't seem to notice him.

Billy's thoughts could not depart from Myrredith. "She's in trouble."

"What's that?–"

"Who's in trouble?"

"Lady Myrredith."

"Your friend?"

"Yes. I've got to save her."

"How is she in danger?"

"I saw her ... in a grave."

"Then she is dead."

"No!" Billy raised his voice. "She's not dead. Not yet."

"Oh?" The Witan turned around.

"I—she can't be—I know she isn't. I can feel it."

"What else did you dream?"

"What else?"

"Yes, quickly–"

"before you begin to forget."

"Who else did you see?"

Billy rolled the dream around in his head. "I saw my mother ... and father ... and many others who have passed."

"He's been walking with the dead," Gwylith whispered.

"Surprising, for one so young and inexperienced."

"What else did you see?"

"I saw Castle Orgulous." He realized that the memory of the dream was fading fast. It was almost gone. "I—I—Oh, I'm forgetting!"

"Tell us–"

"what did you see–"

"in Orgulous?"

Billy closed his eyes, gathered his will, and concentrated. Forthwith, there came an image of his mother's grave in the Queen's Garden of Orgulous. As in the dream, he could see the thorn bush surrounding it, and—mentally—he pushed it away. At last, he opened his eyes. "My mother showed me her grave."

The Witan again huddled together and mumbled.

"What is it?" Billy asked. "What does it mean?"

"What do *you* think it means?"

"Yes–"

"what do *you* think it means?"

"I think it means ... I must go to Lyonesse."

"Then so you must."

"I don't know what trouble she's in, but I've got to save Myrredith."

"And Tirn Aill."

Saving Lady Myrredith had been the only thing on Billy's mind. "Oh yes ..." He felt somewhat ashamed at his selfish concerns. "I must save Tirn Aill first."

"Perhaps–"

"perhaps not."

"How can I know what's right? If I stay here, I could save Tirn Aill."

"Perhaps–"

"perhaps not–"

"or, perhaps, you will find what you are looking for in Lyonesse–"

"or along the way–"

"or perhaps not."

"But if I stay ... Lady Myrredith will die."

"Perhaps–"

"perhaps not."

"You must choose."

"But if I choose wrong ..."

"There is no wrong way to choose."

"Only follow your heart."

"Perhaps, your mother has shown you the way."

Gwylid's words struck Billy, as if he had lifted the hood on a lantern and the dark unknown before him was illuminated. His mother *had* shown him the way.

"She has, Gwylid. She has. It's quite clear to me now."

"Good–"

"then you've decided."

"Wonderful!"

At that moment, Billy remembered the great black book, but it was nowhere in sight. It had been before him on the table, but no more. He eyed its shadowy cubbyhole. Empty.

Gwylith noticed Billy's searching eyes. "What is it?"

"What? Oh, nothing,"

"Have you lost something?"

"No, n-nothing," Billy said.

"Then what is wrong?"

"Nothing." Billy rose from the table. "I must leave now."

"Well, if you must–"

"Yes, if you must–"

"Goodbye."

"We'll see you–"

"when you return–"

"as king."

Billy nodded, his eyes still scanning the room for the mysterious black book. By the time he reached the door, he'd convinced himself that he had slipped it into another hole and was just too tired to remember where.

He put his hand on the door. "You've been most helpful. Thank you."

The Witan bowed as he opened the door. "'Til we meet again."

Billy stepped through the narrow door and into the brisk outdoors. All around him, piles of brown and yellow leaves slept beneath a layer of frost. His elfish bodyguard waited directly in front of the door, on the roots of the great tree. To his right were pixies, dwarves, satyrs, sprites, and gnomes, and on his left, the dark elves, spriggans, and a wide variety of goblin kind. Both sides stared across at each other, their teeth and weapons bared.

Billy exhaled, and his breath steamed on the crisp air. On cue, those on the left shouted at him, accusing him of bringing a curse upon them. They stomped their feet and beat their shields. The clamor heightened, and so did tempers. A spear flew from the crowded goblins, and Onian knocked it from the air. Billy's elves drew back their bows, and the dwarves raised their weapons.

"Stop! Stop!" Billy shouted over the din. "Stop!"

Elzgig appeared next to Billy in a crash of thunder. The little wizard waved his staff about, and suddenly all was quiet. Both sides backed away and lowered their weapons.

"Now, I think His Highness has something to tell us."

"Thank you, Elzgig." Billy looked at the sullen crowd. "My friends ... fellow citizens of Tirn Aill, I believe I have discovered a way to save our beloved land." All eyes focused on Billy. "It seems that in order for me to save Tirn Aill, I must leave it."

A grumble rose from those on the right, and a cheer from those on the left. Billy held up his hands for quiet, and then continued.

"There is something I must retrieve from the world of men. Tomorrow, I leave for Lyonesse."

CHAPTER TEN

Captive

The Lady of Cyndyn sat in what was once her garden, staring at the roses that now belonged to someone else. The blooms used to bring her pleasure, but today, their transitory beauty only reminded her of how fragile life can be—their sweet scent a naïve lie.

In distant memories, she had been truly happy surrounded by this fragrant garden. The last time was with Billy, and before that, it was Hugh, but now she had lost all hope of ever seeing Billy outside her dreams, and Hugh was dead.

Across the table sat Prince Hereweald of Gwythia, Hugh's killer. He too was staring, but not at the flowers. All his attention lay on his stubborn but beautiful prisoner.

*

Lady Myrredith had not made a move or said a word beyond those required by etiquette. Hereweald, on the other hand, had gone out of his way to make her more comfortable. He allowed her to read books, listen to musicians, and sit in her garden. He even invited her to sup with him. All this, and still she showed him only contempt.

She hates me with every fiber of her being. With each breath she takes.

Her unbending hatred annoyed the prince, but what gnawed at him night and day was the growing sense that she was right to hate him. *This icy silence of hers is something akin to a scream. In fact, I think I would prefer it if she would scream, or cry, or something—anything but this blasted silence!*

Hereweald's entire body shook. He became aware of his taut muscles and relaxed back into his chair. *Ha! You're being drawn in by the very tricks Father warned you about. Women, and particularly courtiers, are adept at provoking men to weakness.*

"You will not provoke me," Hereweald blurted out.

Lady Myrredith looked up. "I beg your pardon, Your Highness."

"I said ..." Their eyes met, his anger petered away, and with it, his resolve. Was she playing him for a fool? The prince was unable to tell. He began again in a more cordial voice. "I said: you will, please, excuse me, Lady Myrredith. Many tasks await."

Hereweald felt quite awkward, and stood as if to leave, but instead of walking away, he waited for some kind of acknowledgment from her. Something that would release him—dismiss him. While he stood there, he felt more the fool than the prince. At last, she nodded to him.

Hereweald turned and took three steps before turning back to face her. "Lady Myrredith, is there something I can arrange that will make you more comfortable?"

Myrredith looked hard at the prince, and for a moment he thought he could read her thoughts. "Aside from dropping dead," he added with a smile. "Is there anything?"

Still, she said nothing.

"Lady Myrredith." The prince took a step closer to her. "I know that we are at odds with one another, but I don't see why you should be made uncomfortable."

He studied her and could see in her angry eyes that she wanted desperately to say something. Then, she closed her eyes and turned away.

"I ... I would like it very much if you could allow me my maids."

"Yes, of course." Hereweald nodded.

"And my gardeners."

Hereweald scanned her visage, looking for signs of deception.

"It's just that this garden is in desperate need of attention." Lady Myrredith motioned to the flowers.

Hereweald examined the roses, the shrubs, and trees. His eyes fell upon Myrredith once more, and he recognized in her something that reminded him of his mother. She, like this lady, had been quite fond of gardens, but he had always been too busy learning the art of war to worry about such things. *Someday ... someday I will have time for this.*

"Very well. Your gardeners can tend to your garden for one hour each day."

"While we are on the subject, I would like my own cooks and kitchen staff returned to their duties."

"What?" Hereweald's patience crumbled. "What's wrong with my cook?"

"Well, nothing, if you're feeding an army, but ..."

"He is a cook from the royal kitchen!"

"Then, I guess Gwythian food is not to my liking."

Hereweald's temper snapped, and all the anger and frustration he had been feeling for days came pouring out. "Not to your likin'? Not to your likin'? I doubt that there is anything much to your likin'. I have bent over backwards tryin' to be gracious and hospitable, but you will have none of it without complaint! When we part your head from your body, you will probably complain that the axe was too cold!"

Myrredith gasped and turned away from her captor. Prince Hereweald had tastefully avoided conversation concerning her execution since his proclamation, but in his anger, forgot his efforts to be less callous.

Hereweald's fury carried him from the garden but fizzled in the shade of the first corridor. His forward momentum stopped, and he felt himself drawn backward toward the door. He turned and smashed his fist against the wall. "Damn!" he hissed.

"What is it, my prince?" Snegaddrick appeared around the corner of the hall.

"That woman is so damned frustratin'."

Lord Snegaddrick nodded sympathetically.

The prince continued to rant, his face reddened by his fury. "I have done nothin' but show her all manner of courtesies, and still she treats me like-like-like a messenger boy!"

"You shouldn't waste your time on that one, my prince. Although, I must admit, you have good reason to hate her, it isn't good to dwell on it. Besides, she will be dead soon enough."

"I don't *hate* her."

"Then what is it? Loathing?"

"No, I ..." Prince Hereweald stared in the direction of the garden. "I guess if I had to put a word to it, I'd say that I *admire* her."

"What? Must I remind you of what she has done?"

"What you say she has done."

"You doubt my word, Your Highness? May the gods strike me down with lightning ..."

"No, no, no." Hereweald held up his hand. "No oaths of gods or lightning bolts, my heretical friend. I know you believe her guilty, but I am not convinced."

"But you heard ..."

"I am not convinced."

"You must believe me ..."

"Must I?" Hereweald fixed the little man with a cold glare.

Snegaddrick stiffened and blanched at the prince's tone. It was a tone that his father, the king, often used to debone uncooperative lords—a tone heavy with irony and sharp as the executioner's axe.

Hereweald continued, "Must I remind you, that I am the prince and you the advisor?"

"No, Highness." Snegaddrick kept his head bowed. "But I am concerned. Will you still go forward with her execution?"

"For the time being, Snegaddrick. For the time being."

Lord Snegaddrick frowned. Hereweald caught his expression and smiled. "May the gods strike you down with lightning? You old fraud!"

"Well ..." Snegaddrick smiled a little. "... It sounded good at the time."

"When you go before the gods, you'll wish you hadn't been such a blasphemous nonbeliever."

"When that day comes—and I hope to see many days before then—and I'm face to face with ... *Him*, on that day, I'll be á believer."

"A bit late then, don't you think?"

"What? You don't think there's any room for negotiations?"

Hereweald laughed. "If anyone could finagle his way in, it would be you, Lord Snegaddrick. You're just lucky that Father doesn't believe in burning heretics, or you'd already be pleading your case."

"Yes, Highness. But, Your Highness, I have not come to debate religion. Our scouts have spotted an army advancing in this direction from Nyraval."

"Nyraval?"

"It is confirmed, my prince."

"How large?"

"It's hard to say, Highness."

"How large?"

"At last count, Your Highness, there were some two thousand men, but it will have grown since then."

"How far?"

"By now, they will be three to four days' march."

"Assemble my staff. Order a general alert."

"Yes, Highness."

"And I wish to speak to the scout who spotted them."

"Yes, Highness. I shall send for him at once."

"We will crush this new army to send a message to Nyraval! Soon, they will know that we are here to stay."

CHAPTER ELEVEN

A Stitch in Time

The rhythmic crunch of soldiers' boots grew louder. The sound echoed deep into the darkness, and became songlike, as it penetrated Hugh's consciousness. It spoke to him, beckoned him. The darkness surrounding him was cold, but undemanding.

I'll stay here.

The darkness silently agreed, snuggling like a chilled lover, becoming more comfortable. And yet Hugh felt alone.

He pulled the darkness in around him but, again, the song of marching feet thrust its way into his awareness. It was, in fact, the only thing outside the infinite, accommodating darkness. The only stimulus. The only thing with an edge in the void.

"Go away." Hugh tried to turn from it.

But the song followed. Everything he tried made the song's edge sharper, more defined. Nuances and variations sprung from the simple monotonous rhythm. Hugh attempted to ignore it, but the harder he tried, the more it called to him.

Frustrated, unable to evade his tormentor, he reached out to push it away and touched its jagged edge. It bit into him—a barbed hook. Then ten hooks, twenty hooks, a hundred hooks, all dragging him upwards. The darkness resisted. He could feel its yearning, seductive arms slipping away. A pale light pierced the darkness above him, like a single star. It brightened as he approached. All at once, he was ripped from the darkness. Hugh was awake.

Pain flooded Hugh's brain like a rain-gorged gutter. He clenched his eyes against the searing light and inventoried his body. His entire being ached; however, the pain in his abdomen dominated. It felt like wounds he had received before, except much deeper.

Hugh cracked open his eyes to have a look at the belly wound. He found a dirty old blanket covering him and pushed it away with a grunt. A gentle hand pushed the cover back over him, and another touched his lips. He looked out the corner of his eye. Someone crouched beside him.

"Shhh," his nurse whispered. "The Gwythies will hear ya."

The rhythmical sound of hobnail boots crunching over cobblestones filled the tiny chamber. Hugh looked toward the source of the thunderous marching. Across from him, no more than two feet, sunlight flowed in through a canvas scrap, which covered a man-sized hole in the wall. The light flickered as the shadows of soldiers crossed the thin canvas screen.

A distinct odor impacted Hugh's nose and he turned to examine his companion. He could discern little about his apparent savior, except the slight build of a young boy or girl. He or she was wrapped from head to heel in rags, only revealing a single sharp eye and calloused feet. Despite the wrapping, Hugh could see that the wretched creature's hands were horribly crooked and nearly useless. A dainty silver ring, with a delicate purple stone, protruded through the wrappings upon the smallest digit. In the opposite hand, Hugh glimpsed a small, slender blade. As for the rest of the body, it was difficult to tell if it was misshapen or merely contorted beneath the low ceiling. It took a copper trinket from within its wrappings, kissed it, and put it back. Its eye, the only feature asserting its human nature, never strayed from the canvas.

Together, Hugh and the stranger waited for the army of Gwythia to march by. Time seemed to stop as the enemy legions passed.

Hugh felt dizzy as the thundering boots pounded at his head. The very noise, which tore him from Death's embrace, now resounded in his skull with the Reaper's terrible rage. Every Gwythie soldier on Lyonesse soil was a gnashing tooth in Death's maw. Gwythian banners rippled and snapped with the flexing of his timeless, adamantine muscles. In each footfall, his ancient voice croaked the names of the countless dead to come; a rollcall of the damned. And Hugh heard each name. He wanted to scream; he could not. He wanted to run; he could not. He wanted to die; he could not.

At last, the maddening sound faded into the distance. Hugh's host slipped the knife away and shambled over to the canvas screen. The unfortunate was, as Hugh had suspected, a cripple.

"You're a beggar?" he asked with a hoarse voice.

The pitiful creature peeked through the side of the canvas flap. It lowered its head to examine itself.

"Yes," it hissed.

"Please, forgive me. I did not mean to … I am no better than you, my friend. In fact, I am in your debt."

"No. Save your wind."

"But I am. And now that I have hurt you, I am doubly so."

"Hurt me? Ya can't hurt me."

"I did not mean to draw attention to your situation. You cannot help the circumstances you were born to."

The stranger turned around. The keen eye fixed itself on Hugh's eyes, and for a moment, the former champion found his own pain insignificant.

"I wasn't always like this." The beggar held out its claw-like hands.

"You are a boy?"

The beggar gave an ironic chortle and asked, "Is it that hard to tell? Yes."

"Again, I am sorry," Hugh said.

The boy held up his crooked hands. "Save your wind, I say! You'll need your strength if you don't want to be dead again by mornin'."

"Again?"

"Aye."

"I was dead?"

"Aye."

"How is it that I am alive?"

"Do not ask me that. Please, rest now."

Indeed, Hugh felt quite tired, and the pain in his innards told him that his scrape with death wasn't over, but the quiet darkness of sleep was less inviting than ever before. It was a smoky reflection of death—a shadow, with only a flimsy barrier separating the two. It would be all too easy to fall asleep and then slip beyond it unaware. Hugh still felt little love for life, but having sampled the alternative, he was not yet ready to face it again. He remembered the cold emptiness and wondered if all men's deaths were so lonely.

"What manner of disease has done this to you?" Hugh fought to stay awake.

The beggar shushed Hugh again, but then seemed moved to answer. "'Twasn't sickness what done this to me. Well, not the kind you're thinkin' of. The thing what done this to me walks among men on two legs. Two fat, healthy legs."

"A man did that to you?" The very thought of such cruelty turned Hugh's stomach.

"Aye, Sir Hugh. He were a man."

"You know my name?"

"Aye." The beggar looked away. "And I know *his* name too."

The beggar's words were as chalk. Hugh's throat tightened as if he had breathed them in. His stomach knotted. He managed to keep its contents down, but the exertion was too much, and he succumbed to sleep. A restless sleep, fraught with dark, formless terrors that only a man once dead could imagine.

***

For two days, Hugh stumbled in and out of consciousness. Each time he came to, the nameless beggar was there by his side. With amazing consistency, the boy provided food, water, and even medicine. Hugh did not know why he was alive. He only knew that he should be among the dead. This knowledge rooted in his mind and grew into a compelling question. The same question he was told not to ask. This in itself added strength to the thought and forced him into a mental tug of war.

Hugh found his strength returning, but he wondered about the wisdom of his cure. Life—his life—hardly seemed worth living, much less saving. Yet somehow, while living in that wee dirty cave—which was literally a hole in the wall—he was recovering. Something in him, which he could not fathom, wanted to survive. It was in constant conflict with the dark part of him that had already surrendered.

"Why do you do this?" Hugh asked his ragged host.

The boy glanced over his shoulder but did not answer.

Hugh looked around him and observed that several items were missing. The large copper kettle had been replaced by a smaller one of iron. There had been some knives and cups as well. The small silver ring that had adorned the boy's finger was gone.

Hugh saw a tremor in the boy's hands. "You haven't eaten since I arrived."

The beggar's only response was to hide his hands.

"You've sold nearly all your belongings to buy me medicine, haven't you?"

"What of it?"

"Why?"

"I didn't need those things."

"You could have used them to help yourself. Why are you helping me?"

"It doesn't matter."

"It matters to me!"

"Why?"

"Because ... because you should have let me die."

"I ..." The boy arched his back. "I could not."

Hugh became frustrated. Stuck between his sudden anger at the beggar's impassive philanthropy, his pain at being alive, and the braying melancholy that ruled his days. For an instant, the pain won out. "You should have let me die!"

The beggar turned to face him. His young, wise eye stared out through the bandages. An eye full of hurt, anger, and empathy—which reminded Hugh once again of the boy's humanity and his terrible suffering.

He could not bear to look into the boy's eye. He had often scolded himself because of his penchant for self-pity, but he had never felt such profound shame over it before. It cleaved down his middle like a great sword cutting him in two.

"I could not," the boy said with some finality.

Tears fell from Hugh's eyes. He closed them to suppress the flow.

"I couldn't let you die, Sir Hugh, because of a boy who once looked up to you as the greatest of men."

Hugh's conscience would not let him sleep. All his anger turned inward. He was ashamed of his weaknesses and angered by his failure to perfect himself. His life was meaningless. He had squandered it. But what angered him most was that the wrong done to Billy, Myrredith, his mother and father, and to him, would never be righted.

The two of them sat in silence for hours. Finally, it grew dark. The boy stoked the small fire and prepared the evening meal.

Hugh broke their silence. "I'm sorry to be such a disappointment."

The boy only shrugged.

"That doesn't matter to you either."

Again the boy shrugged.

"But you've helped me. And you said you once thought of me as a great ..."

"It wasn't me."

"You weren't the boy?"

"No."

"The one who looked up to me?"

"No."

Hugh took in the laconic beggar. "He was a friend of yours."

The boy nodded. "And yours."

A notion snatched Hugh from his melancholy. His eyes focused on the beggar, then on the fire and, for a moment, he saw a face. "Billy," he muttered to himself.

The beggar's head turned to look into Hugh's face. "Aye."

Hugh glanced up from the fire and caught the meaningful look in the boy's eye.

"Billy! You knew Billy!"

The boy nodded.

"And you ..." He paused for a moment to allow his mind to catch up with his mouth. "You are the boy who helped him. Aren't you supposed to be dead?"

The boy's eye shifted from side to side before he nodded.

"Did you also help Billy find his way through the Cyndyn catacombs?"

"Joukery-paukery if I knowed how, but he done that on his own. He's one o' two blokes ever done that, and him a green country lad at that."

"Who was the first?"

"Only the single best burglar Dyven has ever known! Though he was in much better condition when he done it."

"So only one man has ever stole into the old orchard graveyard, navigated the catacombs to Cyndyn Hall, and come back again?"

"More boy than man."

"Yes, of course, but that is what happened, right?"

"That's the shortest tale of it, aye."

Hugh stared into the fire. "And is it possible ... for this same person, and perhaps a friend, to wander into the old orchard one night, find themselves in the catacombs, and ... ?"

"Look, I know where yer goin' with this, and it's a bad idea, even if you weren't half in the grave."

"Perhaps, but is it possible?"

"Possible? Yeah, but you'd have more luck askin' Billy to do it."

"Billy is dead."

Hugh pulled back his tongue, narrowly avoiding his teeth. He wished he could draw back his last breath and remove the words hanging so heavy on the air.

His companion stared into the fire. "I know."

"You know?"

"Aye." The boy's voice came out barely above a whisper. "I heard it in the street."

They watched the fire in silence.

"Stitch? Your name is Stitch."

"It was."

"Was?"

The boy held out what passed for his hands and said, "Before this, it was."

Hugh nodded in understanding. "I too have a new name."

"A new name?"

"Now, I am only Hugh, nothing more."

The boy, who had been called Stitch, considered Hugh with raised brows.

"I am no longer a knight. I have been stripped of all titles and land—everything."

"Everything?"

Hugh nodded. "I am what you see."

The former cutpurse and former king's champion stared across at one another. They both had attained what they thought was something worth having, only to have it stripped away by another. They were without friends, family, or direction, and now even their homeland seemed lost. They each felt alone. In the silence, an agreement passed between them. They had no future, and no past that mattered now. They both had only the moment, and so they were not alone.

***

The next day, Hugh learned that Stitch now wanted to be called "Aeth," a name he claimed his long-dead mother had given him, along with half a lover's locket containing the picture of his father—a man whom Stitch had failed to find in seven years of searching the streets of Dyven. He also learned that his disfigurement was due to a spiteful man named Derian.

"After Derian caught me, he took me to the cells under the tower. It were there that he done this to me."

"Tell me ... how did he ... ?"

Aeth paused for a moment to peek out of his little canvas door. A single raindrop splattered against it, and Hugh heard the scuff of a shoe in the street. Other than that, it was quiet. The sky had donned its dull grey raiment. Gwythian soldiers were scarce.

"First, it was the rack. He was desperate to find Billy. I told him I don't know such a bloke and that he ought to look 'round Apple Hill; if'n he wanted a boy instead of a girl. That really pinched him off, so he stretched me out a bit more. Again, I tell him that I don't know any such bloke, but he already knowed that me and Billy was mates."

"But you still didn't tell him."

"Naw. But then he gets the idea that I'd tell him what he wants if I knew that he knew I knew Billy, and that if I know what's good for me, I better tell him you know what."

Hugh's brow creased in confusion.

"Well, it don't matter." Aeth shrugged. "What matters is that's when he goes to work with his tongs and thumbscrews."

"And you still didn't tell him, did you?"

"Naw. It's odd, but I actually laughed at him."

"Laughed?"

"Yeah. It just sorta come over me. I think I went over the moon."

"And that angered him, didn't it?"

"Ha!" Aeth gave a chortle. "He's got this little vein on his forehead what swells when he's mad. ... Damn near exploded!"

Hugh chuckled at the image of the little tyrant with his red pulsing forehead.

"That's when the other bloke hands him his hammer."

"His hammer?"

"Yeah." Aeth held up his hands. "His hammer."

"He used a hammer on your hands?"

"Among other places."

Hugh shivered. "Wait! There was another man present?"

"Aye. Stuck to the shadows, he did."

"Who?"

"Just some bloke. Talked funny."

"Funny?"

"Yeah. Foreign like. Derian called him ... Spaniard."

"Don Miguel Scarosa," Hugh muttered.

"You knowed him?"

"You don't have to worry about him, ever again."

"Dead?"

"Billy killed him."

"Really?"

Hugh nodded, and half a grin crept onto his face. "With the Spaniard's own knife."

"I didn't think Billy had it in him."

"Neither did Scarosa."

Hugh and Aeth fell quiet, remembering their lost friend. Finally, Hugh broke the silence.

"So Scarosa was there," he mused. "And he's the one that made Derian use the hammer."

"But I still didn't budge."

"No?"

"No. I don't know how I done it, but I kept my tongue and only tells 'em lies. I was runnin' out of oomph. I think Derian saw that then, and I realize that mostly he's been playin' with me, except maybe for the hammer. He would'a killed me with that damned hammer if Cap'n hadn't come along."

"The captain of the guard was there?"

"Well, he come in then. He was real upset at first, but then Derian tells him I knowed where Billy is and he shuts up. The three of them whisper for a minute or two. Not long enough for me. After Cap'n left, Derian brings out the fire and the coals."

Hugh closed his eyes. "Please, no more. I'm sorry..."

"It's awright. I still never told him the whole truth."

"I know." Hugh offered a half-smile.

"You know he's workin' for the Gwythies now?"

"Derian?"

"Aye. He's in tight with them he is. He was once a great man, great burglar. Now he's a pet rat. I seen him with them many times. Onced, he looks right at me, but he don't even know it's me."

"How did you escape from the tower?"

"Well, after I tells them what they think is all I know, they takes me from the tower. The captain tells Derian to let me go, but Derian has his own plans. He tells me he's gonna drown me in the bay and let the fish have my bones, but before he can get me there, I stomp his foot and jump from the wagon. Unlucky for me, there's this other wagon comin' by right then."

"Unlucky?"

"Yeah, 'cause the driver don't see me and runs me over like a rotten melon in the road."

"Ouch!"

"Yeah, ouch. Broke my leg, but then I gets real lucky, 'cause Derian thinks this kills me."

"He didn't check...?"

The voice of a girl outside their little shelter stopped Hugh short.

"Hello? Is there someone there?"

Aeth and Hugh exchanged glances and shrugs.

The girl continued, giving them a larger taste of her strange, melodic accent. "I need to speak with the man living there."

Again, the two occupants exchanged a series of glances and rapid-fire gestures, the result of which was Hugh volunteering to speak.

"Yes. I am here. Who is it?"

"I am called Precilla."

"Why are you here, Precilla?"

"I was told that I would find you living in a hole in the wall. I have been searching for a hole in the city wall since yesterday, and now here you are. May I ... come in?"

"Who told you this?"

"Oh, a voice!"

"A voice?"

"From beyond. May I come in?"

"Beyond? Beyond what?"

"I am Precilla. I speak with the world beyond this one."

Aeth straightened. "You're the spaewife—the Egyptian?"

"Who is that? Is there someone with you?"

Hugh and Aeth exchanged glances, but did not answer.

"Is there a spirit in there with you?"

"No. Just a ... another man."

"Oh. I did not expect to find two men."

"What do you want?" Aeth asked.

"I have a message for the man who lives in the hole in the wall."

"Which one?"

"I am unsure now, but he is a man who has lost much."

"That's you," both men answered in unison.

"No, it's you, Aeth."

"I think it must be you, Hugh."

A raven-haired woman with dark skin and a sheer, pale veil stuck her head through the opening. Her eyes were older than her voice had let on. "I'm sorry, but I can't just wait out here forever. Show me your hands."

Hugh and Aeth exchanged glances.

The seer persisted. "Show me your hands."

Hugh and Aeth held out their hands. She glanced at Aeth's bandages, and then decided to examine Hugh's hands first. Gently, she turned the palms face up and held them up to the light.

"Mmmm," the spaewife murmured, examining the former champion's left hand. "Yes, very promising."

"What?"

"You have great passion, and Saturn favored you at birth with a gift."

"Saturn?"

"Yes, you were destined for greatness. Now, let us see what the other says ..."

Precilla rubbed Hugh's right palm, then brought it closer to her. "Yes," she said, running her thumb over the creases. "But such passion can sometimes interfere with greatness, can it not, my handsome friend? And here ..."

Hugh blushed, but then noticed that Precilla had stopped. The caramel-skinned woman shook, her nostrils flared, and her eyes widened in the same manner as a green horse in battle. She dropped Hugh's hand and turned to leave. Hugh lunged out and caught her by the wrist.

"No, no," she screamed hysterically. "Del preserve me! Let me go!"

Hugh pulled her back into the little cave and grabbed her other wrist. Aeth snapped his hand over her mouth and begged her to hush. Precilla fought them—her face still contorted in equine-like terror.

At last, the woman stopped struggling, and Hugh released her wrists. His hands went immediately to his abdomen, which had begun to bleed again. The spaewife sat up and pushed Aeth's hands aside to stare at Hugh's wound.

"Then you are mortal?" Precilla remained cautious.

Hugh looked at the blood on his hands and said, "It would appear so."

"I do not understand. I saw in your palm that your destiny had come to an end. That you were dead!"

"He was dead."

Precilla's nostrils flared again as if she scented danger on the air. She turned to Aeth. "How is that possible?"

Aeth didn't answer.

"How is that possible?" Precilla placed her hand on the boy's shoulder. "I must know."

"Adwythane." Aeth hung his head.

"The wizard who lives beneath Cromllech Dunom?"

"The same."

"What was the devil's price?"

Again, Aeth didn't answer.

"What was his price, boy? That one always has a price, and for this it would be very high indeed!"

With his one good eye, Aeth stared at Precilla and Hugh, then turned away.

Precilla released the boy's shoulder and turned to face Hugh. Her face was grim—a thin veneer over her fearful core. Slowly, she backed toward the exit. Before Hugh could move to stop her, she spoke. "I will tell you the message I have for you." She held up her hands. "But then you must promise never to seek me out."

Hugh nodded.

"You have lost something very important, something given you by one very close to your heart. When you have recovered it, you will be empowered to reclaim your former self."

Hugh thought for a moment. "My sword! … Is it my sword?"

"Perhaps. I do not know. Now, swear that you will never seek me out."

"My sword was lost at sea. It is impossible! I will never recover it."

"My message is one of hope, Sir. It only *seems* impossible, for in my vision, I foresaw that what was lost will be recovered. Now, swear what I have asked of you."

"My father's sword." Hugh stared into the smoldering fire and watched as a thin wisp of smoke formed into the shape of a sword. "Father left it behind for me, and Mother kept it safe until I was ready to wield it ... and I lost it. I broke faith. That is why I have failed ..."

"Swear it."

"Why, I am damned." Hugh's eyes snapped up from the fire. "I must get it back!"

"And you will." Precilla scooted away until she was half out the small opening.

Aeth held out two coins to her, but she refused them. "The people of Lyonesse have shown me much kindness. When he is restored, he will more than settle the debt with this lot of Gwythies, for me and all my friends." Then she turned to Hugh. "Now, please, Sir, swear to what I have asked."

Hugh looked at the frightened woman hesitating in the doorway. "I am sorry, but first, I must understand one thing, then I will swear never to seek you out for as long as I have life in me."

"What is it?"

"Why are you so frightened of me?"

"Because Death has taken you under his dark wing."

"But I am alive!"

"You are not the Holy Son, nor one of His blessed miracles, and so you are here by most vile, unnatural means. Necromancy! You do not belong here. You belong to the grave."

Hugh looked down from the woman's face and noticed for the first time the tiny cross hanging from her neck. "You are a Christian?"

"Yes, but the blessed Savior still allows me my visions. Now, please, I beg of you, swear for me and let me go."

"Thank you." Hugh looked into the curious woman's black eyes and held up his hand. "I swear with my own blood, before the Spirit of the All Mighty, that I will not seek you out in any way."

Precilla's taut features relaxed slightly, and she pulled back to leave. However, before she could clear the canvas flap, she stopped and stared at Hugh. She squinted, and he could see her mind trying to grasp something.

At last, she spoke. "I can see you are a good man. At least, you believe yourself to be, and that is a hopeful beginning. So, I will give you a bit of advice."

"Please."

"As I said before, I saw in your palm that your destiny had come to an end. Your future—your new destiny—be it for good or evil, is yours to choose. There is an ancient saying among my people that a man given a second chance should be given a third if he uses the second for the good of another. But be warned, I also see The Reaper's owl riding upon your shoulder. You could easily be made to serve him."

Without another cryptic word, the flap dropped and Precilla disappeared. Her escape was so hasty that even her shadow failed to appear on the canvas stage.

Hugh laid back on the floor. The pain in his middle had lessened somewhat, but the weariness in his bones had increased. He rested on his back and stared at the ceiling until Aeth's face appeared over him.

"There, that should staunch the bleeding."

Hugh tried to make eye contact with Aeth, but the boy kept his eye on the wound or the fire. Finally, Hugh reached up, grabbed his nurse's ragged tunic, and pulled him close. The former knight stared at the keen but tired eye and marveled at the boy's bravery.

"You gave your eye so that I could live. I won't forget that. Somehow, someway, I'll find a way to make it up to you."

"Free Lyonesse."

"What?"

"That's really why I done what I done. I knowed you was the only one who'd rid us of these cursed Gwythies."

"But I can't ..."

"But you will."

"I am nothing!"

"You are the greatest knight in the kingdom."

"Not anymore."

"But you will be again. Now, I know you will."

Hugh looked the former cutpurse in the eye and remembered Precilla's words about a second chance. Aeth's request was, indeed, the only way to make this reprieve count for something.

But how? I don't have a horse or a sword, and I don't have the strength anymore. God has abandoned me. But maybe ... maybe if I could somehow recover my father's sword. ... Then God might restore my courage, and allow me to save my beloved Lyonesse and Myrredith. Yeah, and maybe the devil's a flounder, this hole is a palace, and Billy's still alive.

CHAPTER TWELVE

Return of the *Gyldan Mene*

"So, you can see ..." The captain of the *Dragonfly* had his mouth full of apple. "... I couldn't possibly take on a journey to Lyonesse."

Thortan scowled at him. "But you just sailed in here two days ago, ya green-skinned, flop-eared oaf!"

"Precisely." The captain nodded.

Billy's mind strayed as he allowed his eyes to wander over the marvelous ship docked behind the captain. From her pale chestnut woods and delicate gold railings to her silvery spider-silk ropes and iridescent gossamer sails, the *Dragonfly* was utterly breathtaking. She was nothing close to the clunky ships of men, and much more than their shipwrights could hope to achieve. She floated on the water as still as a cloud on the horizon, and as inviting and patient as Billy's old climbing tree.

Elzgig's irritated but restrained voice yanked Billy back to the business at hand.

"I don't think you understand. Take a good look about you, Toady Brimstone. Go ahead. Tirn Aill is going into winter for the first time in memory!"

The captain scrunched up the right side of his face, closing up his steel-grey eye. Then, with his mint-green left eye, he looked around from face to face and scratched his scaly neck. "Yeahr." He wiped his mouth on his sleeve. "Maybe it is, maybe it isn't."

Onian leaned over Billy's shoulder. "It is! Have you not seen the forest or Shiny Brook? Nothing but brown leaves and frozen water."

"Ice," Thortan said.

"Whatever!" The lean elf sighed. "The water isn't moving!"

"And our future king, here ..." Elzgig strained to remain calm. "He needs to get to the world of men so that he can bring back what will fix it all."

The captain seemed more interested in slicing his apple than in what they were telling him. He cut out a piece in the shape of a star, and then ate it from the point of his knife. Then, with slow, deliberate actions, he looked Billy over, starting from his feet and moving up. "Seems to me," he mumbled through the apple, "that a future king could come up with a better way to get to the world of men if he really is—"

"Billy is Eleanor's son."

"See." Thortan pushed Billy's hand forward. "He's wearin' the ring."

"Oooo." Brimstone rolled his eyes. "I'm all impressed."

Elzgig stepped in front of Billy. "He hasn't yet learned the ways of his power."

The captain said nothing.

"Oh, it's hopeless talking to his kind." Thortan threw his hands up and turned away. "Let's go. Maybe the Witan will have a suggestion."

Onian turned and followed Thortan, leaving Billy and Elzgig with the stubborn captain. Billy watched curiously, as the captain continued the odd dissection of his fruit. Elzgig took a deep breath and opened his mouth, but then sighed and walked away.

Now, Billy stood alone before the captain, his arms crossed. He rummaged through his mind for something that might convince the old sea dog, but Elzgig had already exhausted everything, and to no avail. Billy was about to give up and walk away when the captain spoke.

"Well, boy—" Suddenly, he jumped forward and thrust his knife at Billy. "Why don't you get out o' here?"

Billy didn't budge. Instead, he stared directly into the strange faerie's eyes.

The captain held the knife steady, and a wide, green-toothed smile spread itself across his face. Then he chuckled.

"Humph. Perhaps more than a boy. I knew me a pirate once, named Billy."

Toady withdrew his knife and ran it over one of his droopy, pig-like ears. The numerous rings all along its edge tinkled when the blade touched them. He stopped on a large gold ring and held it up with the knifepoint.

"I stole this from him while he slept." Toady laughed and leaned back against a mooring post.

Upon seeing the captain relax, Billy laughed too. The innocent, joyous sound of it struck the warty little sea captain like a sack of grain and took the wind out of him. He stared up at Billy, his hands hanging by his side.

"What is it?"

"You've got yer mother's laugh," Toady muttered. "And I never dreamed that I'd hear it again."

"You knew my mother?"

"Quite well, don't ya know. She picked me to take her to Lyonesse. Damned awful place, but she insisted. There's another good reason for me not to go there, and you should do the same."

"But I must."

"Look, Your Highness." Toady took Billy by the arm. "I'm an old sea lover, see? And I've seen much in my time at sea. This winter-thing, it'll pass. You'll see, and then we can get back to the way things were before."

The captain seemed quite friendly now, and so Billy risked being a little familiar. "I don't know, Toady."

"Look, just because I'm talkin' to ya doesn't make us friends. See?"

"Yeah, I see. But regardless of what you think of me, or what you think of the others, this 'winter-thing' as you call it, is not just gonna blow over. I know it isn't. I've seen it."

The captain's head tilted to one side and once again he closed his grey eye to stare at Billy. "Do ya have the sight, boy?"

"Aye." It was an odd thought to him, even now. However, there was no denying it: he had precognitive visions. Many of them he didn't understand, but they felt real and were often more disturbing than nightmares. It was most unsettling when they became reality.

Billy's mind flashed with images of a barren, icy wasteland. Frozen faerie corpses, like frosty statues clenched in eternal agony, littered the landscape. It was a painful vision, made doubly so by the uncanny surety that it was their future. Billy had decided not to share this vision with anyone. He didn't want to start a panic. Tirn Aill was topsy-turvy enough already.

Billy measured his words, balancing secrecy against the needs of his mission. "I have seen the future of Tirn Aill, Captain," he whispered. "And it's a cold, dead place."

Toady Brimstone, master of the *Dragonfly* and sailor of the ancient seas, stared candidly with both eyes into Billy's face. Through the facade of his jaded, rough exterior, Billy could see the bones of fear maneuvering under the captain's greenish skin.

Finally, the captain spoke, "I can't see the future. For all my years, I can barely predict the sea from the evening sky."

Thortan shouted from the end of the dock. "Come along, Your Majesty. I could build you a ship before that wart farm will give you a ride on that leak-trap of his!"

Captain Brimstone stiffened and peered around Billy to scowl at the dwarf leader. "The *Dragonfly* does not leak, you filthy old digger! ... Not that you would know a leak from a twig in your ear." He turned his eyes back to Billy and shouted out the side of his mouth, "And Billy—that is,

His Highness—will have the pleasure to witness that for himself ... on our journey to Lyonesse!"

***

Billy and Brimstone agreed that they would sail for Lyonesse on the morning tide, and then went their separate ways. While the captain prepared the *Dragonfly*, Billy returned with Elzgig to the wizard's humble cave and made ready, collecting provisions for his trip.

"I wish I were going with you," Elzgig said.

"No, it's already decided. I need you here, to watch over things and keep the peace until I return."

"Aye." The wizard nodded.

Thortan barged in with a large pack on his back. "Ready to go, Your Majesty."

"Thortan." Billy looked up. "You are leader of the dwarves."

"And they will go wherever I say. We are yours to command, Sire."

"No. I need you and your dwarves here as well. Who else will keep Gulch in check?"

Thortan scowled at Elzgig. "I can see you've mucked up his head with politics. Do you know how long it's been since I went on an adventure? How long it's been since I had a real battle?" Thortan rattled his armaments and growled.

"Calm yourself. Look, my old friend, Billy is quite right. You are needed here."

"But ..."

Elzgig placed his hand on Thortan's arm. "There will be other days for you, I know, but this is Billy's quest."

Thortan dropped his head with a grunt and stepped to the door. Then he turned to face Billy.

"I shall not fail you, Your Majesty." The dwarf bowed to one knee.

"I know you won't."

Thortan rose and drew a dagger from his belt. Gold wire wrapped the grip, and a black sapphire sat in the pommel. The stone matched three others, set in gold down the length of the black scabbard. Thortan reluctantly extended the weapon to Billy.

"Here. You might need this."

"I don't intend to do any fighting."

"Aye." The dwarf nodded. "But you're not the only one who can start a fight. Better to be safe."

Billy reached out and gripped the dagger. *It's warm! That's odd; it should be chilled.*

"Your Majesty." Thortan made eye contact. His hand still held the dagger tight. "This blade has served me well. It will bring you luck."

"Thank you." Billy lifted the weapon from the dwarf's hand. "I'm sure it will."

With that, Thortan bowed and left. Billy looked at the glittering weapon and drew it slowly from the sheath. Nearly ten inches of gleaming curved steel flashed in the firelight. The blade was unusually wide near the hilt but tapered along its sweeping curve to a deadly double-edged point. He strained his eyes to examine the finely honed edges and caught a glimpse of numerous infinitesimal lines running along the blade like hundreds of tiny black waves on a silvery beach. Billy's eyes were captivated by the blade's mesmerizing pattern. He also noted the peculiar markings inscribed at the base of the spine.

Elzgig looked up from his packing. "Its name is Lura Zahn."

"Its name?"

"Aye. A dwarfish craftsman, such as Thortan's father, always names his best work."

"And what are these marks?"

"The runes that make up its name. It means Star Tooth."

"Star Tooth? Why?"

Elzgig sat and placed his hands on the insides of his thighs as if he were readying himself for a long-winded tale. "Well ... the story goes that the metal Fjorel used to make that blade, fell from the night sky."

Billy's eyes shone as he inspected the runes. "Lura Zahn," he whispered reverently.

As if to answer, the dagger vibrated in Billy's hand. The sensation startled him into dropping the weapon, but before he could blink, the dagger was resting in its scabbard. He stared at it for an instant before setting it down on the stone table and stepping back.

Elzgig chuckled and slapped his leg. "The Rune Quencher's blade has some surprises for you, Your Majesty, as I'm sure you have for it."

Billy returned to the table, still eyeing the dagger suspiciously. After a moment, he reached out to take it, and it leapt from the scabbard into his hand.

"It's ... it's ... Wow!" Billy couldn't take his eyes from the weapon.

"I'd say that Lura Zahn has taken a likin' to ya."

"You think so?" He put it back in the scabbard.

"I should say so." Onian made his usual stealthy appearance.

Billy and Elzgig's heads snapped around to look at the elf. Billy was getting used to Onian's sudden, unannounced arrival, but it still startled him. The only comfort was in the knowledge that it had the same effect on others.

"Oh no! I'll tell you what I told the others. I can't take you with me."

"I know."

"Oh. Then why have you come?"

"I have come to wish you a good journey, for Thortan and I must be off on a mission of our own."

Elzgig frowned. "What's wrong?"

"Goblins are massing in the forest."

"Massing?" Billy and Elzgig spoke in unison.

Onian held up his hands to calm them. "I don't know what they're up to, but I will by dawn."

Onian started to bow, but Billy grasped his hand and shook it. The elf stiffly returned the shake.

"Thank you, Onian. I don't know what I'll do without you."

"You will do fine." The lanky elf smiled with a twinkle in his eyes. "Shaldra will protect you. I have already spoken to him."

"Perhaps he should stay here with you."

"No, Your Highness. I have warriors aplenty, but only one king."

Billy grinned.

"Your Highness, if you are set on going to Erin, remember King Finvarra is a crafty one. As I have told you, the Daoine Sidhe are especially well versed in battle, but I don't think asking them for an army is wise."

"Why?"

"Finvarra will more than likely challenge you to a contest for such a favor. Usually, that means combat."

"But aren't we allies?"

"Aye," Elzgig said. "Although Finvarra seldom sees it that way."

"Well, if he does challenge me, I'll politely decline."

"Oh, you mustn't do that." Elzgig shook his head.

"And why not?"

"Politics."

Billy felt befuddled. "Huh?"

Onian crossed his arms. "Because that would infuriate Finvarra. He'd consider it an insult and would probably kill you for such a slight, or have you thrown into his dungeon."

Elzgig held up his hands. "At any rate, it would be most unfavorable, and we may need him later."

"Then what you're telling me is: I will have to try."

"No." Onian straightened his spine. "You do not have to go to him. But if you go to Erin, and Finvarra challenges you, you have to win."

"Can't I just surrender and leave?"

"No." Onian shook his head. "Finvarra never plays for free, and you'd be lucky to escape with your lives."

"Are we allies or not?"

"Well, only when Finvarra wants to be."

Elzgig touched Billy on the elbow and said, "Remember, his wife Oonagh was quite close to your mother once. She might help you."

Onian sneered.

"What?"

"Oonagh has her own games to play." The elf crossed his arms again. "Just hope she's in a good mood."

Billy sighed. "So much."

Elzgig nodded. "Yes, Your Highness; the weight of a crown."

"If I must go against Orgulous," Billy said, half to himself. "I will need the Daoine Sidhe army. I must go to Finvarra."

Onian frowned, but then managed to turn it into a reassuring smile. Then he turned and disappeared through the dark doorway. Billy went to the door to watch him leave, but saw only the glitter of frost on the wind and the telltale smoke-like breaths of his elfin guard. Billy winced at seeing how much the terrain already resembled his dark vision of the future.

"Well..." Billy returned to his packing. "Do you think I'm making the right decision, going to Finvarra?"

"Only you can know that, Your Highness. You must go where your heart leads you."

"At any rate, I think we've heard from everyone tonight."

"Not quite." Shaldra poked his head in the door.

Again, as with Onian, Shaldra's silent appearance gave Billy and Elzgig a start.

"Would you youngsters stop doing that?"

"Doing what?"

"Oh, never mind."

The leader of Billy's guard turned to him. "Your Highness, Sylvys approaches."

Billy and Elzgig went to the door and watched as the satyr made his way up the path to Elzgig's little cave.

"Wonder what he wants," Elzgig muttered.

"Probably wants to wish me a good journey."

"Your Majesty." Sylvys bowed his head.

The slowness of the satyr's movements and the lack of color in his face struck Billy.

"My dear Sylvys." Elzgig waved the satyr inside. "If you wanted to wish His Highness a good journey, you could have met us at the bay in the morning, as everyone else is doing."

"I do not wish to bid farewell to His Majesty."

"No?"

"No. I wish to go with him."

"What?"

"Yes, what?"

"I wish to go to Lyonesse with His Majesty."

Billy and Elzgig exchanged glances. Then Elzgig rubbed his face and massaged his eyes.

"What's wrong? Why can't I go with him?"

Elzgig sighed. "Sylvys ... His Highness travels to the land of men. How do you suppose to-to-to ..."

"To what?"

"Your horns and feet." Billy had to work hard to stifle his grin.

"Thank you, Your Highness," Elzgig said. "I didn't quite know how to say it."

Sylvys looked up from his feet. "I'll hide them."

"Hide them?"

"Yes. Please, please, I must go with you. If I stay here another day, I will go mad or die."

"But—" Billy stopped when Elzgig grabbed his hand. He looked down at the little wizard.

Elzgig returned a meaningful stare. "Remember? Balance."

Billy stared blankly at Elzgig, and then shrugged.

"You have not yet become one with the mysteries of Tirn Aill. Believe me. It would be better if he goes with you."

Billy looked once more at the satyr. "If you say so."

"Great!" Sylvys smiled. "You won't regret this, Your Highness!"

Billy and Elzgig watched as Sylvys skipped down the path to the valley below. Billy thought he heard him whistle as he disappeared into some trees.

"Good," Elzgig said.

"Good? How am I gonna explain him?"

"You're assuming that you'll have to."

"I know I will!"

"You may not. Besides, what I said about balance was true. Sylvys is an important part of Tirn Aill, more important than you know. Giving him hope gives us all hope."

Billy yawned and realized how tired he was. "I had better get some sleep."

"Yes. You go to bed. I'll finish packing for you."

"All right, but if I find you've slipped in another additional member to this little quest in my pack, I'll hang you up by your whiskers."

Elzgig chuckled and shoved a bag of dried fruit into Billy's pack. At last, Billy's exhausted body conquered his wound-up mind. The last thing he heard as he drifted off to sleep was the little wizard humming a quaint faerie tune.

***

Billy awoke early in the morning. It was long before the sunrise or the morning tide, when his tiny band of faeries would depart on what could only be the most important quest of their lives. But rather than getting out of bed, Billy laid where he was. His mind still whirled with thoughts of the future, his mission, his friends, and Tirn Aill.

Eventually, the chill air goaded Billy out of bed, but try as he might, he could eat little of the breakfast Elzgig offered him. His stomach now joined in all the whirling, twisting motions of his thoughts.

"Better eat up. You've a long journey ahead of you."

"Can't." Billy rose and went to the door. "Too many butterflies today, but don't worry: I'm not one to go hungry if I can help it."

Elzgig nodded. "An admirable trait in a king, Your Majesty."

Billy smiled and threw his pack onto his back. He then picked up Lura Zahn and hooked the weapon onto his belt.

"Ready?" Elzgig asked.

"As ready as I'll ever be."

"Nonsense." Elzgig took the lead down the path to the valley. "Ever is a long time. When you are king with many adventures under your belt and you and I are here in Tirn Aill, we will drink and feast as all good faeries do. We will look back at this time, and our fat bellies will jiggle with laughter."

Shaldra and his elves snickered.

"Promise?"

"Aye. I promise."

Billy's entourage walked down the hill into the valley, past the royal court, and along the river, until they came to the gap in the hills that led to Glitter Gilt Bay. Along the way, the inhabitants of Tirn Aill waited to wish Billy a safe journey and to follow him down to the sea. Although not supportive or cheerful in the least, the malevolent faeries were represented by many goblins, hobgoblins, and others of their ilk. By the time they reached the pass, the rabble looked like an army, although not so orderly.

The sun peeked over the horizon and cast its golden beams beneath the grey clouds and across the water. True to its name, the bay gave off a glittering display of light. It was a perfect scene and the perfect way to begin the quest, except for one thing.

Billy stopped, and all his followers stopped with him. He held up his hands to shield his eyes from the dazzling light.

"What is it?" Elzgig squinted to see the bay.

"There's no ship."

Shaldra pointed. "The *Dragonfly* is gone."

"Gone!" Elzgig ran towards the dock.

A grumble rippled through the crowd. Billy felt ill and walked to the dark, rocky shore. The mob followed, growing louder with each step until their chaotic roar rivaled the surf. The noise finished the job on Billy's innards, and he pitched Elzgig's breakfast into the waves.

He straightened, still holding his stomach. "Silence! Silence!"

After a moment, the crowd settled down to a soft murmur of whispers.

"What has happened?"

"The *Dragonfly* left, Your Highness."

"I can see that." Billy fought to remain calm. "Why have they left?"

The only answer was a murmur through the crowd.

Shaldra appeared next to Billy and whispered, "Paryn thinks the goblins had something to do with it."

Billy eyed the elf named Paryn and called him over.

"Yes, Your Highness."

"Paryn, why do you think the goblins had something to do with this?"

"Well, Your Highness ... because Toady Brimstone and his crew are goblins."

Shaldra spat. "Cowards, the lot of them."

Billy's eyes traveled down the beach, across the many faerie faces, and to the end of the dock, where a tiny gnome-wizard and a disheartened satyr stood staring out to sea. His stomach knotted again, and his hands shook with weakness, but then Billy balled them up until they shook with rage. Every muscle in his body tightened, and he threw himself to his knees on a large flat rock. He threw back his head and released a terrible scream.

Billy's mind was aflame. Everything was disjointed and jumbled up. At that moment, he had thoughts that were strange to him. *Show these insects some real magic! Time to show them what you have learned!* His anger was great. Then all was red.

The congregated faeries stepped back from him as he let out an eerie roar unlike any they had ever heard. Then he slumped down on the rock, exhausted.

A moment later, a smoky black form materialized before Billy. It hovered in the air, tugging at his bowed head with its wispy tendrils. He grabbed a shell from the sand and scratched a large white triangle on the black rock beneath him. He surrounded it and himself with a circle, and then threw the shell aside. The dark form solidified into a large open book. Billy raised his head and chanted from the book:

"Come ye infernal power under the sea,

I call on thee in all thy dread.

Keeper of its secrets, guardian of its graveyards,

give up thy dead.

Thou who doest rejoice when the sailors cry out

and the sea drinks of their blood.

Thou who doest strike terror into mortal hearts,

release to us thy bounty from the mud.

And when I knock this ring upon this stone,

to raise a ship in thy feared name,

It shall not rest 'til I please again."

Billy beat the rock three times with his fist. Each time, the rock seemed to ring out like a bell. The sound echoed on the air, and then all was still.

Abruptly, Billy found himself chilled and kneeling on the rock. The tide had gone out some, and where there had been crashing waves, now only rocks and small tidal pools remained. Dark clouds obscured the sun, and the bay was an angry, foamy green. He tried to rise, but his feet were asleep. He sat and turned around on the rock. All before him were the inhabitants of Tirn Aill sitting back from the rocks, on the sand, staring at him. Many of those who had come to see Billy off were gone. Malkry and her mounted warriors had replaced them.

The goblins and hobgoblins laughed and pointed fingers at Billy. He examined himself and found nothing. More and more of the dark faeries joined in the laughter. In their ridicule of Billy, they jeered and made all manner of funny, obscene faces.

The remainder of Faerie visibly shrank. Billy saw in their eyes that they wanted to slink away, and several of them did—fading into the wooded hill behind the beach.

The only ones unmoved were the elves, both those who served Onian, and those that served Malkry. They were more interested in each other than in Billy.

Elzgig approached. When he was a good ten feet away, he stopped and asked, "Where did you learn that charm, Your Highness?"

"What charm?"

"That vile spell you worked there on that rock."

"I didn't work any spell."

"But you did." Elzgig pulled his beard. "And not a pleasant one at that."

"I worked a spell?"

"Aye, ya did." Elzgig looked around him before continuing, "Or, at least, you tried to."

"Me?"

"Aye. Right there on that rock!"

Billy looked beneath him. The black rock he knelt upon was now dry and charcoal grey. There were some faint scratches, which he found vaguely familiar. Then words came back to him as if echoed from a deep gorge. He heard them in a voice that was undoubtedly his, but they were words he would never have said on his own. The Witan's forbidden black tome flashed in his mind's eye, like a spark hammered from a blacksmith's anvil.

Billy stared at Elzgig. "What have I done?"

The little wizard inhaled sharply. His eyes doubled in size and his jaw went slack. The hair on the back of Billy's neck stood on end, and his ring finger tingled. As if on cue, the goblin rabble ceased their mockery and stared to the sea. Billy watched as the remainder of Faerie stepped back from the surf. The only sound came from the waves on the distant rocks.

The tickle on Billy's neck became a chill that playfully danced down his spine, but he was afraid to look back. The absolute horror dripping from hundreds of faerie faces was enough to paralyze him.

With a great deal of trepidation, he forced himself to turn and look into the bay. There, before his eyes, a tall blackened spar moved upright through the dark water, growing taller as it approached the shore. A single pale figure rode in the remains of a battered crow's-nest near the top.

Again, the spar surged forward, and a boom emerged from the bay. Shreds of canvas and rope hung from it, draping into the water. Then more canvas, wood, and rope were exposed, and it became quite evident that what approached was somehow the mast and yard of a sailing ship. Closer and closer the object came, motivated by some unknown force beneath the waves. The lower boom became visible, and then the railing and deck.

Billy squinted and saw several more figures, standing upon the deck where no living man could. Another chill went up his spine, for he saw that the figures were the skeletons of men. They stood motionless, their dark eye sockets staring to the shore. As the splintered hull of the ship came into view, the skeleton at the wheel moved his arm and pointed to the mast. The other skeletons began to climb up the ropes.

Immediately, a commotion arose from the shore as most of the faeries screamed and scrambled over each other to escape the vicinity. Even Elzgig moved back to stand behind Shaldra. The only ones who remained were the elves. However, even these staunch warriors were visibly shaken.

A dank odor drifted on the cold air, assaulting all those in its presence. Behind Billy, the mounts of Malkry's warriors went berserk. Lances and riders came clattering to the ground as flying rock and debris filled the air. Cries of pain burst forth, as the animals overturned stones and trampled their former riders into the sand in their haste to escape the smell of death.

By the time their mounts had fled from the beach, most of Malkry's contingent lay wounded. The dark elves had come in force, but now only Malkry and one other remained mounted and battle ready.

Billy returned his attention to the phantom ship as it pulled in next to the dock. One of the skeleton sailors threw a rope over a mooring pole, the ship coasted to a stop, and another threw down a charred boarding plank.

Everyone still on the beach prepared to run, but nothing got off the ship; in fact, all the ghostly sailors remained motionless. An icy wind blew in during the long hour that passed before anyone got up the nerve to approach.

Billy, towing Elzgig by his staff, stepped onto the first planks of the pier. When nothing changed, he took another step and another. Before long, he was standing beside the boarding ramp, staring at the two sailors that stood on either side at the far end of it. He scanned up and down the length of the heavily damaged vessel for signs of life, but found none.

Dead sailors sailing a phantom ship. It was all too bizarre, but what was stranger was the nagging feeling of familiarity about it. He looked at the skeletons, examined the shape and design of the ship, and then marched down the dock to the bow. There was a name on her—crusted with barnacles, muddy and cracked, but it was still there.

Billy reached up and touched a piece of seaweed hanging in front of the name. It felt real enough, and nothing bad happened to him, so he pulled it away to reveal the name.

"*Gyl-dan M-ene*. The *Gyldan Mene*. The *Gyldan Mene?*"

"What's wrong?" Elzgig whispered.

"What's wrong?" Billy stepped back. "This is the ship I stowed away on when I escaped from Lyonesse. She was headed to Erin when we went down."

"This ship?"

"This very ship."

"This is not good."

"This is a ghost ship that should be sunk to the bottom of the sea! Of course, it's not good!"

"No. A ghost ship is, indeed, not good, but *this* ship, this *exact* ship ... here ... now! This is *really* not good!"

"What do you mean?"

"This ship will lead to something ... something terrible."

"What makes you say that?"

"I don't know, precisely." The wizard tugged on his beard. "But I feel it in my bones."

Billy allowed Elzgig's warning to settle in as he walked aft, along the pier. He looked across the deck at the skeleton behind the wheel. It was missing a few bones and half its rib cage, but was definitely the captain he had seen commanding the *Gyldan Mene*.

Billy cleared his throat. "Captain? Captain?"

With a creaking sound, the captain's head twisted to the side and revealed that half his skull had been bashed in. He still had most of his teeth, including one of gold on the right side, but the missing upper cranial chunk dispelled any imagined humanity. The remaining eye socket seemed to stare back at Billy, and then the ghastly apparition nodded.

"Captain, will you take me to King Finvarra?"

Again, the captain nodded.

Billy couldn't shake the idea that the captain, despite his horrid state, was grinning at him. He swallowed hard. "Then that settles it."

"Settles what?" Elzgig asked.

"We need a ship, right? We must leave as soon as possible, right? Well, here is a ship and a captain willing to take me to Finvarra."

"I wouldn't trust him, Your Highness."

"What choice have I?"

Elzgig clasped his hands behind his back and walked in circles, mumbling to himself. He was clearly frustrated with not only the situation, but also finding a solution.

"Ah!" he said, at last. "We will ask the Witan."

"We haven't the time, Elzgig."

"Aye. Time is wasting."

Billy turned to watch Sylvys walk up the pier. Much to his surprise, the satyr's horns and feet could not be seen. He wore a long robe, tied at the waist, which covered most of his body, and a small helmet on his head. Over one shoulder he carried a sack, and in one hand a short spear with a broad, leaf-like head. The oddest facet of his appearance was the movement of his steps. At a glance, he looked like someone trying to cross some ornery, sticky mud.

Billy scrutinized the area below the robe and caught sight of some boots. He imagined himself a stranger, seeing Sylvys for the first time, and came to the conclusion that he would pass for a man to anyone who didn't look up his robe—granted, a very hairy man, with a gimpy walk, but nevertheless, a man.

Sylvys smiled and tried to act as if nothing were irregular at all. He came to stand before Billy and bowed his head. Billy could see now that the satyr's short horns protruded through the helmet and appeared like horns attached to the outside.

"Good morrow, Your Highness."

"Good morrow." Billy had to chuckle.

Sylvys caught him examining his weapon and helm. "What's wrong?"

"Is that bronze?"

Sylvys grinned sheepishly and looked at the planks beneath him. "Well ..." He chuckled. "It's been a long time since I did anything like this."

Billy noticed Sylvys' occupation with something on the ground. "What's the matter?"

"Oh, nothing." Sylvys turned his head and looked even more embarrassed than before.

"No, tell me."

The satyr looked from side to side, and then leaned forward to whisper. "You probably didn't notice, but I'm having a bit of trouble, and I was wondering: How do you do it?"

"Do what?"

Sylvys hiked his robe up to reveal his boots. "Walk with such big feet."

Billy laughed.

"Did I say something funny?"

"Well ... I never looked at it that way before."

Billy waved to his elfin guard, and they ran to the pier. As they approached closer, they drew their weapons, and he could see their intense alertness. They showed no fear, but a great deal of caution.

"Shaldra. I'm taking this ship to Lyonesse. I will understand if you don't wish to come along."

The hurt shone in Shaldra's eyes.

"Where you go, I go also, Your Highness."

"Please, Your Highness." Elzgig stepped forward. "I beg you to reconsider this course of action."

Billy looked down into the tiny wizard's troubled eyes. He knelt before the gnome and gave him a smile. "I've made up my mind. I know you are worried. I'm going on a dangerous mission, but I'm more worried about what will happen here while I'm gone. You'll look after Tirn Aill for me, won't you?"

"Yes, Your Majesty."

"Hey, I'll be back. I promise."

With that, Billy rose and started for the gangplank. He sized it up and was about to step onto it when Shaldra thrust his hand in front of him.

"Wait, Your Highness. I will go first."

Billy watched as Shaldra climbed the plank. The nimble elf's foot hovered above the deck as he eyed the silent skeletons on either side of the gangway. Finally, he set his foot down.

"It seems safe, Your Highness." Shaldra turned around.

"I'm next!" Sylvys stepped onto the plank.

When both of his questing companions were on the rickety deck, Billy proceeded up the plank. Just as he got to the top, he heard hooves striking the planks of the pier. He stopped with one foot on the plank and one on the railing of the ship and looked back.

Malkry and her last mounted warrior had left their comrades on the beach and rode up the pier to the dock. Their black capes fluttered in the wind, imparting the illusion of flight. They kept their spirited animals tightly reined.

"Come to say goodbye, Malkry?" Shaldra said. "How touching."

"Not quite."

"What do you want?" Elzgig moved forward. "You've never shown any support for his highness's quest."

"Quite the contrary. I applaud Billy's courage. But what a tragedy it would be if something were to go wrong and I could have prevented it."

"Prevent it? Ha! You mean, cause it."

Malkry snapped a burning look at Shaldra and held it for a moment. "I wasn't speaking to you." Then she turned to the leader of the quest. "Billy, I know we've had our disagreements, but let's put that behind us. I would like to send Drif, my finest warrior, with you." She motioned to her companion. "You may need someone who can fight."

"Malkry—!" Shaldra's face turned red.

Billy threw up his hand. "Yes, we have had our disagreements, Malkry, and I'm sorry, but this is one of them. If I thought I needed more warriors with me on this quest, I would have taken my guard."

The elves of Billy's bodyguard straightened with pride.

"Then please, take Drif for my peace of mind."

Billy glanced at Shaldra, who shook his head. His eyes traveled to Elzgig. Like Shaldra, the mighty little wizard was fervently shaking his head. Finally, Billy's eyes came to rest on Malkry's warrior.

There was very little one could tell by looking at the filigreed, midnight-black armor. There was no face to look into, nor hands, nor even eyes. Even the warrior's scant movements betrayed nothing, except perhaps strength and patience.

Elzgig's head wagged from side to side, and Shaldra whispered "no." Billy looked again at Malkry. He could discern little from her face. Her violet eyes and the haughty turn of her brows told him nothing he didn't already know.

"Yes. Drif is welcome."

"What?" Elzgig and Shaldra said in unison.

Malkry batted her eyes and nodded. "Thank you. Now I know my people will be served. ... Drif."

Drif handed Malkry the reins and dismounted, then removed the saddle and tack and placed them on the dock with practiced speed. The caped warrior turned to Malkry and bowed.

Billy noticed that, like Drif, the elegant black armor made no sound. Before he could reflect on this any further, the dark elf marched up the plank with bags, saddle, and weapons in hand. Billy stepped onto the ship and out of the warrior's way.

He looked at the few items Drif had brought on board. "You will need nothing else?"

The warrior's helmet inclined slightly.

Billy scanned the dark elf's equipment again. It consisted of armor, war saddle, crossbow and bolts, javelin, dagger, sword, and the most meager of saddlebags. There was no sign of personal effects or even a bedroll. *Only the tools of a warrior, or an assassin.* Chills tickled his spine.

"You have no one you wish to say goodbye to?"

Again, the answer was silence.

And nothing to lose. But what have they to gain: reign over Tirn Aill—an entire kingdom frozen in perpetual winter? They don't know what I know of Tirn Aill's future. Perhaps it was a mistake to keep my visions secret.

"What is it?" Shaldra asked.

Billy shook his head. "Nothing."

Drif secured the battle gear—save sword and dagger—to a post, and walked to the bow of the ship.

Shaldra now stood next to Billy and leaned down to whisper in his ear. "I won't take my eyes off that one, Your Highness ... and you would be wise to do the same."

Billy turned to his protector. "We have a hard journey ahead of us, Shaldra." He grinned. "I guess this will make your life a little more interesting."

Shaldra returned the smile.

"Good. We have enough gloom and doom around here from Elzgig without you adding to it."

The fiery little gnome grunted. "I heard that!"

Billy looked over to see Elzgig standing on the end of the gangplank. "I thought we agreed that you would stay here."

"Aye, Your Highness." The wizard stared sullenly at what Billy had conjured from the sea. "I hoped that I might be able to prevail on you to do the same, at least until we have come up with a more *suitable* transport for you."

Billy smiled.

"I thought not." Elzgig raised his sheepdog-like eyebrows. "You certainly inherited your mother's ways. Well, as long as I am not accompanying you, allow me to give you something you can carry with—"

"Honestly, Elzgig." Billy indicated his pack. "I don't think I could carry another thing."

"It's not heavy, Your Highness."

"Well, all right. What is it?"

"A word of advice ..."

Billy rolled his eyes.

"All right." Elzgig sounded somewhat put off. "If you don't want my advice, then take my blessing."

Billy held out his hands to the tiny wizard, who placed his hands within them. So much had happened since the two first met. It felt wrong that they should part company so soon. Billy said so, and Elzgig's wrinkled face lifted into a welcomed smile. Beyond this, the wizard's birdlike eyes searched for something that would bring him peace.

"'Twill be all right, my friend."

Elzgig nodded. "You have only to tell me so, my king, and I will believe. Good journey to you, and ... hurry home."

Elzgig's words brought little comfort, for Billy had no faith in them. He had seen a bleak future for Tirn Aill that no amount of words could erase. What's more, he had no visions to indicate that his quest would succeed. The daunting journey ahead, with so many unknowns, loomed before him like a great black wraith awaiting the foolish to enter its sacred graveyard.

Smile, Billy told himself as he released Elzgig's hands and watched him walk down the gangplank. *Smile.*

Once Elzgig was on the dock, Billy turned to the skeleton behind the *Gyldan Mene's* wheel. He stared at the fish-cleaned bones a moment, wondering whether he was being brave or foolish.

"Captain."

The captain's grinning remains shifted, and the empty eye socket regarded its new master.

Billy did his best to take on a commanding voice. "Captain. Take us to Finvarra."

The captain nodded. With a great creaking and clattering of bones, the skeleton crew began to move. They withdrew the gangplank and mooring lines, then scurried up the ropes with uncanny ease, despite the fact that some of them were missing limbs. They deployed the tattered remains of the sail, and the ship surged forward and turned into the wind.

Billy, Shaldra, and Sylvys went to the stern of the *Gyldan Mene* while she swung into the bay. They stared across the growing gap at Billy's elves, who stood still and somber as elms. Elzgig and Malkry were likewise motionless, except for what animation the biting wind provided. The dark, rocky shore and hills behind them seemed a thousand miles away, pressed down by the leaden sky. The wind quieted. The entire scene crystallized in Billy's memory.

Just then, a single snowflake floated into view before Elzgig. Curious, the wizard held out his tiny hand and allowed it to land in his palm.

"The first snowflake," Billy muttered as Elzgig closed his hand.

He remembered that, as a boy, growing up in the Valley of the Yew, he would anxiously await the first blessed snowfall of winter. Now, for the first time, he saw it as cursed. At that moment, another snowflake drifted into view, then another and another, until there were too many to lay eyes on separately.

"What is it?" Shaldra gripped Billy's arm.

"Snow."

"So that's what it looks like."

"Aye, that's what it looks like."

"Seems harmless."

Billy nodded.

The three original questers stared back at Tirn Aill as snow blanched its remaining colors. Voiceless, they watched as the gentle hills, ancient forests, and lonely mountains of their home shrunk further from sight. The mysterious dark elf never once looked back, but stood in the bow and stared ahead into the vast, dark waters of the sea.

CHAPTER THIRTEEN

The Dogs of War

Ergyfel awoke with a start. He cast about at the dim, dirty laboratory, then sighed. *Gone.* Billy had taken the horde of unspeakable monsters and deformed beasts that he commanded in Ergyfel's dreams and vanished. From the day he had sent his mind into the future, Ergyfel's named demon had plagued him.

The sorcerer-king wiped his wet brow and lit one of the brass lamps hanging from the dark oak beams. He leaned forward and examined the experiment in the clay jar before him. He had discovered that the magic flowing through his body when casting spells was feeding the arcane cancer that spread painfully up his arm. Unless he gave up magic completely, the cursed thing would eventually engulf his entire body. But how could he? Spells were food and drink to him. What's more, since he learned of Billy's coming, he had a growing sense that he would need every bit of sorcery he could muster. For this reason, he had started his experiments to find an alternate method to fuel his spells.

Ergyfel had started in the early morning, worked through the day, and now—judging by the darkness—it was night. He had labored like this for several days and nights. Now it was taking its toll. Falling asleep on his stone table was not a choice, but a necessity. He could still feel the impress of its cold surface on his cheek.

He flung his arm out and swatted the clay vessel off the table. It shattered against the far wall, sending shards and yellow sticky ooze in all directions.

His anger sated, Ergyfel muttered, "Another failure."

Hungry. I need food ... and solace. ... I need Maeven.

Still feeling exhausted, but hopeful, he turned to leave his private sanctum. When he reached for the door latch, he felt a magical disturbance. He closed his eyes and concentrated on this feeling.

"Ergyfel. Ergyfel!"

The king's eyes snapped open, and he pulled out the simple medallion that hung from a gold chain around his neck. He concentrated, and a bright spark jumped from the medallion to his forehead.

"What is it, Hengest?"

"Brother, we battle the Gwythies."

"But it's night!"

"Aye."

Through his brother's ears, Ergyfel could hear the thunder of hooves and roar of angry hosts, the mighty clash of steel, and cries of pain as men and animals collided in bloody carnage. Then, through his brother's eyes, he looked about and saw the flash of swords and armor and the momentary dance of silk banners in the moonlight.

"What has happened?"

"My scouts spotted the enemy earlier today. There were only one thousand of them, so we waited for them here, at a place Cairmac calls 'Amaranth Heath.' When they came into the open, we attacked. So far, we are winning, but these Gwythies are a difficult lot."

A Gwythian soldier broke through the line in front of Hengest and charged at him. He stopped talking to engage the warrior. The Gwythian came rapidly to his death when Hengest ducked his blow and riposted by cutting off the man's leg. Once down, the man's head came away with one strike.

Ergyfel found himself squatting low on the floor of his laboratory, his fist outstretched, the smell of blood in his nose. It was only then that he realized he had been mimicking his brother's actions. Even the sensations of the night air, the sword in his hand, and the hot pulse of battle were present. It was as if he were in Hengest's body. This was unexpected. *What if Hengest is killed? How would that affect me?*

Another voice came to Ergyfel through his brother's ears. It was that of Earl Cairmac.

"We've been duped! Look to the trees! Look to the trees!"

Hengest's eyes scanned the tree line around the huge clearing. The pale bluish moonlight reflected off hundreds of helmets. Cairmac's army was surrounded. At that moment, there came a *shooshing* sound, and Hengest looked up to see the moon shuttered by a dark cloud of arrows.

He held up his shield. The first volley of arrows fell like the rain of hell. Cries went up from all quarters of the battlefield as the unholy hail struck down friend and foe alike.

Ergyfel called out. "Hengest, you must get out of there!"

"I have one more task to complete, my brother."

"No, get out of there now!"

At that moment, Earl Cairmac and his bodyguard came into view. The earl was down on his side, holding his leg where the shaft of an arrow protruded. Three of his guard lay dead beside him.

Another swarm of arrows took flight, and the last man of the earl's guard was struck in the neck. He collapsed onto his lord's body and expired with a gurgle.

Ergyfel's view shifted and became more intimate. He now heard Hengest's thoughts, and for all intents and purposes was right inside his head.

Hengest appeared above the Earl of Wyneddhamshire, who struggled to free himself from the corpse of his fallen guardsman.

"Oh, thank God. Help me get out of here."

Hengest remained motionless and stared at the prostrate man at his feet.

"Help me. For God's sake, man!"

"For God's sake?"

"Yes!" Cairmac pushed at the heavy armored body, which lay on his.

Hengest smiled, and in the dim light, his face took on the aspect of Ergyfel. "You're far more valuable as a martyr, milord. The people of Lyonesse will remember your heroic death."

"My death?"

"Yes." He placed his sword on the earl's neck. "Because of your *sacrifice*, they will rally beneath my brother's banner to wipe this scourge from the land."

"Please. ... Please, I'll give you anything, just let me live."

Hengest sneered at the nobleman and sheathed his sword. "You disgust me."

Relief flooded the earl's eyes. Then, suddenly, Ergyfel's brother clubbed him across the face with a mighty blow. Before Cairmac knew what was happening, Hengest had tied his hands behind his back.

"What are you doing?"

"Keeping my word."

"What word? What word?"

"That you would die upon the battlefield."

He thrust a loop of rope around Cairmac's neck. He then tied another loop in the other end and tossed it over the saddle of the earl's horse.

"No!" Cairmac cried. "No!"

Hengest smiled once more. "Do not worry. I will never tell your wife and daughter what a coward you were, no matter how long I must comfort them." With that, he swatted the horse, and it bolted into a gallop.

Hengest didn't wait around to watch the earl's last charge, but instead, dropped low in the brush and scurried into the woods. The forest was full of Gwythian soldiers, and he reckoned that the now-deceased earl had been telling the truth about their strength. *The bastards*, he thought. *They let their archers do all the killing.* He glanced over his shoulder at the carnage that was transpiring on the heath. *They even kill their own.*

Hengest killed two archers and slipped past a dozen swordsmen before hiding under a log-bridge. He waited, breathless, while a large force marched over him to clean up the remains of the earl's troops.

When he was sure they had passed, he rose up and headed farther into the forest. There, he happened across a young officer who had dismounted to relieve himself. Hengest gained access to his back with stealth and planted a dagger in his heart. He scanned the dark woods as he eased the man's body to the ground. The only sound was the far-off ruckus of battle and the last breath of the youth escaping his lungs. Hengest leapt to the back of his victim's horse and disappeared into the darkness.

"Are you still with me, brother?" Hengest urged the horse to go faster.

"Aye, brother." Ergyfel sounded somewhat breathless. "I think I finally understand what it is about battle that you love. But we'll talk more of that later. I will send to you a special mount. It will await you at the Feorrdagas crossroads. Do not fear, brother, the steed will not harm you, and it will bring you here much quicker than any earthly beast."

"But I ..."

"I need you. ... And I'm sure the earl's widow will need comforting."

*

Ergyfel broke the magical contact with his brother and fell to the floor. His muscles ached and his arm burned. He had not expected such an intense contact, or for the magic to take so much out of him.

He rose and crossed his sanctum to a set of bookcases. There, amongst his valuable books, nestled a small statue of a horse. He picked it up and examined its smooth onyx surface.

Ergyfel spoke to the stone steed. "I've been saving you for just such an occasion."

He then placed the figure on the floor and stepped back. Next, he took a bag of silver filings and, with them, drew a large circle on the floor around his feet. Then he chanted:

"The inner eye that found you,

The arcane hands that ground you,

The learned tongue that bound you,

The whole that did confound you,

Now commands you to come forth!"

Ergyfel repeated the rune six times, each time feeling the power in his body build and the sickness in his arm itch. Then he shouted, "Come forth!" The stone statue shattered as the pain in his arm brought him to his knees.

One by one, the tiny black shards sublimated and became smoke-like, sooty vapor that hung in stringy columns on the still air. Ergyfel detected a slight sulfurous odor. The mist stirred, first to the right, then the left. The columns swayed and merged. With unexpected speed, they charged towards Ergyfel and circled his position. Faster and faster the mist circled until its movement created a whistling wind that knocked books from their shelves and sent papers flying around the room. The lamps swung violently on their chains, splashing sporadic shadows and beams of amber light on the walls. The sound rose and fell like a gusting blizzard heard through a window.

Abruptly, the shrill whistle became a whinny, and the mist coalesced into a sleek, sinewy steed with the color and sheen of coal. It snorted and glared at Ergyfel with its red ember-like eyes.

"Finished?"

The shadowy beast shifted its weight from side to side and examined Ergyfel with hot, discerning eyes. It lowered its head with caution, then crooked its front knee and bowed.

Ergyfel smiled. "Good. Then you *do* remember me."

The steed stood.

"Go now ... to the Feorrdagas crossroads. There, you will wait for a man wearing a medallion like this one." He pulled on the chain about his neck. "You will bring the man and all his belongings here to me, as fast as you can, intact and unharmed; or you will learn what an eternity locked in stone feels like."

The steed grunted and pawed at the floor. Ergyfel looked down at the thin silver band around the ankle of its foreleg.

"Of course. ... If you complete my task, I will remove it."

The creature nodded, and became thin and smoky again. It then fled up the laboratory's small chimney as if sucked out by tremendous winds. A shrill whinny echoed from the shaft as the last dark plume vanished.

Ergyfel rubbed his hands together and chuckled. *I can hardly wait to see Hengest's face.* He waved his hand, and all the lamps were quenched. In the dark, Ergyfel laughed again. *Especially when I tell him what I've got planned.*

CHAPTER FOURTEEN

The Proposition

L ady Myrredith dismissed her maid. "Good night, Megan."
"Good night, milady. Pleasant dreams." Megan bowed and closed
the door.

The clank of the key in the door as the guard locked her in rang in
Myrredith's soul. This shadow of existence—a condemned prisoner under
the gallows—had gnawed through her nerves, and it was all she could do
to keep up a facade of calm.

Pleasant dreams. The thought was itself a dream, for sleep did not come
easily anymore, and the life she led when the curtain on sleep did rise was
a hellish play of her demise.

"Please, not tonight," Myrredith pleaded as she laid on her bed.

She stared at the ceiling, the wall to the left, the wall to the right, and
finally again at the ceiling. The flickering firelight soothed her mind, feeding her kind thoughts of long gone yesterdays.

Sleep was almost upon Lady Myrredith when she heard a low grinding
noise. She sat up and scanned the room. The light from the fireplace had
declined to the mere glow of embers.

Suddenly, a shadow crossed before the hearth. Before she could
scream, a large, coarse hand clamped over her mouth, and another at the

back of her head. Her assailant smashed into her with his armored shoulder and threw his mass onto her body.

Myrredith slapped, punched, kicked, pinched, twisted, clawed, and bit the man, but only grew tired under his iron strength.

He forced a dirty cloth in her mouth. "Go ahead, Lyonesse cow. I like it rough."

Myrredith continued to struggle and, by chance, found her hand on the hilt of his dagger. With little thought, she bared the blade and drew it back to stab him. He grabbed her wrist and pressed his thumb into the joint.

"Now, now. No toys for you."

Counter to her will, Myrredith's hand sprung open, and the weapon dropped to the mattress. The warrior flicked the dagger off the bed and riposted with a slap to her face.

He whispered into her ear, "That's just a warning." He then licked her stinging cheek.

Myrredith resisted with all her might, but his was the powerful body of a man who had trained his entire life to battle men and beasts and topple castles. His breath was all wine, gristle, and rotten teeth while his body reeked of smoke, manure, and week-old sweat. His implacable stench was the only equal to the juggernaut's might.

A terror like no other ripped through Myrredith's frame. She felt smothered and helpless in the brute's filthy grip. Even her death sentence was less cruel than this gruesome offense. Her sole desire was to escape. She yearned to leave the bonds of her earthly body and float away on the wind.

With one hand, the despoiler raised Myrredith's arms above her head and tore the front of her nightgown with the other. His eyes widened with lust when he spied her pale torso. He halted for a moment, just long enough that it seemed he would not continue. His tongue absently caressed his upper lip before a lecherous grin crept onto his broad, stubbly face. He lunged into her, biting her neck and moving down to her collarbone.

At that moment, there came a knock at the door. Myrredith's assailant popped up and stared her in the eye. The knock became more insistent. The brute glanced from side to side, and then turned his head around to face the door.

Myrredith managed to spit out the rag and scream. "Help!"

The would-be rapist came back around and slapped his hand over her mouth. "You taupie! You've ruined everything!" He reached to his side, groping for the weapon she had taken. His heavy eyelids snapped open in alarm, then lowered again to glare at Lady Myrredith. His coarse paws gripped her throat. As he cut off her air, Myrredith clawed at his face.

A key rattled in the lock, then the door burst open, and three men charged in, reducing the juggernaut to a scared rabbit. He released his victim and leapt from the bed. Frantic, he searched the floor for his dagger, but to no avail.

Prince Hereweald charged in. "Get him!"

The young soldiers accompanying the prince sprang at the culprit, but he opposed an easy capture. He tossed one, arse over teakettle across the room, smashing a table to kindling. In the blink of an eye, he dropped the other soldier to his knees with a kick. Just then, he spotted his lost dagger and snatched it from the fur rug like a hungry tiger.

The first soldier recovered from his tumble and, seeing the naked dagger, drew his sword. He rushed his foe, tripped on the spilled bedclothes, and ran himself onto his opponent's blade.

The young warrior stared into the old campaigner's face, and then down at the weapon in his chest. Myrredith's attacker was shaken, but true to his years of training and battle, he grabbed the younger man's sword and let him slide off his dagger to the floor.

By this time, the other soldier had regained his strength and stood ready to do battle. With firm hand and grim eyes, he faced the slayer of his comrade.

The two warriors began to circle, but then the prince stepped in-between them. He stood erect, holding his naked sword in a relaxed fashion by his side. He still wore his chain mail and the bloodstained tabard he had worn into battle.

"Decurion, would you harm your prince?"

The man opposite the prince shifted his gaze around the room, look-ing for an escape. The muscles in his jaw flexed. Then he pursed his lips and wrinkled his stubbled chin. Tears welled up in his eyes, and he cried.

"Forgive me, Your Highness," the decurion blubbered. "I could never. It's just that Lyonesse kelpie! She's the enemy, ain't she? And she walks around here like she still owns the bloody place! I just wanted—I just wanted ..."

"Yes, I know."

"I didn't mean to kill Bryan. *She* is the enemy!"

"Yes, of course."

The decurion lowered his weapons. "I am sorry, Your Highness. It'll never happen again."

"Yes, I know, Decurion." The prince paused for a moment. "How many campaigns have we been on together?"

The decurion gave a cautious smile. "Many, Your Highness. Many."

"Aye." The prince nodded. "You've proven a good decurion, but I know you too well."

The decurion nodded with his eyes lowered, and Hereweald plunged his sword into the old soldier's heart. The prince held his flawlessly executed lunge position until the man on the end of his sword raised his head and made eye contact.

"Therefore, I grant you a quick death and no mention of this to your family."

Blood ran from the lips of the decurion as he sputtered and coughed. He crumbled to his knees and rasped, "The battle, my prince?"

"A victory."

The decurion smiled, then slumped to the floor. The prince cleaned his sword on the dead man's tunic and sheathed it.

"Remove these two and send for the lady's maid."

"Yes, Your Highness." The guard moved toward the door.

"And someone to clean up this mess!"

"Yes, Your Highness."

"Now!"

"Yes, Your Highness."

*

Prince Hereweald approached Lady Myrredith as the guard exited. She cowered on the bed against its headboard, staring at the decurion's body, unaware that her breasts were half exposed. Hereweald caught himself staring at her naked beauty, then turned away with boyish embarrassment.

"Milady?" He spoke in soft tones. "Milady?"

Myrredith blinked. She turned her attention to Hereweald and attempted to answer, but couldn't manage. She rubbed her throat, swallowed, and whispered, "Yes."

"Milady ... I do not know how to apologize for such a villainous outrage! I hope that you can forgive me."

Myrredith noticed the prince's awkward stance and looked down to her torn gown. She wrapped the remnants around her and pulled a quilt up to her neck.

"It's very important to me. I can't tell you how much. You see, I ..." The prince stopped when he saw the lady's vacant stare. "This can wait 'til morning."

The young guard returned at that moment with two more soldiers. Megan was on their heels.

"Milady?" The maid rushed to her mistress's side.

Megan then turned and stood in front of Myrredith and, in a fiery pose reminiscent of her ladyship, she ordered the prince to leave.

Hereweald cowed her with a frosty stare, then turned and ordered his men to "Hurry, before they grow stiff!"

After his men had removed the bodies, he turned to leave, but stopped at the door and spoke.

"I know you'll take good care of Her Ladyship, Megan. Stay here the night. If there's anything she needs, do not hesitate to ask. My physician is at your disposal." He pulled the door to him. "Oh, yes. Send for me the instant she is up to a visitor. I have something very important to discuss with her."

Megan bowed her head, and he closed the door.

***

The dawn came to Myrredith as just another moment. If not for the early morning chill, which gripped her bones, the arrival of a new day would have gone unnoticed.

All at once, Myrredith sat up in bed and pulled the quilt around her. She spoke to the maid sleeping in the chair next to her, "Megan. Megan!"

Megan blinked her eyes and hopped up, ready to battle. "What is it, milady?"

"All is well, Megan. Have you been there all night?"

"Aye, milady. Except when the prince came askin' after ya."

"Prince Hereweald?"

"Aye. He said he wished to speak with ya on a most pressing matter. His words, not mine, milady."

"Oh."

"Are you well, milady?"

"Yes, Megan. I will be." Lady Myrredith fell silent for a long while. Finally, she spoke, "What did the prince say?"

"He's so impatient, that one," Megan said in her allegro gossip's tongue. "Kept goin' on and on, really about nothin', and finally says that if you can't be seen this morning, he would see you this afternoon. I tried to tell him that it was simply impossible, but he insisted. Then he orders me to make sure you were *presentable* and downstairs by supper tonight!"

"Ordered you?"

"Aye, milady, and he was none too polite about it."

"Presentable?" A hint of ire shadowed Myrredith's voice.

Megan smiled. "Aye, milady. That's what the prince ordered."

"Well, we shall see about that!"

Megan tried to egg Myrredith on further, but her tiny spark dwindled, and she slipped into brooding.

She rested in the room she had inherited, on a bed that was a wedding gift, under covers her hands had sewn, and yet she was mindful that they were no longer hers. In fact, the world was no longer hers. An awareness grew that the world was shrinking even as she prepared to leave it for the next. Her mind had come to accept the fact that she would be executed soon, and the night's events had gone far to convince her that she was powerless to stop it. Yet she did not wish to die.

It wasn't so much the loss of her life that Myrredith resisted. She felt she had very little left to live for. Billy was gone, Hugh was dead, her people were worse than defeated, her ancestral home had fallen into enemy hands, and Prince Hereweald's army was sweeping across Lyonesse like a plague. No, the thing that chafed her was being executed like a common criminal. That was a defeat, regardless of the accusation's veracity. The victors would write history, and the fact that she, the last Cyndyn, would be portrayed as a wicked, barbaric murderer tortured her conscience.

Lady Myrredith's mind moved with primitive, forbidden thoughts. They were foreign to her, against her very nature, but they made her pulse quicken and the blood course faster through her veins.

She was tired of being the victim in this entanglement. Tired of standing by while her people suffered. She had to do something. With time, she could solve any dilemma through diplomacy, but the current circumstances left only enough room for drastic measures. To end the pain, someone had to die; either her or Prince Hereweald, and since she wasn't scheduled to die for a while yet, that left the prince.

Killing him would end it, and it would be so simple. Myrredith sat up and pondered the idea of murdering Hereweald for a moment. The image sent a shudder through her.

"Oh, what's the use?" She slouched again. "I could never bring myself to do it."

Megan, who was sitting near the window, looked up at the unexpected utterance. "Do what, milady?"

"Nothing." *Besides, it would only give Snegaddrick and Gwythia fuel to do worse things still.*

Myrredith noticed that the window behind her maid was now painting a long narrow band across the floor and up the far wall. It would be dark soon. *Another precious day gone.*

"What time is it, Megan?"

"I reckon it's near supper, milady."

Myrredith stood before the full-length mirror and stared at her reflection.

"Then ready my best gown!"

"But milady, just because he says so doesn't mean you have to. You need more time!"

Lady Myrredith spoke in a dry voice. "More time? More time for what?"

Megan fell into an uncustomary silence.

Myrredith sighed. "I haven't got more time."

The silence stretched out around them like a desert.

Finally, Megan asked, "Your best *black* gown, milady?"

"Of course," came the reply. "The one with the high lace. Tonight, I dine with a prince."

Megan rose with a sullen demeanor and did as her lady commanded. The little life Myrredith had felt was gone. She remembered the famine that had struck Lyonesse a few years earlier. Soon after the fishing lanes had gone dry, she lost the only child she had ever bore. The miscarriage had torn her apart in body and spirit, yet she had risen from bed that very day to stop a food riot in Dyven. Lady Myrredith had taken food from the stores at Cyndyn Hall and distributed it to her people in the market square, and no one had been the wiser. Only Megan, Eadwig, and her physician ever knew that she almost died.

When she had finished laying out Lady Myrredith's attire, Megan sent word to Prince Hereweald that the Lady would be joining him for supper, as ordered. Then, as was her duty, she helped her lady into her clothes. For the first time ever, they accomplished this with neither one speaking a word.

***

The prince welcomed Lady Myrredith into the great hall with a smile and bowed with his arms stretched wide. He wore no armor or weapons and was dressed in a sunny red and yellow tunic and Roman sandals. His step and touch were light as he took her by the elbow to lead her to the head table. He appeared a different man from the swaggering, sword-wielding conqueror of their first meeting.

The hall itself was ablaze with candlelight and colored ribbons. A warm fire crackled in the hearth, surrounded by tables set for a feast. However, the most warming sight to Myrredith was that of her kitchen staff standing along the rear wall. They appeared clean and healthy, and each bore an encouraging smile for their lady as they bowed.

The prince nodded, and the servants went about their labors. Most went to the kitchen while the others remained to serve wine and finish setting the large tables.

Myrredith looked about and saw that, except for Megan and the other servants, she was alone with Prince Hereweald. The only sign of the Gwythian army was two guards at the main entrance and a large banner on the wall behind the head table.

Lady Myrredith spoke with no hint of emotion, "I am here, as you ordered."

"Ordered?" The prince glared at Megan before speaking to Myrredith. "Please, forgive me if my invitation sounded gruff. I was a bit agitated and did not intend it as an order! But now that you are here, please, sit." Then he spoke to Megan in a restrained voice. "Please, leave us alone, gentle lady."

Lady Myrredith nodded to her maid and sat in the seat indicated by the prince. She folded her hands in her lap and gazed at the merry decorations. "Why have you freed my servants? And where is Eadwig?"

"Because you wish it, my lady. As for Eadwig, I'm afraid my physician has the old man confined to his bed."

Myrredith flicked her eyes at the prince, pondering what game he could be playing. "May I see him?"

"Yes, of course. In due time."

"I see preparations for a feast. Where are the guests?"

"I have not called for them yet, my lady."

Myrredith found something distasteful in the manner he said "my lady." From his lips, it had the ring of ownership about it.

"What are you celebrating, Your Highness?"

"Well … that depends somewhat on you."

"Me?"

"Today is my father's birthday. All Gwythia will be celebrating, but in addition, I had hoped to announce our engagement."

Myrredith turned to face him. To her surprise, he was on one knee beside her with his hand on the arm of her chair. She blinked, not certain what to make of his words.

Hereweald charged ahead. "Something has been stirred within me. From the moment I saw you, it's been gnawing at my innards. I've been able to think of little else. Even as I rushed into battle, there you were again. I was knocked from my horse and cut off from my guard. I wandered across the battlefield, an easy target, for my heart wasn't in the fight. My only thought was to get back here to you. I've always thought most clearly in battle, but nothing is as clear to me as the revelation I had that night."

The prince paused his rapid speech and placed his hand on Lady Myrredith's. He swallowed and looked into her face, his eyes ablaze with enthusiasm.

"Myrredith—" He flashed an atypical smile. "You wouldn't know it, but I have longed to speak your name. Myrredith, you have disarmed this warrior's heart, and I stand defenseless against you. Marry me. Give me your hand, and my hand shall always protect you."

Myrredith was dumbfounded. She couldn't believe that the man who had invaded her land, killed her people, burned their homes, and slew her beloved Hugh, now knelt before her proposing marriage and using words of love as if they would sway her heart. And yet, she knew he was just a pawn of his father in these abhorrent deeds, motivated by misguided revenge and age-old hatred.

Myrredith beat a hasty retreat back into her mind, but did not find it as comfortable as she had hoped. The answers she sought did not present themselves in their usual clear fashion. Instead, they knotted together with all the emotions and problems she had been refusing to deal with. As soon as she caught the tail of an idea and tried to pull it from the mess, an unrelated emotion or problem would spring forth and tangle up her thoughts further. She felt panicky under Hereweald's watchful eyes. She feared that she would say something that would somehow make matters worse. Before she realized what she had done, she turned away from him, placing her hands over her quivering mouth.

Hereweald's hopeful lips closed. The muscles of his jaw tightened. His nostrils flared wider as his breathing became forced. His flaming eyes cooled and grew diamond-hard. He watched her for another minute, evidently hoping that she would give him a favorable reaction.

"I see." The prince removed his hand, then rose to his feet. "You do realize that you still stand accused of Gaelyn's murder?"

Myrredith did not answer.

"Please, Myrredith. I'm trying to help you. As my wife, you would never be held accountable. Indeed, I find it difficult to believe that you could be involved. If you would only say something."

His voice reverberated from the rafters.

"This silence will only bring about your death!"

Hereweald closed his eyes and breathed deep, trying to remain calm. He paced the length of the table, shifting his gaze from the floor to Lady Myrredith, and then back again.

"I take it, then." He raised his voice. "That you prefer death over me."

"No," Myrredith said, untangling her tongue. "It's just ..."

Hereweald stopped pacing. "Just what?"

"It's just that—I don't know how to say it."

"Try!"

"I didn't know that you felt this way. ... I never considered—of course, I'm flattered—"

"Do not play your games with me." The prince turned his back to her. "Either you'll marry me, or you won't. If you will not marry me, then you will die. It's that simple."

Myrredith sank back, befuddled by the prince's seesaw proposal. She could see by his trembling fists that he was on the verge of an explosion, so she whispered, "Please, Your Highness—"

"Silence!" he shouted, then spun around, his hand raised back as if to strike her. He shook with fury, his eyes wide, his mouth contorted, his nostrils flaring. He screamed and smashed his fist on the table. Then he gripped the arm of her chair with both hands and glared at her through the fringe of his eyebrows.

"Myrredith." His voice was low, trembling. "I would give you everything. I would go against my father. Build a kingdom for us right here, on these shores. I would worship you."

Lady Myrredith looked Prince Hereweald in the eyes. "If I invaded Gwythia, destroyed your cities, killed and raped your citizens, could you marry me?"

His expression fell. He stared at her like a man who'd crossed a desert, only to find the well dry. All at once, he rose from the arm of her chair and turned away. He rubbed his forehead and temples with the tips of his fingers. "Guard," he said, at last. "Guard!"

"Yes, Your Highness." The soldier ran down the steps.

"Take Lady Cyndyn to her chamber." His hands still covered his eyes, but his voice was calm and clear. "I do not wish to see her ever again."

The guard escorted Myrredith from the great hall. She never looked back at Hereweald, but his eyes were upon her. Despite what he, as a prince, had done to her and her countrymen, she felt pity for the man who had the misfortune to fall in love with his enemy.

That night, as Myrredith lay awake in her bed, she could hear the merriment of the celebration in the great hall. The decayed echoes of laughter and singing came rambling up the stairs to her room, but it was not these sounds that kept her awake. It was a memory brought back to life by the prince: the memory of another man who had fallen in love with her.

"Oh, Hugh." She sighed. "Sorely do I miss you."

Myrredith of Cyndyn, a full-grown woman, a lady of stature, a pillar of strength to those around her, cried like a little girl sent to bed without dinner. And like that little girl, she cried herself to sleep.

***

In the wee hours of the morning, a soggy rain fell over Wyneddhamshire. Pit-a-pat drops and trickling rivulets washed the stones of Cyndyn Hall, rousing Myrredith from her slumber. She lay in bed for some time, listening to a gargling drainpipe as it drank the countless ranks of raindrops.

The rain stopped and Myrredith rose from her bed. She picked up a woolen shawl on her way to the door.

Megan awoke. "Where're ya goin', milady?"

"I need some air."

Myrredith donned her shawl, and Megan jumped to her feet.

At first, the guard stationed at the door denied her ladyship's request, but in the end relented, with the stipulation that he would follow at a discreet distance. "And no funny business!"

Lady Myrredith agreed, and they went up the stairs.

Megan followed close behind her mistress as she made her way to the top of Cyndyn Hall. They had forgotten the guard, like forgetting one's shadow, but neither spoke a word as they walked atop the battlements.

Something had changed in Myrredith that could not be erased or denied. Her entire youth, she had demonstrated mastery over her destiny. She had seen what fate awaited women of her station and balked. Much to her father's dismay, becoming a woman hadn't slowed her headstrong ways. And when, in his senility, he thought to remedy things by marrying her off to the rough and surly Sir Aonghas, she had become all the more stubborn and shrewd. She was the dauntless ruler of her mind and body and, in time, an entire fief. Not to mention her late, bull-headed husband.

However, the previous night had witnessed an end to that self-reliance and certainty. A message had been delivered, in a manner louder than trumpets. She had been helpless to stop the decurion, and every fiber of her being had known it. In that instant, caught between rage and terror, all she had been—ambitions, goals, dreams—all had vanished. She became so utterly empty, only to fill with numbing despair. Now, she yearned to forget. She would forsake all the nights of her lifetime to forget the one.

Myrredith stepped closer to the edge and placed a foot in an open crenel. The crisp, moist morning air caressed her face, and she felt Megan's steadying hands upon her shoulders.

"Would you fetch my cloak?"

"Yes, milady, but perhaps it would be better if you came in."

"No. I'll be fine."

Megan released her mistress and stepped back. She moved away, looking for someone to fetch her ladyship's cloak, but there was no one. Even the guard had disappeared from sight. Megan started down the steps and paused to look back. At that moment, the Lady of Cyndyn Hall stepped up into the notch in the battlements.

"My lady!" Megan ran back up the steps.

Myrredith ignored her maid. Her mind focused on the narrow bit of masonry separating her from a fatal plummet. Just one step and it would all be over: no more worries, no more strife, no more fear, and Hugh on the other side. She closed her eyes and imagined her descent to the distant rocky earth under the shadow of Cyndyn Hall.

"My lady, please!"

Myrredith opened her eyes. She felt dizzy. Her balance shaky. The dark ground below loomed up as she looked down. She lifted her left foot to step back, but the morning rain had made the stones slick. Her right foot slipped out from under her, and down she fell.

CHAPTER FIFTEEN

Dead End

The first night out of Tirn Aill, the seas calmed, and the *Gyldan Mene* floated across glassy green water. The moon and her sister-stars admired their reflections glittering on the rippled surface and, for a while, Billy and his companions relaxed and enjoyed the beauty of the sea.

Within an hour, a fog bank swallowed up the ship, which first dimmed the moonlight, then blotted it out. They lit lanterns, but all they could see was the light surrounding the ship, reflected back at them by the impenetrable fog. The sea grew quiet until the sound of the waves was a whisper. In the eerie stillness, Billy heard the dilapidated ship complain: each creaking board, groaning rope, and squeaking peg.

Shaldra eyed their surroundings as he sharpened an arrow. "I've got a bad feeling about this."

"It's nothing. Just fog."

They sailed through the stillness for hours unnumbered, until all reckoning of time was confounded. The dawn never came. Billy made his way back to the wheel and asked the captain if they were lost, but the captain didn't answer.

Sylvys leaned out over the railing, straining to see something below. "Billy! Come here!"

Billy arrived next to him. "What is it?"

The satyr grabbed Billy by his shoulders and shook him. "There's no water!"

Billy stared at him and crossed his arms.

"Did you hear what I said? There's no water beneath us. Look."

Billy plodded to the railing and found that, indeed, he could see no water. He squinted, trying to see through the smoke-like fog. "It's there. We just can't see it because of this blasted fog."

"No, watch." Sylvys tossed a belaying pin overboard.

They both watched as it disappeared into the fog without a sound.

"Wait, wait, wait. … This can't be. We just have to …"

Billy took another belaying pin and tied it to the end of a nearby rope. Then he dropped it over the railing. He lowered the rope: first ten feet, then twenty, and thirty.

"Something is wrong here."

"Aye!" Sylvys shivered. "That's what I've been trying to tell you."

Billy pulled up the rope. The pin and its tether were dry.

Shaldra came up behind them. "I told you I had a bad feeling about this."

Sylvys nodded. "I prefer to be on water—well, actually, on land—but this …"

Billy turned to them. "What do you want me to do about it?"

Shaldra looked at Sylvys and Billy, then shrugged.

"You see, there's nothing to be done. We appear to be safe for now, so try not to think about it."

"Try not to think about it?" Sylvys stared. "We're sailing on nothing!"

Billy clamped his hand over the satyr's mouth and nodded to his left.

In unison, all three of them looked to the bow. The still fully-armored Drif had made camp there and now sat motionless, staring ahead.

Billy whispered, "I'm not sure I want our friend to know about this."

Sylvys and Shaldra nodded in agreement.

The *Gyldan Mene* continued on what they presumed was a forward course. Billy was counting on the captain to find his way through the gloom, and quickly. He fought to maintain a calm facade for his comrades while his innards squirmed like fresh-caught eels in a basket at the prospect of being forever adrift in that sea without a sea, in that place of the sunless, starless sky.

The fog thinned, and then cleared altogether. Billy greeted the stars in the sky with a smile. But it was not the same sky. There were shadows and strange shapes in the heavens, and then he could see that they had entered a cave of enormous proportions. The ceiling arched far above the tallest mast, with crystals and gems set like stars in the dark bluish rock.

Billy ran back to the stern. "Captain, we've entered a cave! Look out!"

The captain gave no reply. He stared straight ahead and steered his ship further into the cave.

"Is this the way to Finvarra? Answer me, Captain!"

The captain's skull nodded.

Billy returned to mid-ship and spoke to Sylvys and Shaldra, "This seems to be the way to Finvarra."

Sylvys scratched his chin. "How do you know?"

"The captain."

Shaldra scowled. "I don't trust him."

Billy looked at the fierce elf warrior. "What choice do we have? I can't make him tell us the truth."

"I could wring his bony neck."

"And what good would that do?"

"It would make me feel a whole peck better."

Billy smiled and patted him on the back. "Be patient, my friend. First, let's see where this takes us. Then, if it'll make you feel any better, you can try to kill a dead man."

"Good." Shaldra glared up at the captain. "I don't like the way he's been looking at me."

Billy, Sylvys and Shaldra went to the railing to have a better look at the cave. The ship again made a wake in the liquid beneath them, a welcome sight to all, but it was hardly what any of them would call water.

The light from their lanterns, even when lowered, failed to penetrate the inky, brackish liquid, and its smell was without life.

All around them, the cave echoed with a plaintive moaning sound. It seemed to originate from smaller caves, which were no more than black gaping holes in the distant walls. In addition, a number of noises—most of them drips or clicks—scurried across the surface of the lake to their ears.

They sailed for hours into that gloomy winding cave. The only light came from their lanterns and what part of that light winked like tiny rainbow colored stars off the jeweled ceiling.

Despite its unbelievable size and strange beauty, Billy felt claustrophobic. He examined the distance to the ceiling and walls several times to assure himself that the cave wasn't shrinking. Much to his surprise, it grew larger instead of smaller. But then this, too, worried him.

Sylvys came to the railing next to Billy. "What is it?"

"I was just thinking." Billy tried to act natural.

"About what?"

"Nothin'."

"I was just thinking too."

"Oh?"

"I was thinking that only a tiny creature can live in a tiny cave ..."

"Well ... that doesn't mean that only a giant creature would live in a giant cave."

"Oh, no. Absolutely not. Why, there might be a few medium sized creatures ..."

"Or even many small ones."

"Yes, quite. There mightn't be any at all."

"Yes, of course."

Billy spotted Shaldra sitting across the deck, sharpening arrows and staring at the dark elf. "You think he's afraid of Drif?"

Sylvys scoffed. "Nothing frightens that boy; he's fate-born."

"What?"

"Shhh!"

"Shaldra is one of the fate-born?"

"It's very personal. If he hasn't told you, it's not my place."

"But – "

"Shaldra's not afraid, Your Highness. He's just sizing up Drif in case they have to tangle."

Shaldra walked across the deck. "What are you two whispering about?"

"Nothing," Sylvys and Billy answered.

"Good. I thought maybe you saw something."

"No. You?"

"Well, a moment ago, I thought I saw something moving in the lake, but really, what could live in that stuff?"

When Shaldra crossed back to his post, Billy and Sylvys moseyed back from the railing. Sylvys tried in vain to tighten his helmet strap without drawing attention, but he fumbled with the buckle and dropped his spear. Then he waddled forward to pick it up, and his helmet came down over his eyes. Meanwhile, Billy leaned his back against a spar, casually ran his finger over Lura Zahn's grip, and snickered politely at the nervous satyr's antics. He was thankful that, for once, he was not the one playing the fool.

At last, another light glinted on the horizon. From a distance, it looked like a large bonfire, spitting forth occasional sparks at the stony roof. However, as the *Gyldan Mene* approached, they saw that it was no fire at all, but a huge pale palace perched on the peak of an island. The island itself erupted from the center of the greatest part of the black lake, where the ceiling of the cave soared upward higher than a hawk's flight.

The dead captain steered his ship nearer and nearer to the island. Now, all four members of the quest party went to the bow to stare, unblinking, at the approaching chimera.

Beneath the ivory palace, rugged yellow bluffs tumbled down into a narrow gorge. Here, the black waters of the lake became a jagged ribbon, just wide enough for the ship to pass. A lonely dock waited at the channel's terminus, and a torchlit path wound its way up the mountain.

The *Gyldan Mene* coasted into the dock and came to a gentle stop. A skeletal sailor tossed ropes over the mooring spars while his mates finished with the ragged sails. Once the gangplank rested on the dock, the crew became motionless.

Billy approached the captain. "What is this place?"

The captain glared dumbly at him.

Billy remembered to whom he was speaking and rephrased his question, "Is Finvarra here? Will I find Finvarra here?"

The captain nodded and pointed to the shore.

After a long dialogue, Billy was still unable to persuade Sylvys to depart the ship. Only when he feigned seeing something move in the lake did the satyr volunteer to go ashore.

Shaldra, on the other hand, was no trouble at all. After the proud elf saw Drif stroll down the gangplank without a word, it was all Billy could do to keep him from running ahead.

They left the dock behind and started up the chalky trail. All around them a soft, sulfurous stone made up the cliff face and ground they walked upon, and the smell of it stung their noses. The torches seemed to brighten when they passed. Billy slowed to examine them as they climbed.

The head of each torch was an intricately carved iron cage, with no two being alike. Inside these cages, tiny fiery balls darted about and reminded Billy of the faerie hand-fire Elzgig had shown him in Tirn Aill. However, these seemed to have their own will. They flew around their iron cells, sometimes chasing, sometimes clashing, but mostly they would move to the side closest to Billy and hover. Then one of the little fireballs slipped through the roof of its prison and shot straight to the dark, distant ceiling of the cave. It twinkled there briefly before disappearing. A moment later, another blazing sphere appeared in the cage and thrashed about, banging into the black iron bars.

THE PRINCE | 207

Billy looked over the edge of the trail and saw the *Gyldan Mene* below them, looking like a toy boat in a puddle of ink. The hair on the back of his neck prickled and he turned to find Drif not two feet behind him. He forced a smile and reminded himself that Malkry's warrior could very well be an assassin, and that he should be careful not to make himself an easy target. He stepped away from the edge and continued uphill.

Shortly, the party of four arrived at the top of the bluffs. An armored guard stood on either side of the path, silhouetted against the wondrous palace they had seen from so far away. It was the color of bone and illuminated in scintillating shades of red and amber. Billy looked for the large fires that must surely be the source of such lighting, but there were none—only a flat, barren limestone plain.

He hailed the guards, but they made no response. He took a few paces forward and tried again.

"I seek an audience with King Finvarra. I am Billy, son of Eleanor, the High Queen of Faerie."

The shadowy armored figures remained motionless.

Shaldra stepped forward and marched up to the guardians. "Are you deaf? This is William, heir to the throne of Tirn Aill, and your ..." Shaldra stopped just short of shoving the guard on the right. He drew his long sword and spun around to face the other guard. Then he backed away from the guardians until he was next to Billy.

"What's wrong, Shaldra?"

"More skeletons."

"More skeletons?"

Drif walked from their midst and passed between the two guards. Both armored fists shot out from the elf warrior's shoulders and leveled the scarecrow-like guards. They went down with a crash that sent broken bones and armor skittering over the hard ground.

Shaldra crossed his arms. "I could'a done that."

"How long do you think they've been there, Your Highness?" Sylvys asked.

"A long time, I'd wager."

The satyr smirked. "Someone should have told them to come in to dinner."

"Say..." Billy rubbed his belly. "I think someone forgot to tell *us* it was time for dinner."

Sylvys pointed to the huge edifice. "Maybe they'll feed us in there."

"Yeah," Shaldra said. "But what will they feed us to?"

With that said, their appetites shrank to a manageable level, and they continued.

Billy nodded to Drif as he passed. "Well done."

The close-lipped warrior acknowledged the accolade with a nod.

They crossed the open, rocky plain and headed towards the palace. With each step, the edifice seemed to grow larger until it loomed over them in staggering proportions.

Forty-nine steps separated them from the entrance, and on each step, there stood a skeletal warrior. All were girded in armor, tooled by the finest artisans—although now in ill repair, half rusted, bent, and sometimes hewn.

Now, up this stair the intrepid company went. One step at a time, they passed the motionless, dead guardians. All bore blank eyes and no expression except, perhaps, the same bony grin. With the memory of the *Gyldan Mene's* crew still set in their minds, the party kept their distance.

Carved on the riser of each step, in deep relief, was the "dance of the dead," as Billy had seen in the catacombs of Cyndyn Hall. The small chiseled skeletons, depicted in lively dance steps, blew horns and waved banners. Billy read the banners while they ascended, and found that the first seven steps were dedicated to sloth, the next seven to anger. Following these were envy, gluttony, lechery, avarice, and pride at the top.

A row of six thick columns rested ten yards from the last step and rose up like great towers to the gigantic eaves. Beyond these stood a wall of pale red marble, so expertly crafted that the seams were almost undetectable. A broad, intricate knotwork pattern sprawled across the wall. It unraveled in the middle to twist its way around two columns, one on either side of a dark inset doorway. Two massive doors, no shorter than thirty feet tall and hinged on opposite sides, hung in the gloomy orifice. They were forged from black iron, with the sweat, soot, and grease of manufacture still anointing them.

Shaldra grabbed Billy's arm. "I don't like this! This is the sort of place a ghoul would live."

Billy looked up at the edifice and chuckled. "Maybe the king of ghouls." When he looked back to Shaldra, the elf was gaunt. Billy grinned. "It'll be fine, Shaldra. Finvarra is here."

"I am not so sure."

"You can stay here if you like, but I must go in."

Shaldra clenched his teeth and then said, "Where you go, I go also, Your Highness."

When they approached, the doors swung open. Inside, the light was dim, but Billy could see a forest of red pillars spaced in rows, supporting a ceiling that gleamed with gold. The pillars and ceiling were reflected in a glossy ebony floor, giving the illusion of an equal space beneath it.

Billy looked at his shrugging companions, then entered. They allowed him to proceed several paces onto the mirror-like surface before following. Sylvys brought up the rear. When the satyr was ten yards from the entrance, the doors began to swing closed. As swift as he could, the satyr sprinted back to the doors, but he slipped on the smooth floor and crashed into the doors as they came to with a final clank. He pushed and hammered on them, but to no avail.

"Open up! Let me out!"

A light from his left drew Billy's attention from the hysterical satyr. He turned. A grey figure shambled toward him, led by a solitary thin light. As it approached, Billy could see that it was a single candle burning bright as twenty, but the figure carrying it remained grey and hazy as if wrapped in dusty gauze.

Now Drif and Shaldra turned to see what had stolen Billy's focus. They watched as the creature approached. Shaldra stepped in front of Billy and slipped his dagger from its sheath.

The phantom stopped several feet from them. The scent of rot and mold was on the air. Sylvys, finally turning from the doors, gasped upon seeing the specter and dropped his spear. Drif picked up the weapon and handed it back to the quivering satyr while keeping an eye on the figure before them.

"Thanks." Sylvys pressed his back against the large iron doors.

Billy peered around Shaldra. "I seek Finvarra."

The figure made a beckoning motion with its free hand and backed away in the direction from which it had come.

"Will you take us to Finvarra?"

The figure continued to beckon and retreat.

Shaldra glanced back at Billy. "No offense, Your Highness, but you don't honestly think she'd tell us if we were the main course for some ghoulish feast, do you?"

"I suppose not. But what choice do we have?"

"We could turn around and get our bushy tails out of here," Sylvys said.

Shaldra shook his head. "I think not."

"And why not?"

"First, you're the only one here with a bushy tail; second, I don't believe those doors are gonna open for us anytime soon; and third, you are the biggest—"

Billy nudged the elf. "And third, I don't think *they* are going to give us another choice."

Sylvys and Shaldra stopped their bickering. On all sides of them, grey, skulking figures crept from the dim shadows surrounding the pillars. They approached, and the air grew thick with their fetid smell. It was hard to breathe.

"Come on!" Billy rushed through a gap in the shambling mob of specters to follow the candle bearer.

Drif and Shaldra shot after him, but Sylvys hesitated for a moment and only just escaped the grasp of the phantoms. Once the entire party had caught up to the candle bearer, the mob fell behind and ended its pursuit.

"Who were they? What was that all about? Where are we going?" The nervous satyr shut up only after Shaldra flashed him an angry glare.

"As if we should know."

"I was only speaking my mind."

"Well, don't. Your continual babbling is driving me insane."

"I'm sorry—"

Drif elbowed both Shaldra and Sylvys in the gut to quiet them. This was the first physical contact either had received from the mysterious dark elf, and that alone seemed to carry weight enough to hold their tongues.

Billy concentrated on their guide as they marched through the endless red pillars. He caught a glimpse of bone and grey, crumbled flesh protruding through a rough hole in the creature's garb. He shivered at what horrors might lay farther beneath its wrappings.

At last, a well-lit doorway appeared ahead of them. Two gigantic iron doors barred the way, identical to those they had passed through at the main entrance. Their phantom guide stopped some distance from this doorway and motioned for them to continue. It then turned and disappeared into the shadows with its candle.

Billy walked toward the doorway, feeling oddly reluctant to leave behind the ghostly figure that had led them this far. Ordinarily, he would have thought it strange to desire the company of a corpse, but under the circumstances, it only seemed natural. Again, he spotted figures moving in the shadows around them, and all desire to stay put evaporated.

Much to their relief, the doors opened when they neared. Bright light burst out from the room beyond the doors, forcing the party to squint to see inside.

A grand dining hall lay within. Ancient war relics and tattered flags decorated its white walls. Intense white flames licked the air from a wide hearth at the far end and the numerous torches set along each wall. The black and white checkered floor was empty, with all the tables and benches stacked to the sides except for one set just before the great hearth. Four empty chairs waited at the table, their backs to the door. Across from them sat a large, dark throne of oak.

The party entered the hall and approached the only standing table. They each found themselves behind one of the empty chairs, staring at the table and each other.

"Looks like someone's been expecting us." Billy indicated the five place settings.

"Aye," Shaldra said. "But where is our host?"

"And who is our host?" Sylvys asked.

Shaldra looked around the vast chamber. "Aye, who?"

"King Finvarra," a voice bellowed from behind them.

They spun around and beheld a grim procession, which had entered the rear of the hall. Three-score of the grey shambling figures marched in three columns. Those in the middle ranks shouldered a large palanquin of gold.

Upon this lustrous platform, nestled among crimson pillows, reclined a sharp-eyed man with a grey beard. He wore a red cape over a long blue tunic with gold trimming, and his lower extremities were wrapped and sandaled in the fashion of ancient warriors. Unadorned copper jewels of plain but bold design wrapped each wrist, as well as his waist and neck. The only visible gem on him sparkled from the brooch that clasped his cape about his shoulders. Billy observed all this in detail; however, his eye clung on the simple, thin crown, which crossed the man's high forehead on its circular path around his head.

The silent grey spirits lowered the palanquin, and the man—who seemed most colorful against them—descended, using the backs of some as steps. As soon as he was off, the procession bowed to him, then exited with the palanquin.

"Welcome." The man stood tall and proud. "I am Finvarra, your host."

"I am Billy, son of Queen Eleanor, and I am here to—"

"Yes, yes, yes." Finvarra strutted across the floor. "I know who you are. Please, sit. Feast with me, and then we shall discuss your request on full stomachs."

The party glanced at each other, but none moved.

"Please. It's so rarely that I receive guests here who can enjoy a good meal."

Now Finvarra was upon them, and Billy could see what a large man he was. He towered above Billy at more than six feet tall and, though time had engraved deep lines across his features, he did not look feeble in the least. His broad shoulders and ruddy skin were those of a healthy, fit man.

He clasped Billy by the forearm. He had the grip of a blacksmith. "Indulge me, and I promise you a great feast!"

Billy, remembering Onian's warning about a show of weakness, did not let on that Finvarra's grip smarted. He nodded, and the party sat in their chairs.

"Good, good." Their host took up the throne across from them.

Immediately, a group of the grey phantoms streamed into the chamber. Some dished out bread, spiced meat, vegetables, and fruit while others poured wine into their cups. These ghosts went about their tasks, and then stood back from the table and waited.

Sylvys gobbled up some bread and washed it down with a deep drink from his goblet. "M-m-m-m, this is good." He then shoved some fruit in his mouth.

One of the phantoms came forward, refilled the satyr's cup, and then returned to her station.

Finvarra smiled as Sylvys took another drink, then drained his own cup. Again, one of the grey phantoms came forward to fill the empty goblets.

Billy and Shaldra sipped their wine and nibbled the food. The taste was superb, and soon they were eating like the hungry men they were. The only one to abstain was Drif, who refused any offer of food or drink.

"What is this place?" Shaldra asked between bites.

"Ah." Finvarra put down his wine. "Pleasant dinner conversation."

Shaldra looked at his host, then to Billy. "Yes."

"Well, this is my second kingdom."

Billy wrinkled his brow. "Your *second* kingdom?"

"Aye."

"We are not in Knockma Rath?"

"Knockma?" Finvarra belted out a hardy laugh. "No, no, no. This is not my Knockma."

Billy wiped some crumbs from his mouth. "Well, I assumed that we were in Erin; that this was Knockma."

"Why?"

"The captain said he would take me to you."

"And so he has."

"But this is not Knockma."

"No. This is a place very different from my Knockma."

Billy was becoming frustrated by his host's circumspect conversation. Then he remembered Elzgig saying that the Daoine Sidhe would render nothing without a struggle. Everything was a contest to them. With this in mind, Billy pieced together the events that had brought him to where he was, in the hope that it would shed some light on just where he was.

"This is not Knockma Rath, nor even Erin, and we were brought here by dead men ... so this must be a place belonging to the dead."

"Not exactly." Finvarra smiled and shrugged. "You see, by conscription of fate, I am king of these dead; the sailors who drown at sea, the warriors who fall in unworthy causes, the ruthless, the unholy, the wicked—men who die for gold or kill for power. Also, many who are too fat, too lusty, or too envious find their way here. In the grave, I am their lord and master.

"Most nobles come here to serve me, but the jewels of my crown are the kings and princes. Despite their former life experience, I find they make quite adequate table servants, grooms, wine stewards ... though there's not a decent conversationalist among them."

Finvarra let out another jolly laugh and motioned to his left. A shadowy figure skulked up beside him, awaiting a task to perform. Billy gave the poor wretch the first close examination he had dared give any of the servants since entering Finvarra's hall.

He jumped to his feet, staring at the phantom.

Finvarra looked first at Billy then to the corpse beside him. He smiled. "Oh, yes. It's funny, I didn't notice the resemblance right away. Your father is a recent arrival. His soul is not as laden as some, but he will be with us for quite a long time."

"Your father?" Sylvys and Shaldra said.

Billy stared at the haunting phantom of his father. "That man ..."

Finvarra tilted his head. "He's no longer a man."

"That ... spirit was once King William of Lyonesse."

"Murdered his own wife," Finvarra added.

"It wasn't his fault!" Billy cried.

"She was your mother—"

"He's not to blame!"

"—and Queen of Tirn Aill."

"He killed Queen Eleanor?" Shaldra's eyes widened.

"He was under a spell."

Finvarra leaned back in his throne. "Would you like to plead his case?"

"Aye."

"What?" Shaldra rose to his feet.

Billy frowned at the elf until he sat down. He then turned back to Finvarra, who had kicked one leg over the arm of his throne and was grinning.

"Aye. I would like to plead for my father."

"How sweet." Finvarra watched the wine as he swirled it in his goblet. "But I'm afraid it'll do him no good. You see, all who come here are guilty. Once they enter this domain, they must serve until their soul slips its bonds to the flesh. Only then will they find rest in the grave. But not for long: judgment still waits. Many will serve me until the Day of Judgment. I have no say in it, but if I did …" Finvarra paused to stare at Billy. "I would keep your father here forever."

Billy pounded the table with his fists, then swatted his goblet to the floor. He glared at Finvarra with the fire of hate consuming him. Lura Zahn vibrated in sympathy at his side, and he felt the blade's cold thirst for blood. He also became aware of the black tome's presence, like a hand pressing on his back. A clear thought stung through the fog of anger and wine. *Finvarra's trying to provoke me. If I let him, he will kill me.*

Should strike him down with flame!

No!

Billy took a deep breath and stiffly returned to his seat. He and Finvarra stared across at one another as William's specter returned the spilled goblet to the table and filled it.

Finvarra grinned. "I see you have some fire, son of Eleanor."

Billy lifted his cup. "To my mother, Queen Eleanor …"

Finvarra and the others followed suit. "Queen Eleanor."

"Queen, of *all* Faerie." Billy threw back his head and drank.

Finvarra glared at him over the rim of his goblet, and then brought it down on the table with a clank. "What do you want of me?"

Billy sensed the turn in their battle of wits. "Are we done with the pleasant dinner conversation already?"

"Aye!" Finvarra said, through his teeth. "Now, why have you come here?"

"As you know, my mother, the Queen of Faerie, is no longer with the living. Now I must go back to the land of men to collect something she has left there for me."

"What has that got to do with me?"

"I have powerful enemies in Lyonesse, and I may need an army."

"You want me to give you an army?"

"As my mother was Queen of Faerie, and I know you are a loyal—"

"No!"

"What do you mean?"

"I mean I will not help you!"

"But we are allies—kinsmen. Are the Daoine Sidhe afraid?"

Finvarra leapt to his feet, and all the flames in the room changed from white to blue. The temperature became noticeably warmer.

"Watch your tongue, boy!" He leaned across the table, seeming to grow in size.

Shaldra stood and unsheathed the first inch of his sword.

"Put it away, elf." Finvarra never took his eyes from Billy. "Put it away, or die where you stand."

Billy locked eyes with Finvarra. He placed his hand on Shaldra's, and the elf slipped the blade back into its home.

"I know what you Tirn Aill faeries think of the Daoine Sidhe." Finvarra's face was red. "You think you can manipulate us with insults and implied threats, or call us to service by the mere mentioning of a name. Well, the Daoine Sidhe certainly will not kneel to you. You, who can't even secure your own throne! A real king would take what is rightfully his and squash anyone who got in his way, but you ... you're naught but a boy—a joke—a jester."

Finvarra straightened, then turned and started for the back of the hall, followed by his grey phantom servants. The doors opened, and the palanquin procession entered again. They stopped and kowtowed to Finvarra as he approached.

Billy turned to his party. "Come, let's leave this horrible place."

Finvarra spun on his heels. "Leave? You cannot leave."

"And why not?"

"Because I do not will it."

"What about your allegiance to my mother and Tirn Aill?"

"This is not Tirn Aill, boy. Your mother had no sway here, and neither do you."

With that, Finvarra stepped onto his palanquin and started out the door. Billy and his comrades ran to the back of the hall, but a mob of specters blocked their exit. Billy saw the sad face of his father's spirit, and then the great black doors closed.

CHAPTER SIXTEEN

Challenge

Billy paced the length of Finvarra's hall. Shortly after Shaldra and Sylvys gave up attempting to beat down the huge iron doors, the fire fizzled, and the torches waned to a dim amber glow. The rhythm of Billy's footsteps reverberated from the dark corners and vaulted ceiling, coming back to his ears like the murmur of an impatient crowd.

He looked to his comrades, but all he got was muffled whispers from Sylvys and silence from the elves. With each step and each echoed murmur, the situation calcified in Billy's mind and his frustration mounted.

Anger filled him—anger for Finvarra, anger for Ergyfel, anger for his father, and even his companions. He was angry with the whole bloody mess, but especially with himself.

"Finvarra! If it's the last thing I do ... !"

Billy furrowed his brow and ground his teeth, his eyes boring into the hard floor. His footsteps grew heavier. The pacing became a march and finally degraded to childish stomping.

Then, he heard a voice. *Why make it the last thing you do?*

He spun to look behind him. No one there.

Getting even with him should be the first thing you do.

He spun again.

The first thing we truly do together.

Billy realized it was the voice of the black tome, and he had actually been hearing it for some time, mingled with his own thoughts. He returned to his pacing. *No. I don't want to get even. I want to get out of here.*

I have no desire to be trapped here forever. Allow me to help you.

No!

There are many things I can do—wonders I can show you. Let me show you the easy way.

Why is it always the easy way with you?

Why is it always the hard way with you?

There's no prosperity without discipline.

Your father's words.

Good words.

Yes. Your father was a good man, and he taught you well: "There's a right way and a wrong way to do things," and "work hard and you will be rewarded," until the tax collector comes, or a famine … or bad men burn down your inn.

And murder your family. The hot blood of anger rushed to Billy's cheeks.

Yes, they did that. And got away with it.

He was a good man!

That didn't stop his killers.

No, but what he taught me was right!

For him. Not for you.

Why should I be any different?

He didn't know magic!

*

All at once, it got quiet. Sylvys, Shaldra, and Drif looked up from the floor to the still, dark figure of their leader. Shadow hid his face. His arms held something tight against his chest. They looked at each other, and then Billy raised his head and spoke.

The pitch of Billy's voice was abnormally low, and the words he spoke were unfamiliar to them all. The torch flames grew, illuminating his face with a bluish glow, but his features were not his own. His cheeks were hollow, his lips snarling, and his eyes white as ash.

Then he shouted and threw up his arms. The torches exploded, ejecting their flames into the air. A dozen fiery spheres circled the room, spinning ever faster around Billy. He clapped his hands together, and the fire orbs collided above his head with a thunderous boom and a blinding flash. Sparks flew in all directions and burned cloth, wood, stone, and metal alike.

A heat wave struck down Billy's companions like a hammer. Shaldra, alone, strained to look at their leader but found he could not bear to face the intense heat and light. His clothes pressed against him like firebrands.

"Billy!"

There was no answer, only the roaring of flames and the weird howling of an unearthly wind.

A blast shook the entire hall. Strange moaning sounds and the stench of brimstone filled the air as glowing chunks of half-molten iron splattered and skipped across the floor. Then the room became dark, and the air cooled.

Shaldra, Sylvys, and Drif raised their heads and looked toward the doors. There was a large, jagged hole torn through the thick iron and a brilliant shaft of light coming from beyond it. At that moment, Billy's silhouette appeared in front of the hole, and he passed through.

"Stop! Billy!" Shaldra pushed up to his feet.

Sylvys and Drif rose and followed Shaldra to the doors. The giant portal still radiated heat as they passed through the newly hewn exit.

"Look." Shaldra pointed to the edge of the hole. "Like ... claw marks."

Sylvys probed the hole with his spear. "Aye, but from what?"

They looked ahead, and the brilliant orb of fire moved away from them. Thin tendrils of flame escaped the main body of fire to caress the red pillars, but never touched Billy, who marched behind it. He had already put some distance between them, and turned out of view into the vast pillar forest.

Shadowy figures shifted in the dark recesses as the light from the flame receded. Sylvys felt a cold hand groping at his shoulder and sprung forward after Billy.

"Hurry!" Shaldra yelled as he gave chase.

The three of them ran to where Billy had turned and, again, saw him disappear into another copse of pillars. Before they could reach this spot, there was a blast like that inside Finvarra's hall and the same agonizing groans.

A hunk of red-hot iron skittered into their path as they turned the corner. They looked up and saw the burning sphere rip out another piece from the entrance doors and fling it aside. It repeated this several times in rapid succession. The naked iron doors screeched and groaned as the tendrils of flame tore out each section. The door shrieked one last time as the sphere pushed its way to the other side.

Billy strolled through the opening behind the being of flame, and the hall became dark. His companions sprinted for the exit, sensing the silent, shrouded figures closing in on their escape route. The phantoms were swift and soon were upon them.

Shaldra led the way, pushing by the first phantom and the second that stepped into their path, but the dead soon became thick as kelp. The party swept back and forth as waves of lifeless hands pushed, caressed, grabbed, and groped. Each contact with the cold rotting flesh slowed their progress, and the warmth and strength drained from their bodies.

"Shaldra, I can't go on."

"Keep moving, Sylvys."

At that moment, a pale light flooded the chamber, and the dead retreated. Sylvys and Shaldra fell to the floor as the press of bodies subsided. They looked up to see Drif standing over them. The dark warrior held a long black blade in one hand and a glowing crystal the size of a robin's egg in the other.

"Thanks," Sylvys said as he and Shaldra got up.

Shaldra stared at the dark elf for a moment. "We'd better get out of here." He then turned and ran through the gaping hole in the door, with Drif and Sylvys on his heels.

Billy stood alone in the center of the desolate plain. He faced away from the palace in a wide stance with his hands stretched toward the distant cave ceiling. Again, strange words poured from his lips; half sung, half shouted. The creature of flame had vanished.

Sylvys flapped his arms and shouted to Billy, but got no response. Then Shaldra, Drif, and he started down the forty-nine steps, all the time cautious of the skeletal guardians.

Before they could reach the bottom step, the air before Billy shimmered. Then a small ripple appeared, like that of a pebble dropped in a pond. The ripple expanded and rebounded, defining a circular plane just larger than a caravan wheel. Colors danced and swirled on the surface of the disc as it grew and spun. Then Billy's right hand shot out, and the center of the disc moved away from him. The disc became a cone, and the cone grew longer, spinning faster with each second. The vortex whirred as it drew in air.

Now, the small cyclone measured ten feet at its base, and the tip spasmed in the air a hundred feet away. Billy threw up his arms, and the tail raced to the dark ceiling.

At that moment, the skeletal warriors came to life. Sylvys, already moving at a good clip, leapt over the last five steps and hit the ground running. The two elves drew their weapons and followed the satyr.

The skeletons turned and marched down the steps, grinding and creaking. When they reached the bottom, they continued across the plain towards Billy.

Sylvys shouted as they approached. "Billy! We've got to get out of here!"

"Come quickly, Your Highness!"

Billy didn't move. His blank white eyes stared straight ahead and gave no sign of recognition to his companions.

Shaldra approached him and passed a hand before his eyes.

Sylvys raised his voice over the noise of the cyclone. "Is he in a trance?"

"Aye, I guess so." Shaldra looked over his shoulder at the approaching skeletons.

Sylvys grabbed Shaldra's arm. "We've got to get him out of here! Those walkin' piles of bone are almost on us."

"And they're not alone." Shaldra pointed beyond Billy.

Sylvys scanned the plain, to the place where they had first arrived. A mob of grey ragged figures was coming up the path. He glanced behind and saw a similar procession of dead pouring down the steps of the great palace.

Shaldra searched the barren plain for another way out, but could see none. He spotted a small outcropping of white stone and decided to make a dash for it, but he wasn't about to leave his future king.

He made a grab for Billy but stopped when something sharp jabbed his chest. He looked up and saw that the dark elf's black sword hindered him. Before he could act, Drif kicked him in the face and sent him sailing over the rocky ground.

Sylvys helped Shaldra to his feet, and then they turned to face Drif, who now stood between them and Billy.

"I knew you dark elves couldn't be trusted!" Shaldra wiped the blood from his lip and looked for his sword, but he had dropped it at Billy's feet. "You'll pay for this, Deordrif! I swear it!"

Drif forced them back at sword point, as the skeletal warriors arrived. Sylvys and Shaldra tried to circle around, but there was no way to get by the dark elf and avoid the bony specters.

Shaldra pushed Sylvys away. "Split up!"

They circled in opposite directions to force Drif to defend a larger area, but it was too late. The first of the armored fiends approached their defenseless leader.

"No!"

Billy pointed at the whistling cyclone. The skeleton turned and walked towards it. As it reached the mouth of the phenomenon, the structure of its bones and armor changed. They appeared to fracture into granules the size of table salt, and yet its menacing visage remained. Then, as the wind steals sand from the dunes, it disappeared, grain by grain, into the vortex. The entire creature took only seconds to evaporate.

The second skeletal warrior fell in behind the first, as did the third and fourth. In a couple of minutes, all forty-nine had vanished, and the horde of forlorn spirits formed into lines behind them. Shambling corpses stretched across the plain in every direction—all lamenting their past transgressions and awaiting their turn to enter the vortex.

Countless dead vanished in this way, and still the lines appeared endless. Billy seemed safe for the moment, so Shaldra and Sylvys relaxed and stepped back from Drif. The dark elf tossed Shaldra his dropped weapon.

Shaldra sheathed his sword. "How did you know?"

Drif, true to form, turned and walked in the opposite direction.

"Sorry, Deordrif. I'm sorry!"

Sylvys came to stand beside Shaldra. "How could Drif know?"

"I don't know. How many spell weavers do you know that can make a wind to send a graveyard's worth of corpses into the sky?"

Sylvys shrugged. "I don't even know why you would want to."

At that moment, there was a crash like thunder and a bright light exploded from the mouth of the vortex. It flashed against Billy's face, and the cyclone collapsed, becoming a thin ribbon of smoke, which hung in the air and then dispersed.

Shaldra, Sylvys, and Billy stood flat-footed, staring at each other, surrounded by an army of the dead. Billy opened his mouth to speak, and all the phantoms turned and marched back in the direction from whence they came.

***

When the dead seemed a safe distance away, Billy turned to Shaldra. "What just happened?"

Shaldra relayed to Billy the events that had landed them on the plain, all to Billy's astonishment. The only thing he could remember was talking to the black tome, but he kept mum about it. The elf had just explained about the strange cyclone, when they heard a thunderous crash, much like the one that had shut it down. A blinding stroke of lightning crackled across the ceiling of the cave and bolted to the ground ahead of them. It disappeared, leaving Finvarra brooding on the smoking spot where it had touched down.

Shaldra and Billy waited for Finvarra to speak. But he seemed to be waiting as well. In the end, Finvarra broke the silence, "What do you want?"

"I want you to let us go."

"Let you go? Let you go? Do you realize what you have done?"

Billy held his tongue.

Finvarra shouted and wagged his finger at the cavern ceiling. "You have brought havoc to my Knockma and terror to the whole of Erin with your child's prank! Don't you realize that people could die! By unleashing that mob of shabby, rude, moaning, groaning, unhappy, not to mention putrid smelling refuse on the world, you have ruined everything!"

"Then let us go."

"Let you go? I'll do no such thing! This is my kingdom. I say when you leave and when you must stay, and you are staying."

Billy pushed up his sleeves and cracked his knuckles. "Perhaps you would like another demonstration?"

"Wait." Finvarra held out his hands.

Before either of them could say or do anything more, a soft, pale beam of light drew their attention. It shone with the color of pink roses and flowed from the ceiling of the great cave to the stone plain between them, like honey from a spoon.

Finvarra's shoulders sank. "Now you've done it."

Tiny scintillating flecks of light fell lazily within the beam like autumn leaves and came to rest at their feet. The beam became hazy and brightened. Then the light coalesced into a beautiful woman. The beam faded away, but the luminous lady remained.

An unearthly beauty shone about the lady with such mesmerizing radiance that Billy could do nothing but stare slack-jawed at her. She was more beautiful than Lady Myrredith, more beautiful than Princess Kathryn, and even more beautiful than his mother, the Queen of all Faerie.

The lady smiled, and Billy's knees turned to pie dough. He caught himself and bowed, but never did his eyes leave her. In return, she lowered her sea-blue eyes and bowed to Billy.

"Welcome, cousin. I am Oonagh, cousin to Queen Eleanor, and wife to Finvarra."

"King Finvarra," her husband grumbled.

"Yes, of course, husband." Oonagh batted her eyes. "King Finvarra."

Billy remained entranced.

"And you are William, our cousin; here on a ... visit? Although, why in the name of Tirn Aill did you come to this place?"

Billy still could not answer.

"That was a naughty, naughty trick you played us for." Oonagh grinned. "'Twill take some time for my husband to collect all his charges and bring them back here where they belong. I'm not even thinking of the sheer chaos into which you threw Knockma. Ha! Things will never be the same again. And the people of Erin shan't either. Well, at least the dead livened things up a bit. It has been tiresome lately."

"Oonagh!" Finvarra did not look happy.

"Yes, dear husband."

"I have business with him, if you'll excuse us."

During this interaction between husband and wife, Billy managed to shake himself free of the hold Oonagh's beauty had over him.

"Business? What business?" she asked.

"I have asked your husband to let us go."

"Let you go?" She glanced at Billy's companions, taking in Shaldra, Sylvys, and finally holding on Drif. "Oh, I see."

Though her voice was warm as mother's milk, Billy felt a cold bite to her words.

"You see nothing!" Finvarra shouted.

"I see well enough, husband! And I know your appetites even better."

"Aagh, you don't know what you're talkin' about, woman."

"Then let them go."

"No."

"And why not?"

"*I* am the king. *Me.* And I do not choose to give them their freedom. They must earn it."

"You're just envious … and rutting."

"Earn it?" Billy asked.

Finvarra turned to him. "Aye, earn it. You have not proven to me that you are worthy of my favor. Why, then, should I give you your freedom?"

"Because we are kinsmen."

"Not good enough." Finvarra scowled.

Billy thought a moment. "So, it's a challenge you're after?"

"Aye." Finvarra slapped the hilt of his great sword and smiled. "If you think you're up to it."

"Aye." Billy straightened his spine. "I'm up to it."

"Great." Finvarra ripped his long, broad blade from its sheath.

"Stop!" Oonagh and Shaldra both screamed.

Billy stood his ground. "But not with swords." Lura Zahn vibrated against his chest and hurried his already rapid heartbeat. *Be still. Be patient.*

Finvarra squinted one eye and glared at Billy, the business end of his weapon pointed—unwavering—at Billy's head. "There's only one challenge, after battle, that's worthy of a king, and that's chess."

"Then chess it is."

"Ha!" Finvarra sheathed his sword. "Pity. I haven't had a decent battle in years. But wait. What will you wager?"

"Beg your pardon?"

"Your wager, boy. No challenge is truly worthy of a king without something at stake on both sides. In battle, the stakes are quite clear, but in a game of chess—well, winning isn't enough." Finvarra stroked his beard. "If you win, I promise to release you and your men. Now, what have you to wager against that?"

"But—" Oonagh attempted to speak.

"Hush, woman!" Her husband leaned towards her with dark intent in his eyes. "Billy is about to make his wager."

Billy thought for a moment and came to the unhappy realization that he had nothing to offer, *except perhaps a bluff of sorts.*

"I wager ..." Billy straightened with confidence. "That I will not release the dead on your kingdom on Knockma again."

Finvarra sneered.

"And further, that I will be your willing hostage."

"Very well. It's a wager, and I will hold you to it when you have lost!"

Billy grinned. "Justly so, for I will hold you to your wager when you lose."

Finvarra's hardened exterior cracked, and he grudgingly returned Billy's grin. Then the king of the dead threw back his head and let out a right jolly laugh. Billy liked the sound of Finvarra's laugh, but its echoes returned from the farthest corners of the great cavern distorted, perverted, and menacing.

Finvarra led the way back to his great palace, pausing to frown at the doors Billy's fiery servant had demolished. Oonagh followed right behind, chatting brightly with her newly arrived cousin and paying no attention to her husband.

When they reached Finvarra's great hall, Shaldra pulled Billy aside and whispered in his ear, "What are you doing?"

"What do you mean?"

"Chess, Your Highness? Why, the Daoine Sidhe practically invented the blasted game! And no one, faerie or mortal, has ever beaten Finvarra. You would have a better chance against him with Thortan's blade."

"I have no training in arms. You would only end up guarding the two separate halves of me after he cut me in two. I *do* have some knowledge of chess, ya know?"

"Some?"

"Prince Gaelyn taught me."

"Swell, a mortal."

"A prince!"

Shaldra crossed his arms. "Are ya any good?"

"The prince thought so."

"Your Highness, maybe it's not too late to take back the challenge. Unlike his wife, Finvarra has no affection for you. Perhaps Queen Oonagh can still persuade him to let us go."

"No. There's more at stake here than our freedom."

"Is there a problem?" Finvarra seated himself on his throne.

Billy and Shaldra walked towards the table where a chess board was already waiting. Billy turned to Shaldra and whispered, "Don't worry, my friend. Prince Gaelyn taught me a trick or two."

Billy came to the table and sat across from Finvarra. The king had set up the pieces, giving Billy the white side. He surveyed the board and pieces and found that they were very similar to the ones he and Prince Gaelyn had used.

Finvarra motioned to the board. "You are the white."

Billy stared at him.

"That means you go first."

Billy feigned surprise. "Oh. Then I'll move this one."

"No, no, no. You can't move that one."

"Why not?"

"Because, that is a deruwid! You can't move him until his path is clear. You must first move your feuar."

"My what?"

"The little ones in the front row."

"Oh, yes."

"Do you know how to play or not?"

"Well, I've seen it played."

"Seen it played?"

"Yes, I remember now."

"Perhaps you should not ..." Oonagh said.

"No, cousin." Billy smiled. "I have made an agreement with your husband, and I shall stick to it."

"But—"

"But nothing, wife. Now, be quiet and let the lad have a go."

The room was still for a moment as everyone concentrated on Billy. He reached out and moved a feuar, or pawn, as Gaelyn had called them. Finvarra countered with a move of his own. Billy moved another piece, and then Finvarra. The faster Billy moved, the more Shaldra chewed on his thumbnail.

Finvarra relaxed into his throne as he took the first of Billy's pieces. Billy retaliated in kind, and then lost another. They exchanged two more pieces in rapid succession before Finvarra resumed his reclining position, and Shaldra moved from his nail to his knuckle.

Billy looked up as Finvarra settled back again. The king twirled a tiny game piece in his hand and smiled, but he did not seem focused on the game. He was, however, very interested in something over Billy's shoulder. Billy looked behind him and saw the metal-encased dark elf standing alone like an obsidian statue.

Billy moved another pawn, and Finvarra glanced back at the board. The smug king leaned forward and moved his queen to capture the pawn.

"Cyning weard."

Billy surveyed the situation on the board and saw that, while his king was in danger, his strategy had worked. His shamming had lulled Finvarra into a trap, and now he would take advantage of it. Billy watched

Finvarra's eyes as he made his next move, but the king of the Daoine Sidhe was still staring away from the table.

Billy once again turned his head and glanced at Drif. As he turned back, he noticed Oonagh standing behind her husband; her arms crossed, her lips pursed, her beautiful eyes seething. She too was taking an interest in the dark elf, but her burning stare held no admiration the way her husband's did.

Billy shifted in his seat. "Perhaps you would like to battle Drif?"

"A fight is not what he's after," Oonagh muttered.

Finvarra turned to face her. "Oh, be quiet, wife!"

Billy made his move. "Knight takes queen."

"What?" Finvarra spun back to the board.

"And, um, cyning weard, I believe."

Finvarra leaned forward and glared across the board at Billy. With nostrils flaring and jaw muscles twitching, he ran his narrowed eyes over Billy's face, dissecting him down to the pore. He then let out a growl, leaned back in his throne, and studied the game board. At last, he reached out and moved his king from harm's way. A move he did with a great deal of reluctance, as if never having done it before.

Billy moved his knight back. It was the last move that either contestant would make in haste.

The battle of wits dragged on. Each man maneuvered his pieces around, trying to catch the other off guard, sometimes giving, sometimes taking, but always on the hunt for the opening that could bring victory. Time crept on. On occasion, Oonagh grunted her displeasure when her husband's eyes wandered to the dark figure behind Billy. Finvarra seemed oblivious to his wife's labors, but it proved quite distracting for Billy.

Suddenly, Finvarra leaned forward again. A thin smile crept onto his lips as he made eye contact with Billy. His hand moved over the pieces and hovered. His grin widened as he picked up his knight and took Billy's deruwid.

"Cyning weard," Finvarra said, showing his teeth.

Billy frowned and tugged at his hair.

Finvarra chuckled. "You see, Billy ... anything you can do, I can do better." His head rolled to the side, and he let out a laugh. Still laughing, he leaned his throne back, in order to get a better view of Drif. "And anything I want, I get. You might as well give up now."

Finvarra's words circled in Billy's head until they were nearly thoughts of his own. "*Give up ... give up ... give up,*" they echoed. It seemed senseless to continue. What chance did he have against someone like Finvarra in the first place?

Billy reached out to move, but Oonagh intercepted his hand.

"I think it is time to give our guests a break to refresh, husband."

Finvarra stared at his wife's hand, which stayed Billy's move. He then looked to her face.

"They need something to drink and eat, husband. Or must I listen to the satyr's gurgling stomach for another hour?"

All eyes turned to Sylvys, who grinned and shrugged.

"Very well, very well. Let them drink and eat all they like. We will continue our game in two hours."

Finvarra marched from his hall as a bevy of grey spirits brought in food and drinks. Oonagh remained and played host to Billy and his followers.

Billy drank some ale and worked on a piece of spiced beef, all the time staring at the game board. His cousin did what she could to take his mind off the game, but with all that was riding on it, she had no luck. Finally, she took him by the hand and brought him to the side of the hall.

"You must be careful of my husband."

"Yes, I can see that." His mind was still focused on his next move.

"Do not worry about your next move," Oonagh said, reading his face. She leaned forward and whispered in his ear, "Relax, and I will tell you how to beat him."

"What?" He looked into his cousin's jewel-like eyes for her motives.

"I want him to lose."

"Why?"

"When he loses, you will leave."

"Won't he be angry?"

"Yes, of course, but he needs to be taught a lesson. Besides, I'm your cousin, and your mother was very dear to me. Just promise me one thing."

"Name it."

"When you leave, you will take the dark elf with you."

Billy glanced over his shoulder to where Oonagh stared. The ever-silent warrior might just as well have been a suit of armor. *What's this all about? Why all the interest in Drif?*

"I don't fully understand your motives, but I know my cousin would not fail me, and I shall not fail you either."

***

When Finvarra returned to his great hall, Billy awaited him at the chess board. "Have you made your decision?" the king asked.

"Yes."

"Then you will surrender?"

"No. I will move this piece."

Finvarra's smile dropped, and then his smile broadened. "Glad to see that you don't give up easily. I like a challenge, but you're only putting off the inevitable."

"The inevitable? You think you can beat me so easily?"

Finvarra made his next move, then rested back in his throne; pleased with the effect his games were having on Billy. He folded his hands behind his head. "Well, I've never been beaten, and I hardly think you ..."

"Why, you puffed up, arrogant churl!"

"Churl?" Finvarra jumped to his feet. He grabbed Billy by his shirt and pulled him over the table. "No one calls me a churl!"

A sound like steel on stone intruded, and Lura Zahn was at Finvarra's throat. The others gasped, as Billy pushed the sharp point of its blade under the king's chin. Finvarra froze, his eyes staring down the length of his face to the dagger in Billy's hand.

"This is Lura Zahn." The weapon hummed in response. "It's been dying to make your acquaintance."

"How did you ...?"

"Nice, huh? This blade was fashioned by Fjoral the Rune Quencher, from a star that fell from the night sky."

"I'm impressed. Takes a rare gift to get the better of me."

Billy nodded. "It moves as I wish, and if I wished it to harm you, it would."

Lura Zahn hummed louder and forced Finvarra's head back with a little jab.

"I'm impressed. I'm impressed!" Finvarra released Billy and raised his hands.

Lura Zahn vanished, and Billy pushed back from Finvarra with a smile.

"But ..." Finvarra checked his chin for blood. "... We are not fighting a battle, we are playing chess."

"And I believe you said you would beat me."

"And I shall!"

"Then, if you're so sure of yourself, why not make it *more* interesting?"

Finvarra studied Billy for a moment. "Ha! You haven't got anything more to offer."

"Oh? Have you forgotten Lura Zahn so quickly?"

Billy watched as Finvarra tried to swallow his greed. It glowed green and lusty, like coals in the bottom of his swollen eyes.

Finvarra's eyes returned to their usual shrewd cant. "What would you like in return?"

In that one statement, Finvarra had handed him the reins. Billy was making the deals now, and best of all, he had the upper hand. It was time to secure what he had come for.

"I want your promise that you'll come to my aid when I need you."

"Against Lura Zahn?"

"Aye. You get Lura Zahn if you win."

Finvarra crossed his arms and studied the chess board. His brows bunched together as his lower lip played with the hairs of his bushy mustache. First, one eyebrow raised then the other. His lips relaxed, and he said, "You are a bigger fool than I thought, and Lura Zahn is practically mine."

"Then you agree."

"Aye. If you're in such a hurry to give me that dagger, why not?"

"I want your word. Your word that you will come to Lyonesse when I need you."

"Yes, yes, yes. I'll bring my whole bloody army if you want. Now, let's get on with it."

Two moves later, Billy moved his queen into sight of Finvarra's king and announced, "Cyning daith."

"What?" Finvarra's eyes darted around the chess board. "It can't be!" He pounded his broad fist on the table, then flipped over the board, showering Billy with the pieces.

Billy caught several pieces and juggled them. It was just a happy habit of his. He hadn't meant for it to insult or aggravate Finvarra further, but it did.

Finvarra drew his sword with a growl and yanked it into the air over his head. He glared at Billy, with his lips curled back, his teeth ground together, every ounce of sinew drawn taut, and his eyes white with terrible rage.

Oonagh caressed Finvarra's shoulder and whispered, "Remember your wager, husband."

The moment Oonagh touched him, Finvarra's body relaxed. It was as if she had cut a counterweight supporting him. His face lost its fierce expression, and he turned his face to her. He stared at Billy, and then back to his wife.

"You!" Finvarra shouted, the intensity returning to his limbs. "You hamstrung me!"

"I did nothing of the kind. You allowed your ego and your loins to rule your head, and our clever cousin took advantage. That is all."

Finvarra's hands tightened on the leather grip of his sword. The muscles of his arms tensed. Lura Zahn fluttered at Billy's breast.

"No!" Finvarra's face turned red.

The king of the dead ripped the long blade of his weapon through the air. Its edge howled like the wind as it wheeled towards Billy. He saw the deadly blow coming and froze. The blade drew nearer. At the last instant, Billy dropped the game pieces and leapt back. There was a horrendous crash as the table splintered and the sword continued through into the stone floor.

"That is not all!" Finvarra spat bits of foam from his lips. He raised his sword and wagged it at his wife. "And furthermore ..."

Finvarra stopped and stared at the end of his sword. Or rather, where the end of his sword should have been, for it was gone—broken off. He examined the jagged metal a moment longer before dropping his vision to the floor.

Billy followed Finvarra's eyes to the section of stones beneath the demolished table. There, amongst the splintered wood, a piece of the shattered blade rose straight out of the floor—a polished steel monument to fury.

"I will honor my wager." Finvarra strode toward the entry of his great hall. He glanced at Billy in passing. "You, the elf, and the satyr may go now." He pointed at Shaldra and Sylvys with his broken sword as he mentioned them.

Billy smiled and stepped towards the door. "Come along, Drif."

"No." Finvarra turned to face Billy. "I said that you and your *men* could go. My wager said nothing of Drif."

"What are you talking about? Drif *is* one of my men, and he's coming with me."

Finvarra stared at Billy, and then a smile crept onto his face. Before long, he was laughing and pointing his finger at Billy and then Drif. His laughter grew until it shook the hall. "You didn't know? You really don't know! Nobody told you ..."

"Told me what? What's so funny?"

Finvarra grabbed his side and stumbled over to Billy, still laughing, looking more like a drunken sailor than a king. He slipped his arm around Billy's shoulder and turned him to face Drif. He waved the broken sword at the dark elf, and all the buckles and clasps on the black armor unfastened. Drif's protection fell to the floor with a crash, followed by Billy's jaw.

"You really didn't know." Finvarra walked towards Drif. "Now that's funny!"

"Drif is a woman?"

"Aye. And since she doesn't quite qualify as one of your *men*, I am not obligated to let her go."

"Finvarra!" Oonagh shouted at her husband.

The king of the Daoine Sidhe turned to face his wife; all the mirth had evaporated from his visage. "What is it, wife?"

Oonagh marched the distance to Finvarra, her smoldering eyes locked onto him. She stopped a foot in front of him. "I know you want the girl, my love. I know about all the other girls, my love, but if you think I'm going to let you have this one ... I think you have forgotten the last time you made me really angry."

Finvarra's entire face slackened. After a long moment, his face returned to its hardened, crusty frown.

"You wouldn't dare."

"Oh, wouldn't I?" Oonagh raised an eyebrow. She turned her back to him, nodded to Billy, then strode to the exit. Before she disappeared through the doors, she said, "And the last time, I wasn't nearly this angry."

Billy motioned for Sylvys, Shaldra, and Drif to follow him. "Let's go."

"No!" Finvarra stomped the floor.

A crack appeared in the stone beneath his foot and shot across the floor in front of Billy.

"*I* am the king here! And I alone say who will come and who will go."

Billy stepped forward, and the crack in the floor widened into a chasm ten feet across. Far below, in the pit, shadows churned and amorphous black things writhed about.

He felt Shaldra at his shoulder and turned his head as the elf whispered in his ear. "Your Highness, this is a chance to be rid of her. Think of the quest. Malkry could say nothing."

Billy examined Drif, and then addressed Finvarra. "Look, I know now that I should never have come here. I was a fool to think you would want to help me."

"Yes, you were."

"But you lost the wager, and now you owe me."

"I will come to you if you call upon me in Lyonesse, nothing more."

Billy clenched his teeth and fought back the urge to attack Finvarra, despite Lura Zahn's insistence. He felt himself losing control the way he had before. The black tome stirred, and Billy had to force himself to relax. Then an idea sprung into his head.

"I'll make you a deal."

Finvarra snorted. "A deal? I am tired of you, and I am tired of your deals!" He turned to leave.

Billy shouted after him. "I will release you from your obligation to aid me in Lyonesse if you will release Drif to me."

Finvarra stopped and turned back to face him. Inch by inch, the dark chasm in the floor closed until it was but a crack and the two negotiators were face to face. They stared at each other in silence. At last, Finvarra's mouth curled up on the ends. Billy returned his grin.

Finvarra let out a great laugh and slapped Billy on the shoulder. "You negotiate like a king already! I accept!"

Finvarra was so pleased with himself that he escorted Billy, Shaldra, Sylvys, and Deordrif back to their ship and saw them off. As the *Gyldan Mene* sailed away from the dock, Billy looked back and waved goodbye to the king of the dead.

CHAPTER SEVENTEEN

Sacrifice

"Summon the royal huntsman!" Ergyfel bellowed.

Within minutes, the puffy-eyed man arrived at the king's great hall. His rumpled brown shirt hung out; untucked from one side of his trousers. And his trousers, in turn, lingered half-tucked into his boots. A ridiculous red nightcap still rested on his groggy head. As he approached the dais, the man remembered the cap and snatched it off, then attempted in vain to straighten his knotted hair with his fingers. He bowed ten paces from the dais.

"Ah, Tod. My brother has just returned from battle, and we need to relax."

The royal huntsman glanced at the corner next to the dais, where the king's brother skulked in the shadows. Hengest threw back his head and gulped from a large jug of ale. He appeared paler than Tod had remembered.

"Very good, Your Majesty. I will make arrangements for a hunt tomorrow, or if you desire, I could—"

"No! You will make arrangements for a hunt to leave tonight."

"But Sire, … " Tod gave a nervous laugh. "It's already late."

"I wish to be on our way by midnight."

Tod bit his lip when his eyes met Ergyfel's. "Yes, Your Majesty." He bowed, then turned to leave.

"Just a moment." Ergyfel bid Tod forward; gesticulating with his fingers.

Tod went rigid and turned to face his king.

"What do you think, Brother? Should we invite someone to come along with us on our hunt?"

Hengest took another long drink. Though it was cool in the great hall, sweat rolled off his brow.

Ergyfel smirked. "Tod, besides my personal guard, I want you to invite each lord of my war council. We'll make camp on the north side of Loch Nyraval."

"At once, Your Majesty."

"And, Tod ... I will take down the first hart before nightfall tomorrow."

"Yes, Your Majesty."

***

That night, the woods known as Nyraval Grith echoed with the sounds of a royal hunting party. Clomping hooves and grumbling voices echoed through the trees and vales. Each pampered noble on the war council knew what it meant to refuse their king's invitation, no matter how baffling the hour. So, with blurry eyes and slumped shoulders, they tramped along on their horses, whining about the dark, dank cold and whipping their servants who marched along beside, no more able to remedy the situation than their masters.

Only the king and his brother enjoyed this unusual outing. They galloped into the darkness ahead of the mob, at times visible between the trees as shadows on strips of moonlight.

At last, they came to a wide meadow near the loch with a brook meandering through its middle. Tod and his men set up tents and lit fires while the nobles huddled together, peering across the tall grass at their king. They waited to be summoned and wondered what form of lunacy this was. They muttered over a smoldering fire, asking what each knew.

"The king has not been himself of late."

"'Tis strange to be out about on a hunt, when we are at war."

"And with the enemy not so far away!"

"The king simply might have brought us here for a hunt," the youngest of them said. "Perhaps it will restore his ease."

"Aye," the oldest said. "But this is also a good place to see our throats cut."

Each lord present stared at the last speaker and wanted to argue, but found they didn't have the wind to speak. A sudden thirst overtook them, and they drank in silence.

Finally, without a word to his nobles, Ergyfel retired to his tent. His numerous guards took up their positions around it, and the nobles were forced to go to bed without answers. None was able to sleep.

***

The next morning, tired hunters stumbled through the woods. Though glad to be alive, they dragged along, fatigued by their lack of rest. At noon, the king, aggravated by the lack of prey and abundance of noise, sent his nobles back to camp. Ergyfel, Hengest, and Tod continued alone.

It was late evening when Ergyfel turned to Tod. "I told you I wanted to kill a deer by nightfall."

"Yes, Your Majesty."

"The sun is about to set, Tod, and I still don't have my deer."

"Yes, Your Majesty."

"Tod, if I don't get my hart by nightfall, I will be very upset. Do you know what happens then?"

"I lose my job, Your Majesty?"

"No, Tod. You lose your life."

The royal huntsman swallowed hard. "I think I know a spot where you might find a deer, Your Majesty, but we must hurry."

Ergyfel raised an eyebrow and gave the man a crooked smile. "Must we?"

Tod swallowed again. "Yes, Your Majesty."

"Very well. Then let us be off."

The king produced a small jar from his game-bag and sipped a thin, dark liquid from it, then handed it to his brother. Tod turned and took off at a dead run. He leapt over logs and split bushes, the king and his brother just steps behind him. They ran over a ridge and into the next valley where a small creek trickled its way to Loch Nyraval.

As Tod descended into the valley, the sun disappeared from view. The sky became golden-orange and the entire valley submerged into shadows. The royal huntsman jumped down into the creek bed and raced down-stream across the boulders and rocks.

He stopped abruptly. A huge, ancient pine fell over the creek like a bridge, and beyond it lay a quiet meadow surrounded by a dense curtain of trees.

The royal huntsman slipped under the fallen tree and crept to the edge of the grass. He spotted a large log on the ground near the clearing and made his way to it. Ergyfel and Hengest were soon by his side.

The light in the sky was fading. Tod mopped the sweat from his face and scanned the meadow for his prey.

"It's nearly dark, huntsman."

Tod glanced at the king, and then back to the grassy clearing.

"Hengest ... "

The king's brother pulled out an arrow and nocked it. Without warning, he placed his foot on Tod's back, forcing the side of the man's face into the rough bark of the log. He drew back on the string and pointed the arrow at Tod's feral eye.

"Your Majesty. Just wait for a moment, please!"

Ergyfel looked out over the meadow and sighed. "I don't see any deer here, Tod."

Hengest's bowstring creaked, and he pressed his full weight on Tod's back.

"Let me pin his head to this log."

"My brother can't hold that arrow forever." Ergyfel turned back to look Tod in the eyes. "I'm afraid you're about to meet with a rather unfortunate hunting accident."

At that moment, Tod's eye caught something moving near the edge of the clearing. "Look, Your Majesty. Behind you!"

Ergyfel glanced over his shoulder. He squinted and saw the shape of a young doe tiptoeing into the dark meadow. He turned back to Tod. "It's not the hart I was hoping for, but I guess you get to keep your job for another day, huntsman."

Hengest turned his bow on the clearing and loosed the arrow. It sang through the twilight and thudded into the unsuspecting deer. As Hengest lifted his foot and released Tod, the doe collapsed.

The king's brother leapt over the log and ran into the meadow with Ergyfel right behind him. Tod rose to his feet, took a deep breath, and headed into the tall grass.

By the time the royal huntsman arrived, Hengest and Ergyfel had split the doe open and spilled her hot innards onto the ground. Her legs twitched and kicked, but she was dead. Ergyfel stood and turned around. His arms were slick with blood to the elbows. He held the deer's heart in his hands. Tod watched his king place the dark, slippery organ into his bag.

Ergyfel saw the queer look in Tod's eyes and smiled. "Be glad this isn't your heart, huntsman." He then walked to the creek to wash his hands.

Tod stood gawking at his king. The smell of fresh blood filled his nose. His heart pounded in his neck.

Hengest appeared behind the huntsman's shoulder. He leaned close and whispered, "Your heart, a deer's heart, it's all the same to me. Remember that." Then he, too, went to wash up.

When they were finished, Ergyfel and Hengest walked downstream. Tod, still by the doe, shouted after them, "Your Majesty, Your Majesty! What am I to do with this deer?"

"Finish dressing it and take it back to camp, you fool!"

"Yes, Your Majesty."

Tod shook his head and did as he was told. He didn't want to know where they were going. He didn't want to know what they intended to do with that heart. He just wished he were home, in front of a warm fire, his wife beside him, their children playing at his feet.

***

Ergyfel stood high upon a boulder that erupted like a leaping whale from the shallows of Loch Nyraval. He looked to his feet at the ancient, weathered carvings in the stone. Countless ages past, when magic shaped the world, a powerful wizard had placed the symbols there. It was long before King William tamed the land, so there had been no thought of good or evil, only power—pure, unclouded, undiluted intent. Ergyfel craved this kind of power.

He remembered how, as a young man newly arrived in Lyonesse, his powers had drawn him to this spot. He had discovered the runes atop the boulder and felt their magic, which had been untapped for a millennium. He had copied them, studied them, painstakingly deciphered them, and now—finally—put aside his fear to draw on their power.

He glanced behind him, at the shore, where his brother and a small campfire waited. The cool breeze raised gooseflesh on his all-but-naked body. The smooth stone was icy beneath his bare feet. His eyes wandered to the waning moon floating in a star littered sky. Ergyfel felt the ebb and flow of power that heaved unseen to the mortal eye beneath the still waters of the loch. This was the perfect night and the perfect place. He imagined his predecessor carving the runes and reciting the ritual on such a night.

The king breathed in and chanted the ancient words. He had never given voice to them before, and so they clashed like daggers in his ears. On and on he chanted. His voice grew hoarse, and his body ached with fatigue. The words and their long hidden meaning were lost to their very sound, becoming ordinary as wind. Ergyfel filled his mind with the sound of his voice, and it became dark. Something in the darkness stirred, and he felt the tide of power creep up infinitesimally. He took the heart from his bag and cut the string he had tied while the heart was still beating in the deer's chest. Blood poured out onto the boulder, filling the runic carvings, overflowing them and running down the boulder's smooth surface to the waters below.

"Great Dheumon, dweller of the hidden darkness, knower of secrets, father of storms, ruler of the deep, come to me, I summon thee from thy ancient sleep."

He sensed a hunger from the shapeless dark. He was tapping energy, as raw and feral as the Earth's first days. Something unknowable yearned for that power he was holding back. It bubbled up within him—drawn through him towards the darkness. He had to maintain control. The power grew until it filled his being, threatening to rip him apart, and still he held it.

Just then, the Magister's mind contacted something in the darkness: alien, repulsive. His instinct was to flee. In the panic, something primeval touched his mind: *I am here.*

Shocked, Ergyfel released the magic. The power, white hot and wild, crackled through his body, igniting his senses. The cursed wound on his arm stabbed like a thousand teeth, and he dropped the heart. It fell like a stone and disappeared into the water as Ergyfel collapsed.

A moment later, he dragged himself to the edge and watched in disappointment as the last ripples subsided. He waited there, naked, cold, and in excruciating pain, until he could stare at the water no longer. He rolled back onto the boulder and closed his eyes.

"Another failure."

"No," came the answer from the darkness.

Ergyfel sat up and spun around on all fours. He searched the still waters of Loch Nyraval. Its black surface was void of movement and light, like an infinite, gaping pit. He glanced up at the clear night sky. The moon and stars still littered the heavens, but neither deigned to cast reflections on the loch.

"Why are you in such a hurry to fail, Ergyfel?"

"Fail?"

"You pronounced your 'failure' before I had escaped the confines of my timeless slumber. Are you afraid?"

"How is it that you know my name?"

"How is it that you do not know mine?"

Ergyfel collected his wits, before pronouncing, "Dheumon?"

"That name will do."

"Is there another you prefer?"

At that moment, something invaded his mind. He tried to resist it, but all his skill and power were useless against the dark, probing tentacle. The invader picked up his barriers and toyed with them before crumpling and tossing them aside.

"You did not summon me to garner names, Ergyfel."

With the pronouncement of his name, Ergyfel felt the probe sink deeper into his mind. It encircled his brain, squeezing knowledge from it like a sponge. The oppressive darkness seeped into the voids surrounding his thoughts, searching without mercy.

"No!"

"Tell me why you have summoned me, Ergyfel. Do not waste my time."

Again, his name brought pain and a deeper probing. He struggled to remain in control of his thoughts. "I summoned you to bargain for a task."

"Good."

The probing ceased, but he could still feel the invader's presence in his mind. His thoughts struggled to swim in the syrupy darkness.

"Do not wait for me to ask, Ergyfel."

Ergyfel continued, spurred on by the new pain his name was causing. "Great Dheumon, I have but one task to ask of you ..."

"I tire quickly of your mortal pleasantries. What is this task?"

"I want you to kill someone."

"Ah." Dheumon sounded pleased. "The one whose crown you have stolen."

"It's my crown!"

"I only speak what is in your mind."

"It is mine!"

"I do not care!"

Pain coursed through Ergyfel's head, dropping him to the stone.

Dheumon continued while Ergyfel tried to recover. "What matters to me is your offering. What will you give me in return for this task?"

Ergyfel gasped. "Anything. I'll give you anything you want."

The pain in his head subsided, and his thoughts returned to their previous state.

Dheumon laughed. "You are weak. Your predecessor drove a much harder bargain. The one you wish me to destroy has, indeed, grown powerful—more than you think, but I will accept the task at the agreed price."

"I want you to destroy him and his followers while they are still at sea."

"As you wish, but I will do nothing until you have given me what is already mine by your promise, and for such a task, the price will be high."

"What is the price?"

"You must sacrifice to me something very important."

"What?"

"Something very dear to you."

"Now who is wasting time with mortal pleasantries?"

"Ha! I hadn't realized how pleasing it can be."

"So, what is your price?"

"You must sacrifice to me the daughter of Feolaghe."

Ergyfel's mind reeled. *Maeven,* he thought, *my love.* "No! Anything but that!"

"'I'll give you anything you want.' Those were your words, Ergyfel; your promise to me, and I accepted."

"But I—"

"Once you promised me, Ergyfel, we had a contract. There is no turning back. Someone with your learning should know that."

Ergyfel listened in shock as the demon he had summoned explained the method by which he must kill the only person he had ever loved. It seemed inescapable, that Maeven must die, and so each word the demon uttered stabbed at his heart.

When Dheumon had finished describing the proper sacrifice rites, he burned them into Ergyfel's mind. "Remember, Ergyfel, she is already mine. You may change your mind, your heart, your will, but you cannot change that. If you fail to do as I have said, then I shall take you instead."

***

The royal hunting party let out a cheer at the return of their king. Many of the lords commented, "Good hunting, Sire," or "What a magnificent beast, Your Majesty." However, the subject of their adoration entered his tent, paying no heed to their shouts of praise.

Hengest stood outside his brother's tent and called for Lyart, the king's page. When the boy appeared, he said, "Ready the king's horse and mine, on the double!"

"Aye, sir." The lad bowed, and then disappeared behind the tent.

Next, Hengest addressed the royal huntsman. "Tod, strike the camp. We return to Orgulous now."

"Now?" Tod stepped aside to show Hengest the doe, already spitted and roasting over the fire. "But what of the venison, milord?"

Hengest glared down the length of his long straight nose, and Tod remembered his words: *Your heart, a deer's heart, it's all the same to me.* His throat constricted as he tried to swallow.

"Aye, milord."

Tod turned to his men. "You heard him! Now, get crackin' before His Majesty sees what useless oafs ya are!"

The camp exploded into a panic, as noble and commoner alike scrambled to gather their belongings. Hengest frowned and shook his head at the chaos, as his brother emerged from his tent. A moment later,

Lyart brought the king and his brother their horses. They mounted and galloped from camp alone.

***

Ergyfel paced the length of the ante-room to his chambers. At odd turns, he looked up at the door to his bedchamber and bit his lip. The hall door opened, and Hengest entered.

"Did you find the clearing?" Ergyfel asked.

"Aye."

"And the horses?"

"Three, just as you said."

"No one has been alarmed?"

"Most of the castle still sleeps. Also, the first of the hunting party is now arriving at the gate. With all the stragglers, there will be plenty of commotion to cover us."

"Good." The king turned to face the door leading to his bedchamber and froze.

"What is it, brother?"

Ergyfel did not answer.

"Is she in there?"

Ergyfel wrung his hands. The pain this caused the magical wound brought him back to his senses. "I don't know."

"You haven't gone in?"

Ergyfel spun to face his brother. "I haven't opened the door!"

Hengest raised his hands in apology.

Ergyfel watched the door for a sign. When nothing happened, he approached and placed his hand on the latch. Again, he paused to calm his nerves.

In all his life, Ergyfel had never felt such trepidation for such an easy task as opening a door. He had never been one to be afraid, but beyond that door lay the greatest trial of his life.

He closed his eyes and pressed down on the latch. Much to his dismay, it snapped open effortlessly. Careful not to make a noise, he opened the door. Ergyfel stood his ground as the pale shaft of light broadened and crept across the room to illuminate the peaceful figure of his beloved Maeven. Then he noticed his own menacing shadow already stretching out to touch her pale skin, and he stepped into the shadows.

From the dark, he watched her supple arm rise and fall with her breathing. Ergyfel moved closer, each step taking more will than the last. The beauty of her form filled his eyes while nights spent in her arms filled his mind. He closed his eyes and forced himself to take the last steps, stopping when he felt the bed against his legs.

His mind raced to think of a way out of his predicament. He tried to hypnotize himself into a trance that would allow him to proceed without emotion, but could not get past his feelings for Maeven. His entire body vibrated like a bell. Finally, he decided to open his eyes and hope that, somewhere in him, he would find a ruthless scrap that did not love her. However, when he flung open his eyes, he saw only the image of his love.

Ergyfel snapped a hand over his eyes, then scraped it up his forehead and tugged at his hair. A firestorm raged in his mind. He wanted to scream from the absolute torment threatening to burst him.

She has made me weak. Surely, I should despise her. He pulled his head up and forced himself to look at her, but again her beauty and the memory of her generous love smote him.

At that moment, Ergyfel noticed another form in the bed next to Maeven. His eyes shot to it, and he recognized Caenne, Maeven's younger sister. She was the baby of the family and quite a number of years younger, but the resemblance was unmistakable. His entire body pulsed with his heartbeat, and he turned to flee from the room before he could be discovered.

A notion caught him and held him fast, despite his acrobatic heart. In the confusion of that moment, he wondered what had brought the younger sister to his bedchamber that night. He had only seen the girl twice before and hadn't thought the two were very close. Perhaps Maeven or Caenne had been lonely. *It doesn't really matter; the fact is, she's here.*

Ergyfel's notion matured. Caenne was the daughter of Sir Feolaghe, just as Maeven. Dheumon had asked for "the daughter of Feolaghe," nothing more. Furthermore, Ergyfel felt no attachment for the younger daughter. This, in Ergyfel's mind, made her the perfect candidate for the demon's sacrifice.

"Chance becomes providence."

Ergyfel held his hand out over the two sleepers and recited one of the first incantations he had ever learned. The minor amount of power this cost him only tingled in his wound—a tiny itch. Once the charm was in place, he slipped to the opposite side of the bed. He pulled Caenne closer to him and grabbed her up in his arms. The girl never roused from her sleep, and Ergyfel strode from the room. Hengest closed the door behind them.

Within minutes, Ergyfel, Hengest, and Caenne emerged from one of Orgulous' many secret passages and were bound for Loch Nyraval at top speed. They kept to a concealed path and arrived at the loch's shore in record time. Before long, they were at the spot where Ergyfel had summoned Dheumon.

Again, Ergyfel stripped to his loincloth, and then ripped the sleeping gown from Caenne's innocent body. With some effort, he toted her over his shoulder out to the ancient altar-rock, but could not carry her to the top. After some coaxing, Hengest waded out, hoisted the girl up to his brother, and then returned to the shore to wait with the horses.

Ergyfel tied the girl in the manner prescribed by Dheumon and prepared for the rite. When all was ready, he turned Caenne over onto her back. He was about to awaken her from her charmed sleep when his eyes beheld her pale young face. By the light of the waning moon, how like Maeven she appeared. He pushed back a lock of the girl's hair and allowed his hand to brush her cheek. Then he noticed the black knife in his grip.

"No!" He clenched his fists to his eyes.

"Brother," Hengest called. "Are you hurt?"

Ergyfel held his position for a moment, feeling the cold iron of the instrument in his fist. He lowered his hands and stared at the shore. "Hengest, I need you."

His brother ran across the rocky shore and, once more, waded out to the whale-like rock. "What is it?"

"Come up here. I need you."

Hengest climbed up the rock. He stared at the young girl, who lay helpless on the stone, and then turned his attention to Ergyfel.

"I need you to kill her."

"Me?"

"She looks too much like Maeven. I cannot—"

"She's a girl!"

The two men locked eyes. "You have killed women before."

"But never so young, and certainly not trussed up like a pig!" Hengest edged away.

"It's required for the ritual."

"I will not help you with this!"

"She will be awake."

"If I were to kill her like this, I would prefer that she were asleep so she would not see the shame on my face."

"If you are so ashamed of this, then why have you helped me so far?"

"Because ..."

"What are you holding back?"

Hengest stared at him. "Because, my brother, I do not think you are capable of such a thing."

"You don't understand my predicament."

"Perhaps not, but I understand you."

"You do not understand me! No one understands me! You all are afraid of me and always have been. *That* is why you have helped me."

"No. I don't understand your ways, and your powers *have* frightened me, but I do not fear the brother who protected me from a drunk father. I know that brother would not harm me now ... nor kill this child."

"You know nothing."

With that, Ergyfel thrust out his palm with a grunt, and an invisible force blasted his brother off the rock. Ergyfel's anger allowed him to ignore the pain in his arm.

"Go back to the shore. Can I count on you to hold the horses?"

Hengest held his abdomen and glanced up from the water at his brother. He gasped for breath and could only answer by nodding.

"Good. Now, run along."

Ergyfel turned back to the girl at his feet. He knelt beside her and waved his hand over her face. Her eyes opened, and she looked at her captor. The cold stone at her back made her shiver, and then she winced at the rough bite of the ropes as she attempted to move.

"Your Majesty." Caenne's eyes widened. "What are you doing?"

Ergyfel spoke not a word but raised the shadow-like dagger over his head. The girl screamed. Before he could lose his furious resolve, the Magister performed the prescribed rite. He avoided looking into her face, his eyes drawn to the streams of blood that ran down the giant boulder. And still she screamed on. Her voice reverberated off the water and bounced back from the surrounding hills—the shrill sound distorted and angry. In Ergyfel's head, the echo formed the words of a terrible curse.

The king closed his eyes and covered his ears, but the girl's cries still entered his mind. Shortly, they weakened and subsided. Ergyfel cowered for a moment on the rock-altar before opening his eyes. Caenne's small, pale face and eyes stared back at him. She looked more than ever like his beloved Maeven.

He rose to his feet and stared, stunned by his handiwork. He dropped the foul blade, which chimed once against the altar, and was swallowed by the loch in a single gulp.

"What have I done?"

A clap of thunder answered him.

Ergyfel trained his eyes on the far end of the loch and saw a strange black cloud hastening across the heavens. It spat out a lightning bolt, striking the surface of the loch, which was again black as soot. The thunder clapped and a cold, hard wind leapt off the water to slap his face. Before he knew it, the cloud was overhead, pelting his naked body with icy grey rain. He looked down as the rain washed the blood from atop the stone and into the loch.

The storm redoubled its ferocity and the hair on his body rose up. He fled from the rock and headed for the shore. Still standing in the inky water, he turned back as white-hot lightning struck the top of the altar-stone. The concussion threw him back into the water. A moment later, he sat up: numb, half-blind, and a ringing in his ears. When his sight returned, he saw the rock had been swept clean—no sign of the body.

The rain beat down even harder as Ergyfel dragged himself onto the shore. Hengest stood waiting for him, holding the reins of their horses. Ergyfel dressed hastily and turned to take the reins. For the first time in many years, he saw fear in Hengest's eyes.

Now you fear me. Now you understand what I am capable of.

The words rippled through his mind. *What I am capable of.* They toppled edifices, overran barriers, crumbled plateaus, and finally, lapped against a strange and foreboding shore. *Capable.* Ergyfel realized he had ventured beyond the bounds of ordinary men and dared to step upon that forbidden shore for a dizzying moment. *Fear me.* In that instant, he wished he could take it back, but regret was futile. Once that sand had recorded his tread, no ocean could erase the deed. Even if no one else ever knew what he had done, he would know. *I am capable.* He could never forget Caenne's screams or the accusing stare from her dead eyes. He would forever know that he was not a man, but a hideous, brutal monster. *Now you understand.*

CHAPTER EIGHTEEN

Hanging On

Myrredith fell. The shadows beneath the towering walls of Cyndyn Hall seemed to suck her down. Her mind flew into top speed, only to jar to a stop when her head smacked the stone battlements. The world became a disjointed blur before turning to blackness.

"My lady! My lady! Help!"

The words floated in her mind like unidentified vegetables in a heavy stew. She couldn't tell who was saying them. The pain in her head clouded the issue further.

"Please, my lady! Please!"

A vague pain in her shoulder caused her to open her eyes and examine it. She followed her upward stretched arm and saw a round blur of a face staring down at her.

Her wits became sharper along with the pain in her head. The dark stones of the wall before her gradually came into focus. She tipped her head forward to look between her dangling feet. Myrredith opened her mouth to scream but her lungs greedily held the air within them.

"My lady, take hold of my wrists."

She looked up and grabbed the woman's pudgy wrists. "I'm sorry, I—I don't think I meant to ..."

"Hold tight, milady. I'll pull you up."

She tried to find footholds, but her feet only slipped on the smooth stone wall and treaded the air. Megan pressed against the wall with her thick legs and heaved with all her might. She tugged and tugged, but to no avail.

"One more time, milady."

"Yes, one more time."

Megan took a deep breath while Myrredith put her toes into a joint between stones to lend support. They pulled and pushed and for a moment, she moved upward. They smiled at their progress, sure that the end was in sight.

At that moment, Megan's footing slipped, Myrredith screamed, and over the battlement they went. Their fall stopped abruptly when Megan's matronly figure became wedged in the crenel. Myrredith reached the end of their arm's reach and slapped against the cold, hard wall.

"Help!" Megan gasped for breath. "Help!"

The only reply was the far-off wail of a dog.

Myrredith fought to bring the wind back to her lungs. A tear bled from her eye as she looked into Megan's reddening face.

"I'm sorry. You will live if I let go."

Megan felt Her Ladyship's grip slacken. "Oh no you don't! You've got Cyndyn blood in ya. 'A drop of which can scare away dragons or stubbornly erode a mountain.' Now, you can do this!"

"No one is coming. Let me go."

"You are a Cyndyn!" Megan struggled to hold her grip. "And Cyndyns do not give up!"

A queer expression crossed over Myrredith's features. "Both of us will die."

"Not true." The maid gasped, still struggling to hold on.

"Let me go."

"I know what you're doin', milady, and it's very noble, but I think ya have many more noble deeds ahead of ya, if you'll just..." Megan mustered her strength for another yell. The stone crenel squeezed her ribs. "Help!"

"Let me go." Myrredith's voice was so soft, so serene.

Megan closed her eyes, squeezing out tears that fell on her mistress. "No, milady. I cannot."

At that moment, one of Hereweald's soldiers appeared next to Megan. "Hold on!"

"Thank God," Megan muttered.

The guard grabbed Megan's legs and pulled. He put his feet against the wall and heaved until her broad hips cleared the crenel. He then lunged over her and slapped a grip on Lady Myrredith's forearm. His strong fingers squeezed her flesh as he dragged her up the wall.

"Let her fall."

The voice surprised the guard, and Myrredith slipped through his grip. Instantly, he snatched her wrist with both hands. The young soldier craned his neck up against his armor to see who was speaking.

Lord Snegaddrick stood watching them from atop a nearby crenel. He posed with his arms crossed; wrapped in a long fur cloak, a goblet in one hand, his serpent-like eyes smiling at them.

"Lord Snegaddrick, lend me a hand!"

The prince's advisor sipped from his cup, and then tipped it forward, allowing the remaining wine to pour out. He watched idly as the wine fell to the distant earth. "Let her fall."

The soldier returned his eyes to the lady, whose life dangled in his hands. She was the enemy—a prisoner with a death sentence on her head. Her life continued for the mere pleasure of his prince.

Snegaddrick flicked some crumbs from his cloak. "I will testify that there was nothing you could have done,"

"Don't let go." Myrredith looked into his dark brown eyes.

"She's dangerous. She has bewitched our prince."

"It was my prince who personally ordered me to watch over her."

"I tell you, these Lyonesse wenches are treacherous. She will do everything in her power to bring about his destruction, just as she did Prince Gaelyn! Let her go. There isn't much time."

260 | K. C. HERBEL

The guard hesitated. "I cannot lie to my prince!"

"I will say all that must be said. It is for his good that you let her fall. Trust me."

The soldier was one of Hereweald's personal guard and had sworn to protect the prince with his life. He froze, and Myrredith watched his eyes shifting back and forth. She opened her mouth, but before she could say another word, his face resolved and he began to haul her up again.

"A pox upon you," Snegaddrick muttered.

"You talk too much, milord." The soldier grunted. "My *trust* is solely in my prince."

The guard struggled to get his charge back onto the wall while the ex-ambassador looked on. A few moments later, the guard, Lady Myrredith, and Megan were sitting behind the battlements, laboring to catch their breath.

Snegaddrick stepped down from his perch and strode to the soldier's feet. "The castle still sleeps. If this Lyonesse witch and her maid jump to their death now, who will be the wiser? Who will care?"

"You poor excuse for a piss-pot!" Megan put a protective arm around her mistress.

The guard got to his feet and straightened his armor. Without warning, he stepped forward so that his breath struck Snegaddrick's face. "I told you before, I trust my prince, and like any fool in Cyndyn Hall, I can see that she has become the prince's heart."

"*Your* prince's heart, perhaps, but *my* prince's heart is war, honor, blood! Your prince lacks resolve. Your prince is weak."

"Perhaps I should tell him you said so. Perhaps I should tell him of all your behavior here."

Snegaddrick's face, like leather under the flame, curled and buckled into a crooked smile. His lips split open, and he spat out a laugh.

"Yes. Why not? I'm sure our prince will be most interested. Of course, he will be angry with me, maybe even chastise me for my indiscretion, but he understands my motives. As for you ... your lack of vigilance will more than likely be rewarded by having the royal sword placed, ever so gently, between your neck bones."

The guard stood his ground.

"So, by all means, let us hasten to inform our prince." Snegaddrick laughed again.

"Wait!" Myrredith struggled to her feet.

They turned to face her.

"I think it would be better for all of us if the prince did not know of this incident."

The guard stared at her, and then at Snegaddrick.

"Please," Myrredith said.

"As you wish." The guard bowed to her.

Snegaddrick spun on his heels and strode away.

Myrredith put her hand to her head then collapsed into the guard's arms. He sat her down on the battlements and knelt before her.

Megan jumped up and went to her lady's side.

"Are you well, milady?"

Myrredith placed a shaky hand on the guard's. "I didn't have the chance to thank you, sir."

He bowed his head. "Not at all, milady. I think you should return to your quarters now."

"No, please, just a while longer."

He looked to Megan, then back to Lady Myrredith. "As you wish, milady." He stood and walked to a discreet distance.

Myrredith grabbed Megan's hand. Her entire frame quaked. "Help me."

"What is it, milady?"

"I'm so frightened."

"You're safe now, milady. Everything will turn out. You'll see."

Myrredith began to cry. "I don't know who I am."

"You are still Lady Myrredith of Cyndyn, milady. No prince or slimy lord come out of Gwythia can change that!"

"Lady Myrredith of Cyndyn?"

Megan smiled. "Yes, milady."

Myrredith stared at her maid. "Nothing you've just said means anything to me."

"What, milady?"

"I don't know how I came to be on this wall or in what land this fortress lies. I don't know who you are. Until you told me, I didn't even know my name."

Megan stared back in stupefied awe.

"All I know is that if I'm here because I was going to jump ... I must be in some kind of terrible trouble, and I've no way of helping myself."

Megan eyed the newly vigilant guard, and then turned back to her lady. "We mustn't tell anyone about this, milady."

"Why not?"

"Because they would take advantage of you."

"Who?"

"The prince and Snegaddrick."

"Who is this prince? Why would he try to take advantage?"

"Trust me, milady. It'd be better if you kept this to yourself."

"I don't know if I can do that."

"You must."

"It's too much. I—"

"Milady, you must trust me."

"You saved my life. I will do as you say."

"Good, milady."

Myrredith patted Megan's hand. "Please, I need a moment alone."

"Yes, milady."

Megan approached the guard and hooked her hand around his elbow. The soldier looked down at her hand.

"What is it?"

"I can't thank you enough." Megan looked back at her mistress. "She means everything to us."

The warrior smiled at her. "Of course—as my prince does to me."

The guard then trained his eyes on Lady Myrredith, who stared out over the battlements towards the rising sun. "You don't think she would try it again?"

Megan shook her head.

"Good. If I allowed harm to come to her, the prince would feed my innards to the crows. Now, please, I think it best that you take her ladyship back to her quarters. I will send for Prince Hereweald's physician."

"But—"

"Have no fear. Her ladyship fell in her bedchamber, nothing more."

Megan mulled it over before nodding to the guard. She then left him and did as he suggested.

***

The prince's physician was still examining Lady Myrredith when the prince burst through the door. Hereweald charged across the floor and up the short steps to her bed.

"How is she? Why wasn't I informed immediately?"

The physician looked up from his patient. "The lady has a severe injury to her head, Your Highness. As for the other, I only—"

Hereweald stormed towards Megan and grabbed her arms. "How did this happen?"

"I—I—Her Ladyship ..."

Prince Hereweald's face reddened, and he shoved Megan. "Out! Out, you incompetent! No, not you, Doctor—her! Out!"

"Please." Lady Myrredith's voice sounded timid.

The prince stopped roaring to look at her. Her pale, fragile face caught him off guard. "What is it, my lady?"

"Please, do not shout, Your Highness."

Hereweald chewed his lip. "Yes, of course."

"And ... I would like her to stay."

The prince looked over his shoulder as Megan meandered to the door. He observed her; taking in her deliberate tardiness in leaving. "Oh, very well. Megan, you may stay."

Megan spun around with abrupt speed, her face beaming. She took one look at the prince's stern features and stoppered the smug smile that was dying for release.

CHAPTER NINETEEN

Ominous Sky

The demon storm chased Ergyfel and Hengest from the shore of Loch Nyraval. A frigid wind drove them through Nyraval Grith, whipping them with hail and rain and brambled bough. They dared not stop, even after they had entered the secret passages of Castle Orgulous.

While they made their harried flight through the woods, Ergyfel watched his brother. Hengest never returned his glances—never looked up from the trail. He was weighing him, wondering if the scale might tip towards him as it had for the innocent girl left dead in the loch. He was most likely calculating where he should be on that day. He might even be plotting to betray Ergyfel. In the eyes of the king, he was a fearful witness, and this made him a liability. By the end of that inauspicious ride, Hengest's usefulness to the king had diminished, as had the number of his days.

Still breathless, Ergyfel entered his chambers, stripped off his wet, muddied clothes, and slipped into bed. He lay shivering on his back, waiting for his heart to stop pounding like an alarm drum and hoping that its throbbing would not awaken Lady Maeven. As the minutes passed, his pulse slowed, and then a sudden angry clap of thunder scourged it into frantic labor anew.

The king peeked at the lady beside him, expecting the thunder to rouse her, but she did not stir. Her eyes remained closed, her breathing peaceful and unwavering.

"Ah! The charm." He shook his head.

Ergyfel laid back into his pillow with a sigh, reassured in the knowledge that she would never know what he had done that night. His heart slowed and became constant despite the battering of the thunderstorm outside.

He turned and allowed himself to gaze upon her tranquil face. How beautiful she was, even when veiled in shadow. How perfect, how loving, how like her sister …

Ergyfel clenched his eyes and teeth in violent objection to the thought. He turned away and ejected himself from the bed. The cold stone floor under his feet felt distant as he stared into space, holding himself and biting the end of his thumb—an adolescent habit resolutely broken years before.

The king paced the floor, not daring to glance at the bed, until shrewdness forced him to return to it. He might need the protection of Maeven's confidence, should Caenne's disappearance arouse suspicion. And so, he slunk into his bed, curled up near the edge with his back to his lover, and pulled the covers around him. He raised a hand, waved it in Maeven's direction, and then pretended to be asleep.

Before long, Lady Maeven's hand found his back.

"My lord, you are so cold!"

She slid over to her lover and placed her ear to his back to listen for his heartbeat. A moment later, she sighed in relief and wrapped her body around his to bring him warmth.

"My lord, you are so cold. … My lord?"

Ergyfel continued to feign sleep. It took every ounce of discipline not to move as he drew his mind into a tight ball.

Again, she addressed him. "My lord? Are you awake, my love?"

He felt his resolve crumbling away beneath the echo of her last word. Each reverberation hammered at his will until …

"What is it?"

"My love, why are you so cold?"

"I could not sleep."

"You were pacing again?"

"Yes."

"The same cruel dream, my lord?"

"Yes."

"You should wear furs, my lord, and the slippers I had made for you."

Ergyfel chuckled. "Yes. Next time. I promise."

"Good."

The intrusiveness of Maeven's touch had disappeared and, instead, the king found it most comforting. He pulled her arms in around him and took pleasure in her warm embrace—the feel of her body pressed against his. Without warning, the toils of his long day and night caught up with him, and he dozed off.

"Where's Caenne?"

"What?"

"Where's my sister?"

Ergyfel hesitated. The sounding of one name had snatched him from sleep. His mind was quite clear, and yet the answer to the question was muddied. He needed to answer—to answer before she suspected.

"What do you mean?"

"Caenne was here in our bed. I'm sorry. I probably shouldn't have allowed it, but she was frightened. She had a bad dream, and you were gone."

"A bad dream?"

"Yes. She's always depended on me for comfort when she's had one."

"I see."

"I'm sorry, my lord. I shall tell her she can no longer come to me."

"No, it is … well."

"Thank you, my lord."

"Did she say what it was about?"

"Her dream?"

"Yes."

"No, my lord."

Ergyfel nodded.

"Did you speak to her, my lord?"

"When?"

"Tonight."

"Oh. Um ... no. She wasn't here when I returned from my hunt. Perhaps she went back to her own bed."

"Hmm. Yes. Good night, my love."

"Good night."

Maeven closed her eyes and fell back to sleep. It would take Ergyfel the better part of an hour before utter exhaustion dragged him down to an uneasy slumber.

***

When grey dawn arrived, the castle stumbled awake at a limping pace and steadfastly progressed to a groggy stagger. It was nearing midday before it approached anything like the gait of a listing sailor.

Though their activities turned slow, each inhabitant of Castle Orgulous chafed under masked agitation. There was an undercurrent of tension, as if the whole were expecting some still shrouded and stupendous event to burst through the gloomy tide brought by the drab morning. All the while, the ominous storm wheeled overhead, gaining force and pressing down on the castle, keeping a lid on the cauldron.

And then the storm lifted. Just like that, it swept away from Nyraval and strode like a hungry lion toward the Irish Sea, leaving the bruised spirit of Orgulous to recover. But it was not to be a cheery day, for as soon as the ill-omened storm disappeared, Lord and Lady Feolaghe realized that their youngest daughter was missing.

Maeven rushed to the king's chamber to gain his aid, only to find him still in bed, sick with fever. The festering wound on his hand now stretched to his forearm and was inflamed. The smell attacked Maeven's nose as she bent to feel Ergyfel's forehead.

While the king slept in a fevered dream, Maeven removed the old bandages and washed the wound with wine and water. She then summoned the king's physician and waited by her moaning lord until he arrived. While she waited, she further examined the wound.

Maeven had learned from her mother, the Lady Barane, to care for various injuries—the sort of wounds a caring wife of a knight knew about. In fact, she had learned much while helping her mother tend to her father's wounds. However, she had never seen anything like this. Had never seen a burn that continued to grow and consume flesh long after the initial injury. What's more, something strange was happening deep within the wound, beneath the strange translucent skin. New tissue grew within the wound, but of a color and texture unlike any flesh she could remember seeing.

Finally, the doctor arrived. He bowed to Lady Maeven and proceeded to care for his royal patient.

With the king in good hands, Maeven rose to leave. On the way from the bedchamber, she noticed that his clothes from the night before still littered the floor near the door. She scooped them up, and perceiving their damp muddied state, took them to be cleaned.

Upon finding a servant girl, Maeven handed her the king's clothing and boots. "You must have quite a mess on your hands, today."

"Not more than we can handle, milady."

"Yes, I'm sure. But with the storm last night, you must be up to your elbows in wet clothes and mud."

"Oh that, it has been a bit messy. I'm just glad that the hunting party returned before the storm started. Otherwise, we'd really have our hands full."

"But I thought—"

"Maeven," a voice screeched from down the corridor. She turned to see Lady Barane sailing like a great ship towards her with several servants in her wake. "Where have you been?"

"I have been tending to the king, Mother."

"You'll have time for that later. We've got to find Caenne, now!"

"I only went to the king to see if he would order his men to form search parties."

"And did he?"

"He's too sick, Mother."

"Too sick to make a simple order."

"Mother! The king is in a fever, and I could not wake him."

"Where is his physician?"

"He has only just arrived, Mother."

"Come, then. You have done all you can. We must search for your sister without the king's help."

Maeven and Lady Barane took their servants and split up to search Orgulous. Along the way, they each spread the word and enlisted the aid of any servant who was available. Several nobles joined in, while others volunteered their servant's efforts and, before long, many knights and off-duty guards got in on the search.

**

Two days later, King Ergyfel held court in the great hall. His war council and other influential lords were present, as well as the senior servants of Orgulous, officers of Ergyfel's guard, and his personal physician. Lady Maeven stood near the dais with her weary father and sobbing mother. She appeared red-eyed but held tight to her tears to lend strength and hope to her parents.

"My apologies, Majesty," the seneschal of Orgulous said. "But we have searched everywhere with no sign of the girl."

"Obviously, you have not searched *everywhere!*" Ergyfel shouted. "She has to be somewhere."

"Everywhere in Orgulous has been searched, Your Majesty. Every passage, both common and secret, has been searched. Every room, closet, pantry, trunk, barrel, and well has been searched. I even searched ..." The seneschal stopped.

"What? You even searched what?"

The seneschal cleared his throat and looked from side to side for support from his fellow servants. Finding them sullen and staring at the floor, he continued on his own, "I even searched the royal chambers. I beg Your Majesty's forgiveness."

Ergyfel flashed the seneschal a searing glance that transformed into a smile. "Very well. You have discharged your duty to the letter."

At that moment, Hengest and several guards entered the great hall and strode past Lord Feolaghe and his family to the dais.

"Brother. What have you found?"

"As you requested, I took two-hundred men and searched Nyraval from cellar to rafter. We found nothing of the girl and no sign of Gwythian spies."

"Gwythian spies?" one of Ergyfel's war council exclaimed.

Immediately, a hubbub filled the room.

"Silence!" When they had quieted, Ergyfel turned to the audience of lords. "As a precaution, I had my brother search the town for Gwythian spies while they searched for the girl. Killing two birds ... there's no need to be alarmed."

Another lord stepped forward. "Do you think the Gwythies could have spies here already, Your Majesty?"

"Of course, you twit!" Lord Feolaghe said. "Why else search for them?"

Ergyfel nodded his approval. "Thank you, Lord Feolaghe. You are quite right. As I'm sure you have ascertained, the search for your daughter was a good opportunity to look stealthily for our enemies. Please, forgive me."

Feolaghe bowed. "No need to apologize, Your Majesty."

One of the nobles in the rear spoke up. "Did the Gwythies take the girl?"

Ergyfel held up his hands to preempt the return of chaos to the assembled crowd. "Please, my good lords, let us not get carried away by some imagined threat and go charging into the dark. While Gwythia has invaded and we are at war, we have found no sign of them here in Nyraval. Lord Feolaghe, has there been a ransom demand?"

"No, Your Majesty."

"Now surely, if the Gwythies had kidnapped Lord Feolaghe's daughter we would have heard a demand from them by now."

A general, quiet agreement whispered throughout the hall.

"No. ... The fiends who have done this have even less honor than the Gwythies. It is plain to me that this is nothing less than an attack against me, here in my own home! I am sure that most everyone in Castle Orgulous knows by now that Lady Maeven is special to me and that her family is like my family. This attack against them is an attack upon me! Upon us! Its purpose: to divide our energies and throw us off balance. But they will not succeed!"

The assembly cheered.

"Your Majesty. Your Majesty!"

"Yes, Lord Brabbelyn."

"Your Majesty, perhaps it is the unnamed threat you have warned us about."

Ergyfel stared at the young man, and then settled back into the throne. He stared through his bridged fingers as the audience watched him. The room held its breath.

Finally, Ergyfel exhaled. "Yes. It's conceivable; they could have spies here in Orgulous."

Again, a hubbub filled the chamber, growing louder as each of the lords strained to speak above the lord next to him. This continued until each became aware of the solemn figure of Lady Barane approaching the dais. As she passed, she left only silence in her wake.

The Lady of Feolaghe Tor bowed and waited for the king to speak to her.

Ergyfel acknowledged her. "Rise, good lady."

"Your Majesty." Lady Barane kept her eyes on the floor. "I know I am speaking out of turn, but I only ask for my daughter, Caenne."

"Yes? What would you ask?"

The lady paused for a moment. "I ask that you use your powers to find her, Your Majesty."

"My powers." He paused to take in the anxious faces around the hall. All eyes were on him and the woman before his dais.

In the past, Ergyfel had found it useful for people to speculate about his magical powers. Their fear of him imparted greater influence, and at times, a freer hand than was customarily afforded one of his station. And so, he had allowed their tongues to wag and their imaginations to spin. However, to escape the wrathful hand of a superstitious lynch mob there was a balance to maintain, and uncertainty played counterweight to all his sins—real or imagined. He therefore never felt it prudent to confirm their fears about his magical powers. However, since his coronation, the opinion of the court had become much more *diplomatic*.

Is this the right time?

At that moment, his eyes fell upon Maeven. She bit her lip and stared at her love, her tense body leaning towards him.

"I don't suppose you are referring to my powers as sovereign?" It was the closest to an admission his courage would allow.

Lady Barane bowed her head and cowered ever so slightly. Her husband was beside her now. He bowed to Ergyfel and took his wife by the arm.

"Please, forgive her, Your Majesty. She is distraught."

"Yes. Quite." Ergyfel nodded.

He was, in fact, feeling a sudden rush of relief, for he believed he had once again avoided openly admitting to his magical powers, and sustaining that deep-rooted practice brought him back within his established comfort zone. But his comfort lasted only a breath before his gaze fell on Maeven. He watched with growing remorse as her restrained expression of hope transformed to disappointment, and her expectant stance became listless.

Lord Feolaghe turned to take his wife back to their place in the crowd.

"Wait."

The king's voice clung on the assembly's ears like the first clarion of a tourney. The hall was still. Lord Feolaghe and his wife remained frozen in mid-retreat.

If not now, when? I am the king! Why should I deny the better part of who I am? It will be a relief to stop with this foolish game.

"Milady," he said in a commanding manner.

The Lord and Lady of Feolaghe Tor turned back to face him.

"Milady." Ergyfel softened his tone. "Though my strength is not fully recovered from the fever, I will harness what arcane knowledge I possess to the task of finding your daughter."

Caenne's parents bowed with reverence to their king. A low buzz began in the crowd of lords and spread to the servants.

"Now, leave me." The command had returned to his voice. When he saw that several gossiping lords remained unmoved, he shouted, "All of you!"

The rooted lords bowed, then scurried to catch up with the others at the rear of the hall. All save Lord Brabbelyn.

"What is it, Brabbelyn?" Ergyfel took no pains to disguise his annoyance.

"What of the spies, Your Majesty?"

"For now, leave them to me."

"As you wish, Your Majesty."

Brabbelyn bowed and left the hall with his fellow noblemen. As Ergyfel watched them leave, he became aware of a hand on his wrist. He had almost forgotten the eager physician standing beside him.

"You too, leech. I need peace to prepare for this task."

The last to leave were Lady Maeven and the king's brother. Maeven bowed to her lord, who acknowledged her with a nod before she retired. Hengest then approached the throne, but Ergyfel waved him away. He felt weary.

As Hengest reached the doors to the great hall, Ergyfel called out, "Brother."

Hengest spun to face him.

"Find me a spy."

"A spy?"

"The one responsible for the girl."

Hengest bowed his head and left his brother alone.

CHAPTER TWENTY

The Storm

Billy watched from the stern of the *Gyldan Mene* as the last purple shadows and shining star-gems of Finvarra's great cave passed out of view, and the ship slipped into the unfathomable fog. In the supernatural stillness, he felt alone. He turned to see Sylvys and Shaldra standing at the bow, scanning the way ahead in the frail hope they might see something.

Billy marched across the stern castle and started down its creaky staircase. At the bottom, Deordrif sat amid her obsidian-like armaments, polishing and sharpening. She seemed strangely at home, for a woman surrounded by the tools of war. There it was again, an embarrassing splinter in his eye. *Drif is a woman. How could I have been so blind?*

Deordrif stood up to allow Billy to slip by on the steps.

As he passed her, he muttered, "You might have told me."

"Told you what?"

The sound of her voice threw Billy off balance. His statement had been for his own edification, as he expected her to uphold her usual stony silence.

Billy regained his footing and stepped in front of her. He stared beyond the ornate breastplate to study her elegant features.

Deordrif's slender neck offered her regal head up to the heavens. Her smooth, high cheeks and full lips remained motionless while her catlike, lavender eyes regarded Billy from on high. There was something feral and yet stately in her gaze that made him feel uncomfortable. The visage of the Night Queen stirred up from his memory and settled perfectly over Deordrif's face. Billy's heart froze.

"Told you what?"

Her words shook Billy from his trance.

"That you're a ..." He pulled himself up short when he realized how ridiculous he must appear, to have mistaken her for a man. It was rather obvious to him now that she was all woman. *Any half-wit could see that, with or without armor.* Billy also wondered how he had managed to miss her distinct resemblance to the Night Queen when Finvarra exposed her.

"Well," he said. "That you're a—oh, never mind."

Billy turned, but found Deordrif's hand on his arm. He faced her and watched as her aloof expression muted.

"Would it have made a difference?" she asked.

He looked down at her hand then back to her piercing eyes. The sound of her voice was pleasing to his ear.

Deordrif released his arm. "If you had known, would it have made a difference?"

Billy measured his answer carefully. "Yes."

She smiled. "Ah, an honest answer."

"Aye."

"Well. ... I am no stranger to the application of glamour, and my intent was in it for that end. I'm only surprised it worked so well on the ..." Drif pursed her lips.

"Worked so well on the what?"

Drif regarded him then said, "On the son of Eleanor."

"Ah, an honest answer?"

Deordrif tilted her head and lowered her eyes. "It would appear so."

He found her voice soothing, and felt the tensions of the quest ebbing away. His mind stumbled across the thought that this, too, might be faerie glamour. At this, his back stiffened while his collar pressed tighter against his pulse.

Billy tugged at his collar. *Will I ever be able to trust her?*

At that moment, Shaldra appeared between them. Billy watched as the two elves eyed each other in silence.

"What is it, Shaldra?"

"Something's happening ahead."

Billy followed Shaldra forward to the bow. When they reached Sylvys, the satyr was leaning out over the figurehead, facing ahead.

"I think we're almost out, Your Highness."

The ship remained shrouded in mist. All Billy could see was the light of their lanterns turned back against them.

"I can't see anything."

Shaldra faced the stern. "Don't look with your eyes."

Billy listened, but could only hear the creaking of the ship's timbers. He then closed his eyes and concentrated the way Onian had taught him to do on Tirn Aill.

A sound crept into his ears, at first just a distant whisper, then a soft moan. It was the sound of water, the sound of the sea.

Billy turned to face his companions, but his eyes shifted to Deordrif. The dark elf was practicing a combat exercise with her sword. Her movements were strong and fluid.

"You're right, Sylvys."

"Good. I am?"

"Yes, we're almost out." Billy still stared beyond them.

Shaldra looked over his shoulder to see what had captivated Billy's attention. Drif finished her exercise with a flourish and launched into another.

Shaldra returned his attention to Billy. "Does she trouble you, my prince?"

"Yes."

"Did she threaten you, just now?" Shaldra's hand tightened on his sword as he stared at Drif.

Billy placed a hand on Shaldra's arm. "No. In fact, I think she's reevaluated my worth."

"What makes you say that?"

"I believe she was being honest with me."

"Honest?"

"Sounded like it."

"She spoke to ya?" Shaldra and Sylvys said in unison.

Billy looked at them and shrugged. "Yeah. So?"

"So?" Shaldra made wild gesticulations. "So, she doesn't talk ... to anyone!"

"Least of all us."

"Some kind of oath?"

"Malkry's warriors rarely consider anyone but their kind worthy of speaking to."

Sylvys scowled. "It's a ploy."

"No. No, it's not. I'm sure of it."

Shaldra and Sylvys eyed the dark elf.

Sylvys nudged Shaldra. "It must be the magic."

Shaldra looked at him and nodded.

"What, more glamour? Was she bewitching me?"

Sylvys grinned. "No, Highness. Not her magic, *your* magic."

"My magic?"

"She wouldn't talk to ya unless ya did somethin' to impress her."

Sylvys nodded. "The dark elves have always been impressed by magic—especially the darker kind. The kind you've been tossin' about. Probably the reason she hasn't tried to kill you yet."

Billy swallowed hard. "Yet?"

Shaldra gave him a solemn stare. "Ever since you made that cyclone in Finvarra's cave, I've wanted to ask you: Where did you learn to cast such shadowed spells?"

Billy saw a flash of the black tome and heard himself uttering unfamiliar sounds, and he knew. He knew that the book was affecting him. He could feel its influence seeping into his structure. He didn't want to think about it. "The Witan, I guess."

Shaldra narrowed his eyes. "That was no spell from the Witan. And this cursed ship—"

"It's not cursed."

Shaldra motioned to a passing member of the ghastly crew. "No? What exactly do you call it?"

"Transportation. ... And Toady Brimstone gave me no choice."

"Billy." Shaldra sighed. "You are my king. Tell me, why did you call up this abomination?"

"I can't explain it, but until something else comes along—"

"Something else?" Sylvys said. "How about *anything* else!"

Billy smiled at the satyr. "Look, my friends, I don't like this any better than you. As soon as we find another way, we'll take it."

Shaldra and Sylvys nodded their agreement.

At that moment, the ship broke through the fog bank into afternoon sunlight, and water sprayed up from the bow. The questers scanned the open sea around them for a clue to their location.

"Look." Shaldra pointed aft.

The fog bank lay in their wake, and beyond that, a land of proud green hills.

Billy shaded his eyes against the glare. "Erin?"

Shaldra confirmed, "Erin."

Billy grunted and smiled.

"What?"

"I've never seen Erin before. The *Gyldan Mene* was headed there when she went down. It feels strange to come this close just to show it the rudder."

"We must not tarry, Your Highness."

"I know. I was just wishing."

"Wishing what?"

"That I wasn't in a hurry, that Tirn Aill wasn't in danger, that my friends weren't in danger, and that I was just the son of an innkeeper on a holiday to Erin."

Billy's words floated alone on the wind as the Emerald Isle shrank into the distance. He watched until it merged with the innumerable dark waves. *We will see each other again, Erin. I promise.*

They traveled for an hour with the wind buffeting the tattered sails of the *Gyldan Mene*. Billy marveled at the grey shreds, which pulled at the ship's rigging as if they were whole. He was grateful for the steady breeze and calm water, but his already touchy stomach goaded him when he saw a storm brewing ahead. Billy looked back at the captain, who silently steered his vessel on a straight, steady course.

Billy, remembering the storm that had sunk the *Gyldan Mene*, called to the captain. Once his bony eye socket focused on him, Billy pointed ahead.

"Steer clear of that storm."

The captain looked up and appeared to measure the storm. After a pause, he turned the wheel and coerced the ship to the east.

Within a few minutes, the storm had returned to their bow. Billy cleared his throat, and the captain wheeled the ship to the west. Once again, the storm shifted its course. Despite all the captain's efforts, the storm remained in their path.

Billy joined the captain at the stern. Then scanned the sea behind them. "Can we outrun it?"

The captain reached down and tied a rope to the rudder, then stared straight ahead.

"I see." Billy returned to the lower deck.

A cold wind assaulted their faces, and the waves swelled. Within minutes, the storm had mustered legions of frothy green insurgents to assault the *Gyldan Mene*. The watery horde marched forward relentlessly, row upon row upon row. The ship heaved up over their shields and helms of water and dropped off their backs with a slap. After only a few minutes of this, Billy ran to the rail and hurled the meager contents of his stomach into the sea. In answer, the storm pelted him with icy arrows of rain and hail.

Sylvys came to his side, staring at the dark, billowing front that towered over them. "I sense some power at work here. Is it … is it you?"

Billy glanced up from the side. "It's just a storm, Sylvys. Nothing more."

"No," the satyr said with certainty. "It's more than that."

Billy wiped his mouth and looked to Shaldra for confirmation. The elf scowled at the black clouds, his jaw muscles tensing. "It's not natural." He stared at Billy. "Don't you feel it?"

Up until then, Billy's stomach hadn't allowed him to feel anything but ill. He took a deep breath and searched his feelings. There was something—at the back of his neck—a tingle. Once aware of it, the tingle became an itch and the itch transformed into an impulse—the impulse to guard himself. But against what? He located Drif, who monitored the storm from the far side.

Shaldra stared at Drif from beside him. "What do you sense, Your Majesty?"

"I sense intention—a threat."

"From Drif?"

"No." Billy closed his eyes. "From something … someone … bigger."

"Someone *bigger*?"

Billy opened his eyes. "Someone with power, and reason to stop me."

"Ergyfel."

The name of his nemesis pierced Billy's ears. He turned to face his companion. Billy remembered telling Onian of his struggle with the evil sorcerer, but thought the elf hadn't paid much attention.

Shaldra noticed Billy's surprise. "Onian said I was to protect you from him, but if he can call up a storm like this one …"

Billy nodded. "He is formidable, but not invulnerable."

"And if he's conjured up this storm?"

"If he's conjured up this storm, we'll just have to outlast it."

Both Shaldra and Sylvys scrutinized their rickety vessel. They nodded in agreement with Billy while frowning their dissent.

Billy took some rope and tied himself to the railing. Then he turned aft. "Captain, take us to Lyonesse!"

Lightning struck the water before them with a scolding boom. Then the thunder rumbled into the distance like retreating chariots.

Billy looked to the clouds. "A warning shot?"

Sylvys glanced with wide eyes at Billy, then back to Shaldra, who clenched his teeth and grunted as he tightened the rope around his waist.

"Hang on!" Billy shouted.

All at once, the water swelled and heaved them high above the churning sea. Then it dropped them back into a deep black trough. The next wave rolled over them, crushing them down like tent pegs beneath a giant's mallet. The ship, however, remained unchanged.

The furious sea battered them without pause. Up, down, under, then over again. The ship would slip forward, as if free of the storm's grip, then lurch to a stop as it was dashed against the watery canyon walls. Herculean waves enthralled the vessel, twisting it against the hurricane winds that clawed the rigging. The *Gyldan Mene* groaned with the torturous might afflicted against her structure, but bravely she defied the tyrant.

Below the roar of the storm and crashing waves, Billy heard a strange sound. Like the song of a minstrel who appears hungry at your door, it entered his numb mind on a lark, casting his gloom aside.

He spun around and found Shaldra sitting behind him. He was tired, soaked, and bruised from the relentless and unforgiving storm—as were they all, but he was laughing.

Sylvys appeared behind Billy. He placed his hand on Billy's shoulder. "Oh dear. I'm afraid the cap has slid off his toadstool."

Sylvys then scooted next to the elf, who was beside himself with laughter. Shaldra looked up at the satyr with a comic, toothy grin and slapped him on his shoulder. Immediately, Sylvys grinned back and laughed with him. They turned to Billy and laughed with their arms around each other. They heed and hawed and carried on like two insufferable pranksters enjoying the fruit of their mischievous labors.

Billy grinned. "What? What's so funny?"

Shaldra looked up at him, sober for one breath, then trumpeted his way back into hysterical laughter with a loud raspberry. Sylvys continued to snort and chuckle beside him.

Billy sat down, baffled by their conduct.

Sylvys sat up and turned to Shaldra. "Why are we laughing?"

"Because—because—" Shaldra whimpered between guffaws. "Because I just realized that this ship cannot be sunk!"

Billy scooted closer. "Cannot be sunk? How's that?"

Shaldra collected himself somewhat and continued with a grin, "You know very well, My King. I overheard the words of your spell, on the beach in Tirn Aill. You said, 'To raise a ship in thy feared name, it shall not rest 'til *I* please again.' You brought this ship up by your will, and it will not sink beneath the waves again until *you* will it. A very fine trick you played on us, pretending to be afraid!"

Billy furrowed his brow, remembering the black tome. He had been so angry on the beach that morning and grabbed the book so greedily. And it was so accommodating. It was easy to let it take control and solve his problems.

Shaldra let out a howl to the dark pulsing sky, then threw his arm around Billy and Sylvys and laughed. Sylvys joined in, and before he knew what had taken him, Billy too was laughing and howling with his friends at the storm. The storm doubled in measure with their laughter, but still the ship sailed on, and still the three of them laughed.

In the midst of their mirth, Billy looked up to find Deordrif standing over them. Her eyes scolded him from above her crossed arms. Billy imagined her tapping her foot impatiently on a much calmer deck.

Shaldra shouted at the grim warrior, "Laugh, Deordrif! Laugh! The conjurer of this storm will anger and grow tired."

Her eyes darted down at him, and then she cocked the side of her face to the sky. She glared, steeple-like into the clouds above them.

Drif threw back her head and laughed. It was more of a cackle than a laugh, though the frightful sound of it resulted from lack of practice rather than wicked intent. Again, she laughed at the sky, and the others—stopped dead by the first dread sound—forced themselves to renew their mirth.

The storm surged in power. The sky pulsated with flashes of lightning and rumbling thunder. Then lightning struck the deck. The quest party laughed. It struck again and again, and still they laughed. The clouds roared and thunder boomed, as if to drown out the sound of their laughter, but they would not cower; in fact, they were emboldened.

All at once, a bolt of lightning crashed into their midst. A white-hot tendril grasped Drif by the breastplate and tossed her backward like the blow of a heavy lance.

"No!" Billy jumped to his feet. He arrived by the dark elf's side to see the red glow from the lightning's touch fade to black. He knelt over her. "Drif! Drif!"

He placed his hand under her head and lifted her mouth to his ear. He heard no breath, and turned to face her.

"Please, don't die," he whispered.

Much to Billy's surprise, the proud warrior's eyes fluttered open. She blinked and stared into his eyes. Raindrops, like tears, fell from his face onto hers.

"What are you doing?"

"I-I."

Her hand came up and pushed him back.

"Now that you know I'm a woman, you think you can just take me?"

"No." In truth, her beauty had played a part in his hesitation, but shock had played the larger part. "You were struck by lightning ... and I was trying to ..."

Now separated from him, she placed her hand on the still warm metal of her breastplate. "Be that as it may, you will not touch me again!"

Billy put up his hands. "Fine, fine. I was only trying to help."

"Don't help me!"

"Fine."

At that moment, the braying laughter of Sylvys and Shaldra side-swiped Billy's confused mind. Billy and Drif's audience had found their little scene high comedy. Despite his embarrassment, their contagious laughter soon had its way with him.

When Billy reached the giggling stage, he reached out to help Drif to her feet.

"Don't help me!"

"Of course." Billy recoiled his hand as if from a snakebite.

This redoubled the two's laughter, and she shot them a dark look. They only howled and incited their prince to join them.

Finally, she got up from the deck on her own. She stood erect—as straight as she could on the rickety, bucking planks, and held her chin up. She muttered and abruptly levitated three or four feet above the deck. She then glared at the clouds. "Ha, ha, ha! Is that the best you can do?"

Again, the clouds rumbled and spat out a bolt of lightning at their ship. It danced over Drif's body, through the large hole in the deck below her, and into the sea.

"Is that all you've got? I am laughing at you!"

Lightning crackled on the air and thundered in the clouds. The roar grew and transformed into a furious shout. Then it faded away.

Without further ado, the sea became calm. The black clouds shrank and grew ashen. The rain stopped. Soon, orange beams of sunlight pricked holes through the swirling, smoky canopy of the sky.

The *Gyldan Mene* sailed on under the clouds, creaking and groaning, as was her way. As for serious complaints, she remained as silent as her lifeless crew. Her passengers, too, had little to say, deciding to rest their tongues and heads until circumstance required more.

* * *

This ends Book Three.
The adventure continues with
The King,
Book Four of the
Jester King Fantasy Series.

I truly hope you enjoyed reading this book as much as I enjoyed writing it. If you did, I would greatly appreciate a short review on Amazon or your favorite book website. Reviews are crucial for any author, and even just a line or two can make a difference.

Thank you!
KC

ABOUT K. C. HERBEL

I write stories about adventure, magic, intrigue, danger, defeat and triumph. I also write about things that really matter, like: friends, family, love, loyalty, right and wrong, good vs. evil, patriotism, bravery, duty and honor.

†

K. C. grew up in the American Southwest and spent two decades in Southern California. He has traveled much of the U.S. and Europe (both East and West) and has worked in France, Korea, Japan, and China. Now he lives in the woods near Richmond, Virginia with his family, which includes three dogs.

ACKNOWLEDGMENTS

Over the years, I've had a great deal of advice, encouragement, nudging and badgering from my friends, family and fans. I've been cornered at gatherings, cornered in conversations and even cornered in a few uncomfortable alleys. I can finally say to you, thank you for your advice, encouragement and patience. The book is in your hands. Will you lay off now?

Once again, I would like to thank my village; those cunning, wise, foolish and fun around me. You make the work of writing worthwhile.

Thanks to my talented and ever patient editors Harmony Kent, Kerry Hall, and Jack Mercer. I've learned much from you while you patiently smoothed off my rough edges.

Thanks to my mentors Mark, Raymond and Stiles. You helped me to believe in myself. And to John DeChancie, thanks again for your insightful advice and delightful encouragement – especially on this volume.

I also want to give a special thanks to some very special friends: film maker Hiroshi Katagiri, author Leisl Kaberry, and the fine folks at GameFace Publishing. Thank you for your belief in this project and your support. To Leslie Bobb and Carolene Herbel, I could not have published this book without your most generous support and encouragement. It means a lot to me that you believe in me enough to have my back.

Lastly; thank you, Mary Anne. You are a wonder.

K. C. Herbel
Richmond, Virginia
April 2016
God go with you!

<u>The Jester King Fantasy Series</u>
The Innkeeper's Son
The Jester
The Prince
The King

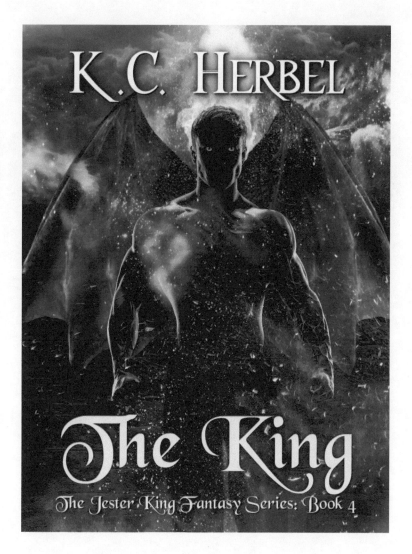

K.C. HERBEL

The King

The Jester King Fantasy Series: Book 4

Look for details at: www.kcherbel.com

Made in United States
Troutdale, OR
01/08/2024